Arthur absentmindedly turned over the drawing and discovered another one on the back. The boy's face lit up.

"I *knew* he had left a sign!" he yelped joyously.

The drawing was a map—to the land of the Minimoys! It was sketched in pencil, rather poorly drawn or perhaps done very quickly.

Arthur stood up and turned the map in all directions. Something about the location seemed oddly familiar.

"So the entrance to the Minimoys' world is here, next to this tree. . . . Wait, I know this tree! And here's the house, and that way's north. . . ."

He ran over to the window and threw it open.

The map corresponded exactly to the view that he had from the study window.

"The large oak tree, the garden gnome, the moon, everything is there!" exclaimed Arthur. "We found it, Alfred! We found it! The Minimoys are in the garden!"

A FILM BY LUC BESSON

ARTHUR
AND THE INVISIBLES

BY LUC BESSON

FROM AN ORIGINAL IDEA BY
CÉLINE GARCIA

TRANSLATED BY ELLEN SOWCHEK

HarperEntertainment
An Imprint of HarperCollinsPublishers

THE WEINSTEIN COMPANY

Library of Congress catalog card number: 2006933180
ISBN-10: 0-06-122726-9 (pbk.)
ISBN-13: 978-0-06-122726-4 (pbk.)

Typography by Karin Paprocki
❖
First HarperEntertainment Edition, 2006

BOOK ONE:

ARTHUR
and the
MINIMOYS

CHAPTER

1

The landscape was green and gently rolling, grazed closely by the hot sun. Above it the sky was blue, filled with small cotton clouds.

It was quiet, as were all of the mornings during this long summer vacation, when even the birds seemed lazy.

In the middle of the peaceful valley was a small garden by a river that flowed past an unusual-looking house. It had a long balcony and was made entirely of wood. To one side stood a large garage with a huge wooden water tank perched on top.

An old windmill kept watch over the garden, much like a lighthouse watches over its boats. It seemed to turn just for the fun of it. In this little corner of paradise, even the wind blew gently.

Nothing on this beautiful morning hinted at the terrible adventure that was about to begin.

The front door exploded open. A large woman filled the entryway. "ARTHUR!" she yelled, in a voice that could make glass shatter.

Grandma was about sixty years old and rather round, even though her elegant black dress, trimmed with lace, was designed to hide her plumpness.

She finished putting on her gloves, adjusted her hat, and yanked violently on the ancient doorbell. "Arthur!" she yelled again. No answer.

"Where on earth is that boy? And the dog! Has Alfred disappeared, too?" Grandma grumbled like a distant storm as she went back into the house.

Inside, the wooden floor gleamed with polish, and lace seemed to have conquered all the furniture, the way that ivy takes over walls.

Grandma put on her house slippers and crossed the room, muttering; "'An excellent watchdog, you'll see!' How did I ever fall for that?"

She huffed up the stairs.

"I wonder what exactly he's watching, this 'watchdog'! He's never *in* the house to watch it! He and Arthur just breeze through!" she grumbled, opening the door to Arthur's bedroom. Still no sign of Arthur.

"Do you think it bothers them that their poor grandmother must run after them all day long? Not at all!" She continued down the hall. "I don't ask for much—only that he keep still for just five minutes a day, like other ten-year-olds!" Suddenly she paused, struck by a thought. She listened to the house, which was unusually silent.

Grandma began to speak in a low voice.

"Five minutes of peace . . . when he could play calmly . . . in a corner . . . without making any noise . . . ," she murmured, gliding toward the end of the hallway. She reached the last door, on which hung a wooden sign engraved with the words KEEP OUT.

She opened the door quietly and peered into the forbidden room.

It was an attic that had been converted into a large office, and it looked like a cross between a merry antique shop and the study of a slightly nutty professor. On either side of the desk were large bookshelves overflowing with leather-bound books. Hanging above it all was a silk banner bearing a cryptic message: WORDS OFTEN HIDE OTHER WORDS. Our scholar was also a philosopher.

Grandma moved slowly into the middle of the bric-a-brac, all of which had a decidedly African flavor. Around the room spears seemed to have pushed through the floor like shoots of bamboo. A fantastic collection of African masks hung on the wall. They were magnificent . . . except for the one that was missing. A lone, telltale nail stuck out of the wall.

Aha! Grandma had her first clue. All she had to do now was follow the snores that were becoming more and more audible.

Grandma moved farther into the room and, sure enough, discovered Arthur stretched out on the floor, the African mask on his face amplifying his snores. Alfred, of course, was stretched out alongside him, his tail beating time on the wooden mask.

Grandma couldn't help but smile.

"You could at least answer when I call you! I've been look-ing for you for almost an hour!" she murmured to the dog, speaking quietly so as not to wake Arthur too suddenly. Alfred put on his best cute and innocent look.

"Oh, don't give me that puppy-dog face! You know I don't want you in Grandpa's room and you're not allowed to touch his things!" she said firmly, reaching to lift the mask off Arthur.

In the light, he had the face of a naughty angel. Grandma melted like snow in the sun. She breathed a happy sigh at the sight of the boy who lit up her life.

Alfred whined a little—perhaps out of jealousy.

"That's enough, Alfred! If I were you, I would make myself scarce for the next five minutes," she said sternly. Alfred took the hint and backed off. Grandma lovingly placed her hand on the boy's face.

"Arthur?" she murmured. The snoring only became louder. She changed her tone.

"Arthur!" she thundered, her voice echoing through the room. The boy jumped up with a start, bewildered and ready for battle.

"Help! An attack! Quick, men! Alfred! Form a circle!" he shouted, half asleep. Grandma grabbed his shoulders.

"Arthur, calm down! It's me! It's Grandma!" she barked.

Arthur shook himself awake and realized who he was facing.

"Oh, sorry, Grandma. I was in Africa."

"I can see that!" she replied with a smile. "Did you have a good trip?"

"Fantastic! I was with Grandpa and a whole African tribe. They were friends of his," he added helpfully.

Grandma played along. "Oh, my. What happened?"

"We were surrounded by dozens of ferocious lions that came out of nowhere!"

"My goodness! What did you do to escape?" she asked.

"Me, nothing," he replied modestly. "It was Grandpa who did everything. He unrolled a large cloth and we hung it up, right in the middle of the savannah!"

"A cloth? What kind of a cloth?" asked Grandma, mystified.

Arthur was already climbing on a crate to reach the top shelf. He took down a book and opened it quickly to the right page.

"There, see, like this! He painted a canvas that he hung in a circle around us. That way, the wild animals saw only the painted scenery, so they turned away and couldn't find us. It was as if we were . . . invisible," he concluded with satisfaction.

"Invisible, perhaps, but not odorless!" Grandma responded.

Arthur stared at her blankly.

"Did you take your shower this morning?" she asked.

"Well, I was about to, but then I found this book! And it was so interesting that I forgot everything else," he confessed, leafing through the pages. "Look at all these drawings! This is the work that Grandpa did for the most isolated tribes. Hardly anyone else has ever seen or heard of them."

Grandma glanced down at the drawings, which she knew by heart.

"What I see is that he was more interested in African tribes than in his own," she replied, smiling.

Arthur was immersed in the drawings. "Look at this one. He dug a superdeep well and invented an entire system with bamboo to transport water more than a mile away!"

"It's ingenious, I know, but to be fair the Romans invented that system long before he did. They are called pipelines," Grandma reminded him.

This was a page of history that Arthur had totally missed.

"The Romans? I've never heard of that tribe!" he said.

Grandma smiled. "It was a very old tribe that lived in Italy a long time ago," she explained. "Their chief was named Caesar."

"Like the salad?" Arthur asked.

"Yes, like the salad," replied Grandma, smiling once again. "Come on, let's straighten up. We have to go into town to do some shopping."

"Does that mean no shower today?" asked Arthur with delight.

"No, it just means no shower right now! You can take one when we get back! Now hurry up!" Grandma ordered.

Arthur carefully rearranged the books that he had scattered, while Grandma put back the African mask. They had a proud look, all these warriors' masks, which had been given to her husband as a sign of friendship from various tribes. Grandma gazed at them a moment, remembering the adventures that she had shared with her husband, who had been missing now for four long years.

She let out a deep sigh, as long as a memory.

"Grandma—why did Grandpa leave?"

The question resonated in the silence. She glanced over at Arthur, who was staring up at the portrait of Grandpa in his helmet and full colonial garb.

Grandma searched for the right words. She moved toward the open window and took a deep breath.

"That, Arthur, is something I would really like to know . . ." she answered, closing the window. She remained there for an instant, looking down at the garden. An old garden gnome smiled up at her from the foot of an imposing oak tree that overlooked the place.

How many memories had this old oak accumulated during its lifetime? It could probably tell this story better than anyone, but it was Grandma who continued.

"Grandpa spent a lot of time in his garden, near that old oak tree that he loved so much. He said that it was three hundred years older than he was, and so it must have a lot of things to teach him."

Without making a sound, Arthur perched on the edge of a chair, anticipating a story.

"I can still picture him at nightfall, with his telescope, observing the stars," said Grandma in a soft voice. "The full moon was shining. It was . . . magnificent. I could watch him for hours when he was like that—passionate, fluttering like a butterfly." Grandma smiled, replaying the scene in her memory. Then her smile faded and her face grew hard.

"And then one morning, both he and the telescope were gone. Disappeared. That was almost four years ago."

Arthur was a bit stunned. "He disappeared just like that? Without a word, a note—without anything?"

Grandma nodded sadly. "It must have been something very important for him to leave like that, without telling us," she said with a touch of humor. She clapped her hands as if she were popping a soap bubble.

"Come on! We're going to be late! Go put on your jacket!"

Arthur ran happily toward his room. Only children seem to have this ability to shift so quickly from one emotion to another, as if the heaviest things do not really have any weight before the age of ten. Grandma smiled at this thought. For her, it was often difficult to forget the weight of things, even if only for a few minutes.

Grandma adjusted her hat one more time. She crossed the front garden toward her faithful old Chevrolet pickup.

Arthur wriggled into his jacket as he ran up to the passenger side. A trip in this vehicle was like a journey on an antiquated spaceship—always an adventure.

Grandma fiddled with two or three buttons and turned the key, which was as stubborn as a stuck doorknob. The motor coughed, crackled, then raced, jammed, became blocked, cleared itself, revved up, and finally started.

Arthur loved the hum of the old diesel engine, which sounded very much like a manic washing machine.

Alfred the dog, on the other hand, kept his distance from the truck, as if he couldn't understand why there needed to be all this noise for so little result.

Grandma addressed him through the window:

"Excuse me, Alfred. Would it be possible, if it's not too much trouble, for you to do me a very big favor?"

The dog lifted one ear. He knew that favors were often associated with rewards.

"Watch this house!" she ordered.

The dog barked, not really sure what he was agreeing to.

"Thank you. That is very kind of you," Grandma responded. She released the emergency brake, shifted the Chevrolet into gear, and rolled toward the road.

A cloud of dust bloomed in the slight wind that blew over the countryside. The truck traveled over the green hills, taking the small, twisting road to civilization, or the nearest thing to it.

The town was not big but it was very pleasant. Almost all of the shops and merchants could be found on the wide main street.

Grandma parked in front of a store that, without a doubt, was the largest in the town. An imposing sign announced the name of the owner and its purpose:

DAVIDO CORPORATION
FOOD SUPPLIERS

Which meant that it covered a lot.

Arthur liked to go to the supermarket. It was the most modern store in this friendly little town, the closest thing he had to a space station. And, since he imagined himself to be traveling by spaceship, there was a certain logic to his thoughts, even if it was a logic that only children could comprehend.

Grandma primped a little before she got out of the car, knowing she would run into her friend Martin, the police officer.

Martin was around forty years old, rather jovial, with hair that was already turning gray. He had the look of a cocker spaniel but a smile that saved everything.

He hurried over and opened the supermarket door for Grandma.

"Thank you, officer," said Grandma politely, pleased by his gentlemanliness.

"You're welcome, Mrs. Suchot. It is always a pleasure to see you in town," he added.

"It is always a pleasure to run into you here, officer," replied Grandma, happy to play along.

Martin twisted his hat in his hands, as if he had run out of conversation.

"Do you need anything out there? Is everything all right?"

"Well, there's no lack of chores, but it certainly prevents boredom! And then I have my little Arthur. It's nice to have a man around the house," she added, ruffling her grandson's hair.

Arthur hated it when people patted him on the head. It made him feel like a stuffed toy. He pulled away with a frown, and this was all it took to make Martin even more nervous and awkward.

"And . . . the dog that my brother sold you? Is he working out well?"

"Better than that! He's a real beast!" Grandma said with a chuckle. "Fortunately my little Arthur, who knows so much about Africa, was able to tame him," she said. "The animal is now well trained, although we know that the wild beast is still sleeping inside him. Sleeping rather a lot, in fact," she added teasingly.

"Good, good—I am delighted," Martin stammered, as if he were not quite sure this was the right thing to say. He continued regretfully, "Yes, well . . . good-bye, Mrs. S."

"Good-bye, officer," Grandma replied with a friendly nod. Martin watched them pass and gently let go of the door, the way one lets go of a sigh.

Arthur used all of his strength to separate two shopping carts, which were evidently madly in love with each other.

He found his grandmother already in one of the four aisles, shopping list in hand.

Arthur let his feet slide to slow down his cart. He moved close to his grandmother in order not to be overheard by anyone else.

"Grandma, wasn't that police officer flirting with you just a little?" he said bluntly.

"Arthur! Where did you learn that word?" she asked.

"Well, it's true, isn't it? As soon as he sees you, he starts strutting like a duck and acting as if he is going to eat his hat. Mrs. S. this, Mrs. S. that!"

"Arthur! Stop!" Grandma said. "Let's have some decorum. We do not speak about people by comparing them to ducks."

Arthur shrugged. He wasn't convinced that he'd been rude. All he'd done was point out the truth.

Grandma calmed down. "He is very nice to me, as is everyone in the village," she explained in a serious voice. "Your grandfather was well liked here, because he helped people with his inventions, just as he did in the villages in Africa.

And when he disappeared, people like Martin were a great comfort to me."

The conversation had turned somber. Arthur felt it and stopped squirming.

"Believe me, without their kindness, I would probably not have been able to stand the loneliness," Grandma admitted.

Arthur remained silent. You don't always know what to say, and that's true whether you are ten years old or a hundred.

Grandma patted his head affectionately and handed him the shopping list.

"Here. I'll let you do the rest. I know you like to. I have to go find something at Mrs. Rosenberg's. If you finish before I do, wait for me at the checkout register."

Arthur nodded, already delighted at the prospect of traveling the aisles aboard his iron vessel on wheels.

"Can I buy some straws?" he asked.

Grandma gave him a big smile.

"Of course, dear. As many as you like."

That was all he needed to hear. He set off down the aisle with a grin.

Grandma left the store and crossed the main street, being careful to look right and left even if it wasn't absolutely necessary, given the rather light traffic in this town. Perhaps it was a reflex from an earlier time, when she and her husband had traveled in the great capitals of Europe and Africa.

She entered the Rosenbergs' small hardware store, where even the doorbell had a story all its own. She was on a mission. It was Arthur's birthday and she had planned a special surprise.

Mrs. Rosenberg appeared, popping out like a jack-in-the-box. She had been at the window for an hour, waiting for her friend to arrive.

"He didn't follow you, did he?" she asked, too excited to say hello.

Grandma gave a quick glance back over her shoulder. "No, I don't think so. I don't think he suspects anything."

"Perfect! Perfect!" The merchant bounced as she went back into the store. She bent behind the imposing counter, took out a package wrapped in brown paper, and placed it delicately on the old wood surface.

"Here you are. Everything's there," she said with a smile that made her look as if she were five years old.

"Thank you. You are wonderful. You cannot know how you have helped me with my surprise. How much do I owe you?"

"What do you think? Nothing! I had a great time!"

Grandma was caught off guard, and her excellent upbringing forced her to insist, "Mrs. Rosenberg, that is very kind, but I cannot accept."

Mrs. Rosenberg was already handing her the package.

"Go on, don't argue, and hurry before he suspects something!" She hustled her friend to the door.

The two old ladies exchanged knowing smiles.

"Go on, out with you!" said Mrs. Rosenberg. "And I am counting on you to stop by tomorrow and tell me everything in the smallest detail."

Grandma agreed with a smile. "I won't forget. See you tomorrow."

"See you tomorrow," said the hardware dealer, returning to her observation post at the corner of the window. Outside, Grandma opened the Chevrolet door and slipped the mysterious package under the seat.

When Grandma met Arthur at the checkout counter at Davido's, he was already emptying the contents of the cart onto the rolling belt, arranging everything in little trains, alternating pasta and toothpaste, sugar and apple shampoo, and a package of straws.

"You found everything?" Grandma asked.

"Yes, yes," replied Arthur, absorbed by the arrangements.

A second package of straws passed under Grandma's nose.

"I was afraid you wouldn't be able to read my writing."

"No problem. And did you find what you were looking for?"

Grandma experienced a moment of panic. Lying to a child can be the most difficult thing in the world.

"Yes . . . uh . . . no. In fact—it wasn't ready. Next week, maybe," she stammered, nervously filling the first bag with packages of straws. She was so distracted that it wasn't until the sixth package of one hundred straws that she finally reacted.

"Arthur! What on earth are you doing with all these straws?"

"You said I could get as many as I wanted, didn't you?"

"Yes, but . . . that was just a figure of speech."

"Well, that's the last one!" he said with a charming grin. Grandma was at a loss for words.

The old Chevrolet, more tired now than during the trip into town, was parked near the kitchen window, where it was easier to unload the groceries.

Arthur began to pile packages on the window ledge.

"I'll do that," Grandma said. "Go play while it is still daylight."

Arthur didn't argue. He grabbed his bag full of straws and ran off barking—or, no, that was Alfred, chasing after him with equal joy. Grandma was now able to remove her mysterious package unseen and sneak it quietly into the house.

Arthur turned on the long fluorescent light in the garage, which crackled a bit before lighting up the room. Out of habit, he grabbed a dart near the door and sent it flying to the opposite side of the room. Bull's-eye!

"Yes!" he cried, waving his arms in a victory sign.

He crossed the room to the workbench, which was littered with bits and pieces of a strange contraption. It consisted of several pieces of bamboo carefully cut lengthwise and pierced with small holes all over.

Arthur enthusiastically opened each package of straws one by one. There were all kinds, in all sizes and colors. Arthur hesitated before selecting the first one, the way a surgeon chooses a scalpel before beginning an operation.

He finally chose one and tried to fit it into the first hole in one of the pieces of bamboo. The hole was just a bit too small. No problem—Arthur simply took out his Swiss army knife and widened the hole. The second attempt was an immediate success. The straw fit perfectly.

Arthur turned to his dog, the lone privileged witness to this memorable event.

"Alfred, you are about to see the greatest irrigation system in the entire region. Bigger than Caesar's, more perfect than Grandpa's, here it is: the Arthur system!"

Alfred yawned, overcome with emotion.

Arthur the builder crossed the garden, carrying his immense length of bamboo, pierced with a dozen straws, on his shoulder.

Grandma, still occupied with putting away the groceries,

saw him pass by the kitchen window and was momentarily struck speechless. She blinked a few times, then shrugged her shoulders.

Arthur placed the bamboo on small, branched tripods he had built for this purpose. The whole thing was perched above a carefully dug ditch, at the bottom of which were small radish seedlings, regularly spaced.

Arthur went back to the garage, found the garden hose, and began to unroll it.

So far, so good.

Arthur, under Alfred's anxious eye, attached the hose to the end of the bamboo, sticking it in place with pieces of multicolored modeling clay. He then turned the bamboo until the straws were positioned above each seedling.

"This is the most delicate moment, Alfred," he said, quoting from one of his grandfather's books. "The calibration must be correct to the exact degree in order to avoid a flood or the total destruction of the crop," he added in a serious voice, as if he were handling explosives.

Alfred didn't particularly care about radishes. He trotted off and returned with his old tennis ball, which he dropped on top of a young seedling.

"Alfred! This is really not the time!" Arthur shouted. "And no civilians allowed on the work site!" He picked up the ball and threw it as far as possible. Alfred took this as a sign that the game had begun, and he charged off, nose to the ground, in pursuit of his prey.

While he was gone, Arthur finished his adjustments and ran over to the faucet on the wall of the garage.

The dog returned, ball in mouth, but his master had disappeared.

Arthur put his hand on the faucet and turned it slowly.

"Please work!" he prayed. He took off running alongside the hose to arrive before the stream of water.

Halfway there, he ran right past the dog, who had come in search of him. Alfred was completely bewildered by this new variation in the game, but he spun around and followed.

Arthur threw himself to the ground and followed the stream of water on all fours as it filled the bamboo and ran through the straws one by one.

Each young radish seedling was happily watered. Alfred put down his ball, intrigued by this machine that could pee on all the flowers at once.

"Yes!" shouted Arthur, grabbing his dog's paw and pumping it up and down cheerfully. "Congratulations! This is a remarkable work that shall be remembered by history, believe me!" he said, speaking for Alfred.

Grandma appeared on the porch, an apron around her waist.

"Arthur! Telephone!" she yelled. Arthur let go of his dog's paw.

"Excuse me, Alfred. It is probably the president of the water company calling to congratulate me. I will be back in a minute."

CHAPTER
2

Arthur was so excited as he entered the living room that he managed, in his socks, to cross the entire room in a single slide.

He grabbed the phone and nestled deep into the comfortable couch.

"I made an irrigation system, just like Caesar! But in my case, it's for *making* salads! It's to help Grandma's radishes grow! With my system, they will grow twice as fast!" he shouted into the telephone without pausing to find out who was calling.

But it was four o'clock and, as was the case every day, it was most likely his mother.

"That's lovely, dear! Who is this Caesar?" asked his mother.

"He is one of Grandpa's colleagues," Arthur said with assurance. "I hope that you'll get here by nighttime so I can show you everything. Where are you?"

His mother's voice was uneasy. "We are still in town, for the moment."

Arthur was a bit disappointed, but today it would take more

than this to wear down his victorious spirit.

"Well . . . that's okay. If you get here tonight you can see it tomorrow morning."

His mother began speaking in her gentlest voice. "Arthur . . . we're not going to be able to come back right away, dear."

Arthur's small body slowly deflated, like a punctured balloon.

"There are lots of problems here," his mother continued. "The factory has closed and . . . Daddy has to find another job," she admitted.

"He could come here! There's lots of work to do in the garden!" Arthur replied.

"I'm talking about a real job, Arthur. A job where he can earn some money so that all three of us can eat."

Arthur thought about this for a few seconds. "You know, Mom, with my system, we can grow anything we want, not just radishes. Then we would have enough for all *four* of us to eat!"

"Of course, Arthur, but people need money for more than just food. We need to pay the rent and—"

"We could all live here! There's lots of room and I'm sure that Alfred would be happy about it. Grandma, too!"

"Listen, Arthur! Don't make things more complicated. Daddy needs a job, so we have to stay here a few more days to look for something," she concluded gently.

Arthur didn't understand why his mother refused even to consider all his sensible solutions, but kids are used to adults not thinking logically.

"Okay," he said.

The subject was closed, and his mother's voice was once again sweet and light.

"But just because we aren't with you doesn't mean we aren't thinking about you, especially on a day like today," she said, "your *b-i-r-th-day!*"

"Happy birthday, Son!" his father boomed into the phone.

Arthur mumbled "thank you" in a monotone.

His father tried to sound cheerful. "So you thought we forgot! Well, we didn't! Surprise! A tenth birthday is not easy to forget! You're a big boy now. My own big boy!"

Grandma was watching from a corner of the kitchen, as if she knew the conversation was painful for her grandson.

"Did you like your gift?" his father asked.

"He doesn't have it yet, you idiot!" his mother growled in a low voice. She tried to cover up for her husband's mistake. "I arranged it with Grandma, Arthur, dear. Tomorrow you will go into town with her and you can choose whatever present you want."

"Not too expensive, though!" added his father.

"Francis!" growled Arthur's mother.

"I—I was joking!" his father mumbled.

Arthur sat like a stone, holding the receiver to his ear.

"Okay, well, we'll let you go, Son, because the telephone isn't free and we can't let your mother go on and on."

Through the telephone it was possible to hear his mother smack his father on the head.

"So good-bye, Son, and once more"—his parents began to sing together—"Happy birthday to you!"

Arthur hung up, almost without emotion. It occurred to him that there was more life at the end of his bamboo pole than at the end of this telephone line.

He looked at his dog, sitting expectantly in front of him, awaiting the news.

"It wasn't the president of the water company," said Arthur. He suddenly felt a real moment of loneliness—a hole inside that was round and dark.

Alfred offered his ball one more time, as a way of changing the subject, but a little song called their attention away from their sad thoughts.

"Happy birthday!" Grandma sang in a full, happy voice. She appeared from the kitchen, carrying a large chocolate cake on a platter, ten proud candles on top. To the rhythm of Alfred's barking—he couldn't stand for people to sing without him—she entered the room and placed the cake in front of Arthur.

His face lit up. Grandma laid two small presents alongside the cake as she finished the song.

Arthur threw his arms around his grandmother. "You are the most beautiful and the most fabulous grandmother ever!" he cried wholeheartedly.

"And you are the sweetest grandson ever. Go ahead, blow out the candles!"

Arthur took a deep breath, then stopped.

"It's too beautiful. Let them burn a little longer. Let's open the presents first!"

"If you want to," Grandma relented, amused. "That one is from Alfred."

"It's very nice of you to have thought of me, Alfred!" said Arthur with some astonishment.

"Well, have you ever forgotten his birthday?" Grandma asked.

Arthur smiled at that and opened the little package.

It was a brand-new tennis ball! He was dumbfounded.

"Wow! We've never had a brand-new one. It's awesome!"

Alfred barked, ready to play. Arthur prepared to throw the ball, but his grandmother intervened. "If you could please wait until you are outside to play ball, I would really appreciate it!" she said.

Arthur nodded, and hid the ball behind his back, between two couch cushions. He opened the next package.

"And that one is from me," Grandma said.

It was a miniature racing car with a tiny key on the side for winding up the spring that served as a motor.

"It's magnificent!" Arthur cried. He immediately wound up the little car and placed it on the floor. With a few growls to simulate the rumbling of a motor, he released the car, which shot across the living room, followed closely by Alfred.

The car ricocheted several times and ended up shaking off the dog by sliding under a chair and out the other side.

Arthur roared with laughter.

"I think he prefers the car to the ball!"

The car ended up against the front door, with Alfred still scrabbling under the chair looking for it.

Arthur looked at his cake again, but still did not want to blow out the candles.

"How did you make a cake? I thought the oven was broken," Arthur asked.

"Mrs. Rosenberg let me use her oven, plus a few of her utensils. She kept the cake at her store and that's the errand I was doing while you were buying all those straws."

"It's wonderful," said Arthur, who could not take his eyes off it. "It's just a little too big for only three of us," he added sadly.

"Don't be angry at your parents, Arthur. They're doing the best they can. I am sure that as soon as your father finds a job, everything will be all right."

"They missed my birthday other years, too. I don't think a new job is going to change anything," Arthur said. Unfortunately, there was nothing Grandma could say or do to prove him wrong.

Arthur prepared to blow out the candles.

"First make a wish," his grandmother suggested.

Arthur did not have to think for very long.

"I wish that on my next birthday . . . Grandpa will be here to share it with me."

It was hard for Grandma to hold back a tear. She touched her grandson's face.

"I hope that your wish will come true, Arthur," she said. "Go on now, blow them out, unless you want to eat a cake covered with wax!"

As Arthur took a deep breath, Alfred found the little car, squeezed next to the front door. But a menacing shadow loomed at the window—so menacing that the dog did not dare get close enough to pick up the toy.

The shadow approached and opened the door, causing a gust of air to swoop through and blow out the candles at the very moment that Arthur was preparing to do so.

The silhouette advanced with slow, loud footsteps toward the living room. Frozen with fear, Grandma and Arthur stayed very still.

The visitor finally moved into the light. He was about fifty years old, an imposing figure with an emaciated face that was unwelcoming, both up close and from afar.

The man removed his hat and smiled a smile that seemed to hurt his face. "Have I arrived at a good time?" he asked.

Grandma recognized him. It was the notorious Davido, owner of the no less famous Davido Corporation: Food Suppliers. This sinister man had been trying to steal Grandma's property for years. He said he wanted to use the land for his corporation, to build apartment buildings—but Arthur and Grandma knew that Davido didn't need this land. He was just being malicious because it used to belong to his family and he wanted it back, and Grandpa wasn't around anymore to stop him. Luckily, so far all of Davido's attempts to get the land had been thwarted. So far.

"No, Mr. Davido. You have not arrived at a good time. You are arriving at the worst possible time and I would be tempted to say *as usual,*" Grandma retorted fiercely. "Even a minimum of politeness requires that when you visit people without prior notice, the least you can do is ring the doorbell!"

"I did try to ring," Davido defended himself, "and I can prove it."

He smugly held up a piece of chain. "One day that bell is going to fall on someone's head," he predicted. "The next time I will blow my car horn instead. It would clearly be safer."

"I don't see any reason why there should be a next time," Grandma replied. "As for today, your visit is ill timed. We are in the midst of a family gathering."

Davido noticed the cake, with the candles all blown out.

"Oh, look at the beautiful cake! Happy birthday, my boy! So how old are you?" He quickly counted the candles. "Eight, nine, ten! My, how time flies!" he pretended to marvel. "I remember when he was that small, running around after his grandfather. How long ago was that?" he said, deliberately turning the knife in the wound.

"It was four years ago," Grandma replied with dignity.

"Four years already? Why, it seems like only yesterday!" he added with barely concealed cruelty. He searched his pockets. "If I had known it was your birthday, boy, I would have brought something, but in the meantime—" He took a candy from his pocket and offered it to Arthur. "Here you go. Happy birthday."

Grandma glanced at her grandson. Her thoughts were clear. Arthur took the candy as if it were a pearl.

"Oh, how lovely. You really shouldn't have. Besides, I already have some just like it!"

Davido controlled himself, although he was dying to scold this impertinent youngster.

"I also have something for you," he said vengefully to Arthur's grandmother.

Grandma cut him off. "Mr. Davido, I don't need anything from you except the chance to spend this afternoon alone with my grandson. So whatever the purpose of your visit may be, I would ask you to please leave this house, where you are most certainly not welcome, immediately."

Despite her polite tone of voice, Grandma left no doubt as to the content of her message.

Davido was oblivious. He had found what he was looking for in his pockets.

"Ah! Here it is!" he said, producing from his pocket a paper neatly folded in quarters. "Since the mailman only comes to your house once a week, I made a small detour in order to save you from having to wait. Some news it's better to have as quickly as possible," he explained with false concern.

He handed the paper to Grandma, who took it and reached for her glasses.

"It's a form stating the expiration of your deed of ownership for this property due to nonpayment of taxes," he said. "It comes directly from the governor's office."

Grandma began to read, her expression already annoyed.

"It had to be taken care of personally," Davido noted. "This matter has gone on for too long."

Arthur did not need to read the document in order to shoot the awful man a poisonous look.

Davido smiled like a snake. "The paper terminates your deed of ownership of this property as of today, and at the same time validates *my* deed of ownership. I suppose that explains why I feel so at home here!" He chuckled evilly.

"But rest assured," he added, "I am not throwing you out tonight, treating you the way you treat me. I will give you time to gather your things."

Grandma awaited the worst.

"I am giving you seventy-two hours," Davido said. "In the meanwhile, please . . . make yourselves at home in my house," he concluded maliciously.

If Arthur could have thrown a dagger with a look, Davido

would have been a goner.

As for Grandma, she seemed strangely calm. She methodically reread the last paragraph of the letter before saying, "I see a bit of a problem here."

Davido twitched, uneasy.

"Oh, really? What problem?"

"Your good friend the governor forgot just one thing in his eagerness to be of service to you."

"What is it?" Davido asked, too casually.

"He forgot . . . to sign it."

Grandma handed him back the paper.

Davido was speechless. Gone were the nice words, the malevolent gestures. He stood holding the paper in front of him, mouth opening and closing like a carp.

Arthur restrained himself from jumping for joy. That would give Davido too much importance.

"So you are still here, in *my* house," Grandma continued, "until you can prove otherwise. And since I do not possess your legendary tact, I am giving you only ten seconds to get out before I call the police."

Davido searched for a clever parting remark, but he couldn't think of one.

Arthur picked up the phone.

"You know how to count to ten, don't you?" the boy asked him.

"You—you are going to regret your insolence! Believe me!"

Davido threatened, backing out of the room.

He turned on his heels and slammed the front door behind him with such force that his predictions came true and the doorbell fell on his head. Half senseless, blinded with pain, he blundered into the wooden column, missed the step, and fell right into the gravel.

Finally he reached his car, slammed the door on his jacket, and took off in a cloud of dust.

The sky looked as if it had been painted orange. As for the sun, it seemed to be trying to roll along the hill, as it did in the marvelous engraving that Arthur caressed with the tips of his fingers. The scene was an African savannah, bathed in the light of the end of day. You could almost feel the heat.

Arthur was in his bed, the smooth headboard smelling of apples, with a large leather book on his knees. He had chosen one of his grandfather's books, as he did every night, to accompany him to the land of dreams. He was especially excited about this one because it had been hidden behind all the others and he'd never seen it before.

Grandma sat down next to him and beamed at the sight of the engraving.

"Every night we witnessed this marvelous spectacle. And it was precisely in this setting that your mother was born," Grandma recounted as Arthur drank in her words. "While I was giving birth in a tent your grandfather was outside painting this landscape for me."

Arthur smiled.

"Tell me again what you were doing in Africa," he asked.

"I was a nurse, and your grandfather was an engineer. He built bridges, tunnels, roads. That is where we met. We were both there because we wanted to help and to learn more about the marvelous people of Africa."

Arthur carefully turned the page and moved to the next one. It was a drawing in color of an African tribe in full official dress, loaded down with necklaces and amulets. All the people were long and thin. They looked like distant cousins of giraffes, with the same strange gracefulness.

"Who are *they*?" asked Arthur, fascinated.

"The Bogo-Matassalai," his grandma answered. "Your grandfather was tied to them in friendship and to their incredible history."

That was more than enough to excite Arthur's curiosity. "Really? What history?"

"Not tonight, Arthur. Maybe tomorrow," said Grandma, who was already very tired.

"Come on! Please, Grandma!" Arthur pleaded.

"I still have to straighten up the kitchen," Grandma protested. But Arthur was shrewder than her fatigue.

"Please, just five minutes . . . it's my *birthday*!" he said in a voice that could charm a cobra.

Once again, Grandma couldn't resist.

"All right. One minute, no more," she conceded.

"No more!" swore Arthur with a grin.

Grandma made herself more comfortable, and her grandson followed suit.

"The Bogo-Matassalai were very tall. There wasn't one adult who was less than seven feet tall. Life is not easy when you are that tall, but they believed that nature made each of them that way and that somewhere there were others who would complement them—a brother that would bring you what you do not have, and vice versa."

Arthur was captivated. Grandma felt herself carried away along with her audience.

"The Chinese call that yin and yang. The Bogo-Matassalai gave it the name 'brother-nature.' And for centuries, they searched for their other half, those who would finally bring them balance."

"Did they find them?" asked Arthur immediately, too eager to leave any time for suspense in the narrative.

"After more than three hundred years of searching throughout all the nations of Africa . . . yes," Grandma confirmed. "They found a tribe that was viewed by many as an object of scorn. This tribe lived right next to the Bogo-Matassalai—only a few feet away, to be precise."

"How is that possible?" marveled Arthur.

"This tribe was called the Minimoys and all of its people measured . . . barely three quarters of an inch tall!"

Grandma turned the page and they found a picture of the famous miniature tribe, posing in the shade of a dandelion.

Arthur was amazed. He had never had an inkling of these wonderful stories. Grandpa had always preferred tales of engineering accomplishments. Arthur flipped from one page to the other, studying the difference in size.

"And—they got along well?" he asked.

"Marvelously!" Grandma assured him. "Each helped to do the work the other could not do. If one was cutting down a tree, the other would exterminate the insects inside it. The extremely large and the extremely small were made for each other. Together, they had a unique and total vision of the world that surrounded them."

Arthur was fascinated. He turned the next page and his gaze fell on a tiny creature that made his heart do a somersault. Two large blue eyes under rebellious red bangs stared back at him with a look that was as mischievous as a young fox, with a small smile that could melt even the hardest heart.

Arthur did not yet realize that he had fallen in love. For the moment, he only felt a glowing warmth in his stomach. Grandma watched him out of the corner of her eye, delighted to be witnessing this magical moment.

Arthur cleared his throat a few times and finally managed to say a few words.

"Who—who—who is this?" he stammered.

"That is Princess Selenia, the daughter of the king of the

Minimoys," Grandma replied. "At least, that is what your grandfather told me. He drew this right before he disappeared. He was always talking about the Minimoys, even long after we left Africa."

"She's beautiful," Arthur blurted out, before getting a hold of himself. "That is, what I meant to say is—very nice—the story, I mean. It's incredible!"

"Your grandfather was an honorary member of the Bogo-Matassalai tribe. He did a great deal for them: he built wells, irrigation systems, dams. He even taught them and the Minimoys how to use mirrors to communicate with each other and to transport energy," Grandma said proudly. "When it came time for us to depart, in order to thank him, they gave him a bag full of rubies, each one bigger than the next."

"Wow!" Arthur exclaimed.

"But your grandfather didn't know what to do with this treasure. He really wanted something very different," Grandma confided. "He wanted the secret that would make it possible for him to visit the Minimoys."

Arthur was mesmerized. He looked first at the drawing of Princess Selenia, then at his grandma.

"And . . . they gave it to him?" he asked, as nonchalantly as possible, although he felt as if the answer could change his life.

"I never found out," Grandma answered. "The war had started, so I returned home to be an army nurse, while your grandfather enlisted to fight in Africa throughout the war. For six years I had no news from him," she said. "Your mother and I were convinced that we would never see him again. As brave as he was, there was a good chance he had died in combat.

"And then, one day, I received a letter with a photo of this house, asking us to come live here with him!"

"And then?" asked Arthur excitedly.

"Then . . . I fainted! It was a bit too much, all at once!" Grandma confessed.

Arthur burst out laughing, imagining his grandmother with all four limbs in the air, a letter clutched in her hand.

"And then what did you do?"

"I came here. And here we stayed!" she said happily.

"Grandpa was very strong, wasn't he?" Arthur asked.

Grandma stood up and closed the book. "Yes, and I am most certainly too weak! The minute is up. Time for bed!"

She pulled down the covers so that Arthur could slide his legs in.

"I would like to find the Minimoys, too," he added, pulling the blanket right up to his chin. "If Grandpa returns someday, do you think he will tell me the secret?"

"If you are a good boy and you do as I say, I will ask him for you."

Arthur hugged her.

"Thank you, Grandma. I knew I could count on you!"

"Now, go to sleep!" she said firmly.

Arthur turned around and threw himself on his pillow,

pretending to be asleep already.

Grandma kissed him affectionately, picked up the book, and turned off the light, leaving Arthur to his dreams of Selenia. She quietly entered her husband's study, avoiding the squeaky floorboards, and returned the precious book to its place. Then she stood for a moment before the portrait of her husband.

She let out a sigh that seemed enormous in the quiet of the night.

"We miss you, Archibald," she confessed. "We really miss you very much."

CHAPTER

3

The garage door was so heavy that opening it was like opening the drawbridge of a castle, and it always took Arthur a few seconds to recover.

He got down on his knees and took his racing car out of the garage. Eight hundred horsepower in only three inches! All it took was imagination, and that was something Arthur never lacked.

He put his finger on the car and rolled it, adding a soundtrack of growls, vrooms, and other noises worthy of a Ferrari. He also lent his voice to the two drivers that he imagined on board, and to their boss, who was guiding them from afar.

"Gentlemen, I want a complete report on our worldwide irrigation system," he said, cupping his hands as if talking through a megaphone.

"Right, chief!" he replied, pretending to be the driver.

"And be careful with this new car! It is extremely powerful!" added the boss.

"Okay, chief! Don't worry," the driver assured him as he left the parking space and drove deep into the garden grass.

Grandma pushed open the front door. She was carrying a large basket full of wet laundry to the end of the garden to hang on the clothesline.

Arthur steered his car as it descended into the ditch and then chugged alongside the impressive irrigation system.

"Patrol car to central. Everything appears to be in order," the driver reported.

But the patrol spoke too soon. All at once an enormous— and brand-new—tennis ball loomed out of nowhere, completely blocking the passage.

"Oh, no! Directly ahead! It's a disaster!"

"Patrol, what's happening? Report!" cried the chief, who could see nothing from his office.

"It's a landslide! No, it's not a landslide! It's a trap! It's Bigfoot!"

Alfred had just put his nose against the other side of the tennis ball and was wagging his tail as hard as he could.

"Central to patrol. Be careful of that tail; it's a dangerous weapon!" warned the boss.

"Don't worry, chief. He seems calm for the moment. We'll take advantage of that to clear the road. Send in the crane!"

Arthur's arm was immediately transformed into a mechanical crane, with all the right accompanying noises. After a few maneuvers, Arthur's hand-claw succeeded in catching the ball.

"Ejection!" cried the driver.

Arthur's arm extended and threw the ball as far as possible. Not surprisingly, "Bigfoot" ran right after it.

"The road is clear and we have gotten rid of Bigfoot!" the driver proudly announced.

"Well done, patrol!" said the chief. "Continue with your mission."

Grandma, meanwhile, had continued on *her* mission as far as the second clothesline, where she began to hang the sheets.

Far in the distance, on the top of the hill, a small cloud of dust signaled the arrival of a car.

But it was not the day for the mailman or for the milkman.

"Now what is it?" Grandma worried.

Arthur, unaware of the approaching vehicle, was still on patrol, where a new drama was taking place. Bigfoot had returned. His paws were on the side of the trench, the ball in his mouth, ready to be released.

Inside the car there was chaos.

"Oh, no! We are doomed!" cried the assistant driver.

"Never!" the driver decreed in Arthur's most heroic voice. Arthur furiously wound the key on the side of the car.

Bigfoot dropped his bomb into the trench.

"Hurry," begged the assistant, "or we are all going to die!"

The ball rolled along the trench toward them. Arthur pointed the car in the direction for escape.

"Banzai!" he yelled, even though the Japanese expression was not exactly appropriate for the situation.

The car leaped forward, propelled by the wind from the ball that was hurtling toward it. The racing car cut neatly across its path, like a fighter plane, shooting swiftly out of harm's way. The ball rolled off into the distance, but, unfortunately, the car was now on a collision course with the side of the trench, which appeared to be an impassable wall.

"We're doooooooooomed," moaned the assistant.

"Hang on!" replied Arthur, the courageous driver.

The racing car arrived at the foot of the wall and shot up it, almost vertically. It flew through the air, landing on the ground in a magnificent series of spins before finally rolling to a stop.

The chain of events had been sublime, almost perfect.

Arthur was as proud as a peacock who'd invented the wheel.

"Well done," said the assistant, exhausted.

"It was nothing, my boy!" replied Arthur with the nonchalance of an old veteran.

A giant shadow suddenly loomed over the little racing car— that of a much bigger racing car, belonging to the sinister Davido. The larger car rolled to a stop, leaving Arthur's car trapped underneath. Through the windshield, Davido looked very pleased with himself.

Bigfoot/Alfred trotted up with his toy again, but from

Arthur's expression he could tell that this was not the best time for games. With a small whine, he dropped the ball, which rolled to the end of the asphalt, crossed under the real car, and came to a stop directly under Davido's foot as he stepped out of the vehicle.

The result was unexpected. Davido stepped on the ball, slipped, fell, and found his arms and legs pinwheeling in the air.

Arthur was on the ground, too, but that's because he was laughing so hard.

"Patrol to central! Bigfoot has just claimed another victim!" announced the driver.

Alfred barked and wagged his tail.

Davido scrambled up as best he could and brushed himself off. Angrily, he grabbed the ball and threw it as far as possible. A tearing sound ripped through the silence and, at the same time, through the underarm seam of his jacket.

The ball landed in the water tank on the garage.

Furious about the damage to his jacket but satisfied with his throw, Davido rubbed his hands together.

"Your turn, 'central'!" he said to Arthur vengefully.

Arthur just looked at him without saying anything.

Davido spun on his heel and headed toward the end of the garden, where Grandma had just hung one of the sheets lengthwise across the clothesline and was turning to get another from her basket.

She found herself face-to-face with Davido.

"You startled me!" Grandma scolded.

"I am so sorry," said Davido, obviously lying. "Spring cleaning? Do you need a hand?"

"No, thank you. What do you want now?" asked the old lady.

"I wanted to apologize. I made a mistake the other evening and I came to make amends," he said slyly.

Once again, Davido whisked a piece of paper out of his pocket and flourished it under Grandma's nose.

"Here, it is fixed! Now the paper is properly signed." He took a clothespin and hung the paper on the line.

"You didn't waste any time," Grandma conceded, sick to her stomach.

"Oh, it was a lucky coincidence," he said. "I was going to church, like I do every Sunday morning, and who should I meet there but the governor!"

"You go to church on Sunday? That's funny, I've never seen you there," Grandma replied implacably.

"I usually stay in the back, out of humility. I was surprised myself not to see you there this morning," he answered. "On the other hand, I did run into the mayor, who confirmed my deed of sale."

Davido took out a new letter that he pinned to the clothesline next to the previous one.

"I also ran into the notary, and he validated the purchase," he said, hanging up yet another letter. "Moreover, the banker and his charming wife have hereby transferred your debt on the property to me." A fourth letter was pinned next to the others.

Unnoticed by the adults, Arthur had begun to climb up the north side of the water tank.

Alfred was watching from below. He did not look very happy about the situation.

Davido continued to hang up letters. He was already on the ninth.

"The surveyor, who authenticated the property lines," he continued relentlessly. "And, finally, the police commissioner, who countersigned the notice for your eviction within seventy-two hours."

He proudly hung up the tenth and last letter.

"That makes ten! My lucky number!" he added with sadistic glee.

Grandma was vexed and speechless.

"There. So, unless your husband returns to do his taxes or you settle your debts within the next seventy-two hours, this house will be mine."

"You have no heart, Mr. Davido," Grandma finally managed.

"Not true! I have a rather generous nature. That is why I have previously offered you a good sum for this miserable property! But you wouldn't hear of it!"

"The house has never been for sale, Mr. Davido!" Grandma

reminded him for the hundredth time.

"See what a bad attitude you have," he replied.

Arthur balanced himself on the edge of the large tank, which was half full of water. The tennis ball floated peacefully on the surface.

Arthur imagined himself as an acrobat. He squeezed his legs around the wooden edge and reached out for the ball.

Alfred began to whine. It's funny how animals can sense an impending drama.

And in fact—there was a *crack*. A small one. Almost ridiculous, but enough to send Arthur plummeting into the tank with an enormous splash.

Alfred trotted off, his tail between his legs.

"Why do you want this tiny piece of land and this 'miserable' house so much?" Grandma inquired acidly.

"I plan to build apartments here, as you know. And I want it for sentimental reasons. This land belonged to my parents," the businessman replied coldly.

"I know. It was your parents who generously offered it to my husband for all of the services he had done for the region. Do you really want to violate the wishes of your late parents?" Grandma questioned.

Davido was clearly ill at ease.

"Late! That's a good word. They are *late*, just like your husband is late, and they left me all alone!" Davido said edgily.

"Your parents did not abandon you. They died during the war," Grandma corrected.

"The result was the same!" he shouted. "They left me alone, and so it is alone that I intend to conduct my business! And if your husband has not paid his debt by noon three days from now, I shall be obliged to evict you, whether your laundry is dry or not!"

Davido lifted his chin, turned around, and came face-to-face with Arthur, who was standing there drenched from head to foot. The businessman clucked disapprovingly, sounding rather like a turkey when it finds out that it has been invited for Christmas dinner.

"You should hang him out to dry, too!" he added in a mocking tone.

Arthur glared at him.

Davido headed off toward his car, still clucking. He slammed the door, turned on the engine, and let the wheels spin, kicking up a thick cloud of dust. The little racing car was knocked out of the car's shadow, somersaulted a few times, rolled backward a bit, and fell into the opening of a drainpipe.

Davido took off, followed by his thick cloud, which settled over all the clothes that were hung out to dry. Arthur and his grandmother were also coated with the yellow dust.

Exhausted, Grandma sat down on the front steps.

"My poor Arthur. This time I don't think I will be able to stop that greedy Davido," she said sadly.

"Didn't he used to be a friend of Grandfather's?" Arthur asked, sitting down next to his grandmother.

"At first he was," she admitted. "When we arrived from Africa, Davido couldn't tear himself away from your grandfather! He stuck to him like glue. But Archibald never really trusted him, and he was right."

"Will we have to leave the house?" asked Arthur worriedly.

"I am afraid so," the poor woman admitted.

Arthur was overwhelmed by the news. How could he live without this garden, the place for all his games, his sole refuge? And where would his grandmother go? He had to find a solution.

"What about the treasure? The rubies offered by the Bogo-Matassalai?" he asked, full of hope. "What did Grandpa do with all that? Couldn't we use it to save the house?"

Grandma pointed to the garden.

"It's out there, somewhere."

"You mean—the treasure is hidden in the garden?" Arthur asked.

"That's what your grandfather told me. So well hidden that even though I have dug everywhere, I have never been able to find it," Grandma confessed.

Arthur was already on his feet. He grabbed the little shovel leaning against the wall and ran to the middle of the garden.

"What are you doing, dear?" Grandma asked.

"Do you think I'm just going to sit back for seventy-two hours while that vulture steals our house from us?" replied Arthur. "I am going to find that treasure!"

Arthur energetically jammed his shovel into a small patch of grass and began to dig like a bulldozer. Alfred was delighted with this new game, barking encouragement and running in circles.

Grandma could not help smiling.

"He is the spitting image of his grandfather," she remarked. Brushing off her knees, she noticed she was covered with dust. She got up with difficulty and went back into the house to change her clothes.

A few drops of sweat had beaded on Arthur's forehead. He was already digging his third hole.

Suddenly, his shovel hit something hard. Alfred barked, as if he could sense something. Arthur got down on his knees and continued digging with his hands.

"If you've found the treasure, you really are the best dog in the world!" Arthur said to his dog, who was wagging his tail almost hard enough to take flight.

Arthur burrowed into the ground a little more, brushed his hand along the object, and pulled it out of the ground.

It was a bone.

"That's not the kind of treasure we are looking for, you wild animal! We need a real treasure!" exclaimed Arthur, throwing away the bone and starting to dig a new hole.

The door to Archibald's office opened slowly. Grandma took a few steps in and looked around at the space. It was a real museum. She carefully took down one of the African masks and looked at it for a moment.

Her eye caught that of her husband, gazing down from his portrait.

"I am sorry, Archibald, but we no longer have a choice," she said bitterly.

She lowered her eyes and left the room, the African mask under her arm.

Arthur reached the bottom of a new hole, where he found yet another bone. Alfred pretended to be surprised, too.

"Did you rob a butcher shop or something?" Arthur asked him in an exasperated voice.

Grandma came out of the house with the mask, which was carefully wrapped in paper so her grandson wouldn't see it.

"I—I have to do some shopping in town," she said.

"Do you want me to go with you?" Arthur asked politely.

"No, no! Continue to dig, that's a good idea! After all, you never know." She quickly got into the old Chevrolet and started the engine. "I won't be long!" she cried over the noisy motor.

The pickup took off in a cloud of dust.

Arthur was somewhat perplexed by the sudden departure of his grandmother, but duty called. He returned to digging.

CHAPTER
4

The pickup came to a halt in the center of a large city. This was nothing like the charming village where Grandma regularly did her shopping. This was a real metropolis, several miles away. Here the shops displayed their wares to hundreds of curious shoppers. Here everything seemed prettier, bigger, richer.

Grandmother held her head high, determined not to let the big city make her feel small.

She stopped in front of a shop and took a business card out of her purse. Verifying that she was at the correct address, she entered the small antique shop. At least, it appeared small from the window, but inside it seemed to go on forever. Hundreds of objects and pieces of furniture of all kinds and from all periods were piled high. Fake Roman gods made of stone stood next to genuine Mexican saints made of wood. Fossils spilled out from porcelain vases like an invitation to a massacre. Old books bound in leather leaned next to simple paperbacks and seemed to coexist peacefully despite their differences in age and language.

Behind the counter, the owner was reading the newspaper. Part antique dealer, part pawnbroker, nothing about the man inspired trust. As Grandma approached, wading through the junk, he did not even bother to look up.

"Can I help you?" he said automatically.

Grandma jumped at the sound of his voice. "Excuse me," she said, nervously showing him the business card. "You were at our house some time ago, and you mentioned—if one day we wanted to sell some of our old furniture or objects . . ."

"Yes, that is possible," he replied vaguely.

"Well, I have . . . an object that comes from a personal collection," Grandma stammered. "I would like to know if it has any value."

The man sighed as he put down his newspaper and slipped off his glasses. He folded the paper and took the mask into his hands.

"What is this?" he asked. "A carnival mask?"

"No. It is an African mask. This one belonged to the chief of the Bogo-Matassalai tribe. It is unique," said Grandma with pride and respect, hiding her resentment at having to let go of such a beautiful artifact.

The antiques dealer seemed interested. He studied it for a minute.

"A dollar fifty," he said with assurance.

Grandma gasped.

"A dollar fifty? That's impossible! This is a unique item, of inestimable value, which—"

The antiques dealer did not give her time to finish her sentence.

"Fine. A dollar eighty. That's the best I can do," he said. "This type of exotic item doesn't sell very well right now. People want practical items, concrete, modern. I'm sorry. Do you have anything else?"

Grandma was bewildered.

"If—perhaps . . . I don't know," she stammered. "What *is* selling well right now?"

The antiques dealer finally smiled.

"Without question . . . books!"

Arthur threw aside his shovel, discouraged. Alfred, on the other hand, was perfectly happy with his pile of bones. The garden now resembled a minefield.

Arthur filled a large glass of water from the kitchen faucet and drank it down in one gulp. Then he went to Grandma's room, took down the key hanging on the bedpost, and headed for his grandfather's study.

He entered slowly, lit one of the beautiful Venetian lamps, and sat down at the desk.

For a long time, he stared at the portrait of his grandfather who, despite his smile, remained silent.

"I can't find it, Grandpa," Arthur said sadly. "I can't believe that you hid this treasure in the garden without leaving word anywhere, any sign or hint, anything that would help us to find it. It doesn't seem like you."

The painting continued to smile. Archibald was still silent.

"Unless . . . maybe I haven't looked for it correctly?" Arthur grabbed the first book above the desk and began to leaf through it.

Several hours passed. Arthur had gone through almost all the books, piling them high on the desk. Night had finally fallen and he ached all over.

He finished with the book that his grandmother had read to him the night before. Once again he saw the drawing of the Bogo-Matassalai, then that of the Minimoys. He skipped a few pages and came across a much more disturbing drawing.

It was an evil shadow, like an emaciated body, only vaguely human-looking. The face had no expression and only two red points for eyes.

A shiver ran through Arthur from head to foot. It was by far the ugliest thing he had ever seen in his short life.

Under the drawing of the shadowy creature was handwritten: Maltazard the Cursed.

Outside, in the darkness, two yellow eyes were trailing their way along the hilltops. It was an ordinary van, piercing the night with its powerful headlights. Guided by the full moon, the vehicle followed the winding road that led to the house.

Arthur quickly turned the pages, trying to forget the

nightmare vision of Maltazard as fast as possible. He found the drawing of Selenia, the Minimoy princess.

This made him feel much better. He touched the drawing with the tips of his fingers and noticed that it was only loosely glued down. Carefully he slid a thumbnail underneath and detached it, so that he could contemplate the princess a little closer.

"I hope that I will have the honor of meeting you one day, princess," he whispered to it.

Alfred sighed pointedly.

"Jealous," Arthur said with a grin. The dog did not deign to reply.

Just then they heard a vehicle rolling up and parking outside. Arthur thought it was probably Grandma, returning at last.

He absentmindedly turned over the drawing and discovered another one on the back. The boy's face lit up.

"I *knew* he had left a sign!" he yelped joyously.

The drawing was a map—to the land of the Minimoys! It was sketched in pencil, rather poorly drawn or perhaps done very quickly.

There was also a sentence that Arthur read out loud: "'To find the country of the Minimoys, trust in Shakespeare.' Who is that?" he asked himself. He stood up and turned the map in all directions. Something about the location seemed oddly familiar.

"So the entrance to the Minimoys' world is here, next to this tree. . . . Wait, I know this tree! And here's the house, and that way's north. . . ."

He ran over to the window and threw it open.

The map corresponded exactly to the view that he had from the study window.

"The large oak tree, the garden gnome, the moon, everything is there!" exclaimed Arthur. "We found it, Alfred! We found it! The Minimoys are in the garden! I *know* they will be able to help us! I bet Grandpa told them where the treasure is!"

He leaped up and down with joy, like a kangaroo that had swallowed a spring.

He turned toward the door, eager to share his discovery with his grandmother, but instead he ran straight into the antiques dealer with his two movers.

"Careful, young man, careful!" said the antiques dealer, deftly steering him aside.

Despite his surprise, Arthur had instinctively hidden the drawing behind his back. The man went out into the corridor again to speak to Grandma.

"It is open, ma'am. Open and occupied!"

Grandma came out of her room and joined them.

"Arthur, I have told you that I do not want you playing in this room," she said nervously. She caught Arthur by the arm and pulled him back so the antiques dealer could pass.

"Please excuse him. Go on in, please," Grandma said politely.

The antiques dealer glanced around the study, like a vulture checking that a corpse is really dead.

"There, now *this* is interesting," he said, with a calculating smile.

Arthur discreetly tugged his grandmother's sleeve.

"Grandma? Who are these people?" he whispered in a worried voice.

She wrung her hands. "It's—the man is here to . . . appraise your grandfather's things. If we have to move, we might as well get rid of all this old stuff," she said, trying to convince herself as much as him.

Arthur was dumbfounded.

"You're going to sell Grandpa's things?"

Grandma paused—a brief hesitation, a moment of remorse—then let out a long sigh. "I am afraid that we don't have a choice, Arthur."

"Of course we do, of course we have a choice!" cried the boy, waving his drawing. "Look! This will help us find the treasure! Grandpa left us a message! It's all here on the map!"

Grandma didn't understand.

"Where did you get that?"

"It was under our noses all the time, in that book you read me last night!" Arthur explained.

But Grandma was too tired to listen to fantasies. "Put that back where it belongs immediately," she said severely.

"Grandma, you don't understand! It's a map to find the

Minimoys! They are out there, somewhere in the garden. Grandpa must have brought them back from Africa with him. And if we can find them, I am sure that they will be able to guide us to Grandfather's treasure. We are saved!" he declared.

Grandma wondered how her grandson could have gone mad in such a short time.

"This is no time to play, Arthur. Put that back where it belongs and keep quiet."

"You don't believe me. You think Grandpa was just telling stories!"

Grandma placed her hand on his shoulder. "Arthur, you're a big boy now, aren't you? Do you really believe that the garden is full of tiny elves who are just waiting for you to visit so they can give you a bag of rubies?"

The antiques dealer whipped his head around, like a fox catching a scent.

"Excuse me?" he asked politely.

"No, nothing . . . I was speaking to my grandson," Grandma answered.

The antiques dealer continued his inspection as if nothing had happened, but his ears were alert. "Of course, if you also have jewelry, we buy that as well," he said, the way you would toss bread out to pigeons.

"Unfortunately, there are no jewels on the horizon!" Grandma answered firmly. Once again she turned toward Arthur. "Now put that drawing back where it belongs, and fast!"

The boy obeyed reluctantly, while the antiques dealer read the banner hanging above the desk like a birthday garland:

"'Words often hide other words. William S.'" The antiques dealer seemed amused by this enigmatic sentence. "S—for Socrates?" he asked.

"No, S for Shakespeare. William Shakespeare," Grandma said.

This rang a bell in Arthur's head and he slid out the drawing again. He reread the phrase on the back: *To find the country of the Minimoys, trust in Shakespeare.*

"Ah? . . . Well, I was close," exclaimed the antiques dealer.

Grandma threw him a sharp look. "Yes. Only two thousand years out of the neighborhood."

"How quickly time flies!" he said, trying to hide his ignorance.

"You are right, time does fly, so please hurry up and make your selection before I change my mind," Grandma answered.

"We'll take everything!" The antiques dealer gestured to his men.

Grandmother was speechless. Arthur started to slide the drawing into the back pocket of his pants, but he wasn't quick enough.

"Tsk, tsk! No cheating, my boy!" said the antiques dealer with an inquisitor's smile. "I said we will take . . . everything!"

Regretfully, Arthur took the paper out of his pocket and handed it to the antiques dealer, who quickly placed it in his jacket pocket.

"That's right, my boy," said the dealer slyly, patting him on the head.

The movers began their work. Furniture and objects disappeared with frightening speed, under the tearful eyes of the poor woman who was watching years of memories slip away. The scene was as sad as a forest going up in smoke.

One of the movers grabbed the portrait of Archibald. Grandma stopped him as he passed, seizing the edge of the frame.

"No. Not that," she said firmly.

"He said everything!" the mover protested.

Grandma began to yell. "And I say everything *except* the portrait of my husband!"

The employee looked at his boss, who decided this might not be worth the trouble.

"Simon! Leave her husband alone! He didn't do anything to you!" joked the antiques dealer. He took the painting and held it out to the old lady.

"Here. Take it, ma'am. A gift on the house!" he had the nerve to add.

The back door of the van was opened and the two movers piled in the last boxes. Arthur lay stretched out on the living room couch, watching his grandmother at the doorway as she finished her negotiations with the antiques dealer.

The man counted out the bills and put the pile in her hand.

"There you go. Three hundred dollars in cash!" he announced proudly.

"That's a small sum of money for thirty years of memories," Grandma murmured.

"It's an advance," the merchant assured her. "If I sell everything, you will have an additional sum of at least ten percent per item!"

"Marvelous!" Grandma replied ironically.

"The antiques fair takes place in ten days. If you change your mind, you can always come and get them before then," noted the antiques dealer.

"That is very kind of you," she replied.

She opened the front door to escort the antiques dealer out, and found herself face-to-face with a short man in a gray suit, accompanied by two policemen. There was no need for a detective to identify the short man as a sheriff.

"Mrs. Suchot?" the lawman asked politely, although the tone of his voice left no doubt as to the purpose of his visit.

"Yes," Grandma replied.

One of the two police officers tried to reassure her with a small, friendly wave and she realized it was Martin, her friend from outside the supermarket. The man in gray continued.

"I am Frederick Sinclair. The sheriff."

The antiques dealer could tell it was time for a quick exit.

"See you soon, ma'am. It was a pleasure doing business with you!" he said, taking off into the night.

The pile of bills that Grandma was holding in her hand caught the sheriff's eye.

"I see I came at just the right time!" he said. He pulled out a letter. "I have a notice against you demanding payment for work done on your house several years ago by one Ernest Davido. It amounts to a sum of one hundred and eighty-five dollars, to which has been added a late penalty of six percent along with the court costs. That comes to a total of two hundred and ninety dollars."

Grandma looked at her pile of banknotes and handed them over, dazed.

The sheriff grabbed them, somewhat surprised at not having to fight for them.

"May I?" he said, counting the bills with lightning speed.

Arthur watched this scene from the couch. He was neither disturbed nor astonished, simply disgusted. He understood that his grandmother had been thrust into a downward spiral from which she could not escape.

"Unless I am mistaken . . . three dollars are missing," said the sheriff.

"I don't understand—I—that should be exactly three hundred dollars!" Grandma replied with astonishment.

"Do you want to count them yourself?" he asked, with great politeness and no doubt. There was little chance that he had made a mistake. He was like an undertaker—if he tells you that his client is dead, you can count on it.

Grandma was overwhelmed. She slowly shook her head.

"No, you must be right."

In his van traveling through the night, the antiques dealer rubbed his hands together with satisfaction.

"That was a nice little deal. Well handled," he confided to his assistant, laughing. He dug his hand into his pocket. "Now let's see what that little monster was trying to hide from us."

He took out the paper that Arthur had given him so reluctantly and unfolded it with pleasure.

It was a supermarket shopping list.

CHAPTER

5

In the living room, it was Arthur's turn to unfold his paper—the drawing of Princess Selenia that he had subtly exchanged. Arthur studied the drawing as if it were his only hope.

The sheriff continued with his business. "In spite of the small sum still due, I'm afraid the law is the law. I am going to have to seize property in order to recover the missing three dollars," he announced.

Martin, the nice officer, felt obliged to intervene. "Wait!" He took out his wallet. "There . . . three dollars. Now the account is clear!" he said, handing over the money.

The sheriff shifted awkwardly.

"That's—well, this is very irregular, but . . . given the circumstances, I accept!"

Grandma was on the verge of tears, but she managed to keep her dignity.

"Thank you, officer. I—I will repay you as soon as . . . as soon as I can!"

"Don't worry about it, Mrs. S. I am sure that as soon as your husband returns, together you will find a way to pay me back," he said with great kindness.

"I'll see to it," Grandma replied.

The policeman grabbed the sheriff by the shoulder and pulled him away.

"You've done enough work for today, sir. We're leaving now."

The sheriff did not dare contradict him.

"Ma'am, my respects," he said as they walked away.

Grandma closed the door and leaned against it for a moment, stunned.

The telephone next to Arthur rang. He picked up the receiver.

"Hello? Arthur, dear? It's Mom! How are you?" whistled the voice in the receiver.

"Great! Things are great," Arthur replied sarcastically. "Grandma and me, we're just great!"

Grandma came into the living room and made signs to her grandson that clearly meant Don't tell them anything.

"What have you been up to?" his mother asked, not really paying attention.

"Straightening up!" said Arthur. "It's amazing how many useless old things one can find in a house. But, thanks to Grandma, we've thrown everything out!"

"Arthur, please, don't upset them!" Grandma whispered.

Arthur hung up the phone.

"Arthur! Did you just hang up on your mother?" Grandma asked, shocked.

"Of course not. The line disconnected," he explained, heading for the stairs.

"So where are you going? Stay here—she'll probably call you back in a minute."

Arthur stopped in the middle of the stairs and looked hard at his grandmother.

"They cut off the phone service, Grandma! Don't you see what is happening? You are caught in a trap. A trap that every hour is getting tighter and tighter. But I'm not going to let them do it. As long as I live, they will not have this house!"

Arthur had probably heard this expression in an adventure film, but he said it very well. He turned around and proudly climbed the stairs.

Grandma picked up the phone and saw that he was right—the line had gone dead.

"It's probably temporary. That happens sometimes when there's a storm," she said.

"It hasn't rained for more than a month," Arthur called down from the top of the stairs.

The doorbell rang.

"You see? That must be the repair man," Grandma reassured herself. She hurried to the door, where, indeed, and much to her surprise, a workman in uniform was waiting.

"Evening, ma'am!" said the workman, tipping the brim of his hard hat.

"Oh, you are just in time!" said Grandma. "The telephone cut off just a moment ago. I think that the least they can do is warn people about something like that, don't you?"

"I agree with you, ma'am," the technician politely conceded. "But I'm not here about the telephone. I'm from the electric company." He pointed to the badge sewn on his jacket as proof. "I have come to warn you that your electricity will be turned off soon because of lack of payment."

He pulled out an official form and handed it to her.

Arthur entered the empty study. Besides a few worthless objects, there remained only the desk, a chair, the banner, and the portrait of Grandfather.

He angrily flopped down in the chair and reread the banner, thinking it was miraculous that it had been left behind. Clearly the bit of cloth was of very little value, even if the advice that it gave was priceless.

"'Words often hide other words,'" Arthur reread out loud.

The puzzle was right there in front of him. He was sure of it.

"Help me, Grandfather. If words often hide other words, what is the secret that these words are hiding?"

The painting remained silent.

**   *   *

Grandma finished reading the blue form and gave it back to the workman.

"And . . . when will the electricity be turned off?" she asked.

"Very soon, I think!" the workman answered. At that exact moment, the lights blinked out through the entire house.

"That *was* quick," Grandma said. "Don't move. I'll go find a candle."

Upstairs, Arthur lit a match and brought it up to light a candle. He placed the candle on the desk and stepped back a few feet, in order to better see the banner, the key to the riddle.

"Now is the time to be brilliant!" he challenged himself. " 'Words . . . often . . . hide . . . other . . . words.' "

The candlelight accented the transparency of the banner and Arthur suddenly thought he caught a glimpse of something.

He took the candle in his hand, climbed up on the chair, and placed the light just behind the banner. Lit from behind, words appeared. Words hiding behind other words! Arthur grinned.

"Of course!" he exclaimed.

He ran the candle behind the banner and read the hidden message. He could almost hear the deep, hoarse voice of his grandfather, as if he were there in the room.

My dear Arthur, I was sure I could count on you and that you would see through this simple charade.

Arthur grimaced. "Not so simple," he answered his grandfather.

The message continued.

You must be close to ten years old now to be so smart. On the other hand, I'm not so smart, because if you are reading these lines, I am probably dead.

Arthur stopped for a moment, a chill running through him. Imagine his grandfather, once so alive, already dead! He could not even bring himself to think about it.

The difficult task of finishing my mission is up to you. If you agree, of course.

Arthur looked up at his grandfather's portrait. The confidence that the old man had had in him made his chest swell with pride. "I do agree, Grandfather," he said solemnly, before turning back to the message.

I expected nothing less of you, Arthur. You are worthy of being my grandson, Grandpa had written.

Arthur smiled, astonished by the old man's clairvoyance.

"Thank you," he answered.

The writing continued: *To find the land of the Minimoys, you must first know on what date the next passage will take place. There is only one opportunity each year. You must take the universal calendar that is on my desk and count the seventh moon of the year. On the night of the seventh moon, precisely at midnight, the light will open the door to the land of the Minimoys.*

Arthur couldn't believe it. Everything that he had imagined was true.

The hidden treasure, the Minimoys, and . . . Princess Selenia.

He let out a small, happy sigh, then took hold of himself and bent toward the desk to find the calendar. Fortunately, the antiques dealer had left it behind. Arthur quickly consulted it and counted the full moons.

"Four . . . five . . . six . . . seven!"

He looked at the corresponding date.

"July thirty-first. The day after my birthday! That's—that's *tonight!*" he realized with alarm.

Arthur turned toward the clock hanging on the wall. It read 10:56 PM.

"That's in one hour!" he cried, panic-stricken.

Grandma, by candlelight, finished signing the paper that the technician had amiably handed her.

"There. The pink copy is for you, the blue is for me. One for the girls, one for the boys," he tried to joke, but the humor fell flat. Grandma remained as hard as a piece of marble. He continued hurriedly, "To have the electricity reconnected, just go to the main office, weekdays between nine A.M. and six P.M.— with a check, obviously."

"Obviously," echoed Grandma, before adding with curiosity: "Tell me, why are you still working at this late hour? It's nearly midnight, isn't it?"

"Believe me, I'm not happy about it, but the head office made me," confided the employee. "They absolutely insisted that I come here this evening. They even paid me triple overtime! You'd think there was someone here that D.G.E. doesn't like!"

"D.G.E.?" Grandma inquired.

"Davido General Electric," the technician explained.

"Ah! I understand now!" Grandma sighed.

Suddenly an odd noise was heard coming from upstairs. It sounded like hammer blows.

The technician uneasily tried another joke.

"Looks like I'm not the only one working overtime tonight!"

"No. Those are our ghosts," said Grandma slyly. "The house is full of them. You should probably go, because they really can't stand uniforms."

The technician looked at himself from head to toe. No one was more in uniform than him. He smiled weakly, but, just in case, opted to leave.

"That's fine! Okay, I'll leave you alone now!" he said, backing into the garden. As soon as he reached the limit of the candle's light, he turned and ran to his car.

Grandma smiled, closed the door, and tilted her head to determine where those hammering sounds were coming from.

CHAPTER
6

Arthur was madly banging on a section of the study wall (with the help of a hammer, of course). He hoped he'd understood the next part of his grandfather's message correctly. This looked like the plank he'd said to hammer on thirty times, but Arthur was not sure what was supposed to happen after all this pounding.

"Twenty-eight . . . twenty-nine . . . and thirty!" he breathed.

The last blow was harder than the others and it made the small plank pop out of the wall. Arthur could see now that the piece of wood was mounted on a pivot. It was the door to a tiny hiding place.

Arthur slipped his hand into the small space and pulled out a piece of paper. He unfolded it and quickly read:

Bravo. You have solved the second riddle. Here is the third and last. Go to the old radiator. Turn the valve toward the right, as many turns as there are letters in your first name. Then turn it back a quarter of a turn.

Arthur squeezed under the window and knelt in front of the old radiator. He grabbed the valve and began to turn it.

"Arthur! A . . . R . . . T . . . H . . . U . . . R!" He had no time to waste. "And now I just have to turn it one quarter to the left." He paused and took a deep breath, as if preparing himself for the worst.

The worst arrived at the door. Grandma burst in and Arthur jumped.

"Now what are you doing? What was that hammering sound?" she asked, exhausted by this endless nightmare of a day.

"I—I am fixing Grandfather's radiator!" Arthur stammered. He wondered if he should show her the messages. But she didn't believe him before—what if she didn't believe him now? And wouldn't she be proud if he found the treasure all by himself? He decided he should probably keep it a secret for now.

"The radiator? In the middle of the night? And in the middle of the summer?" asked Grandma, not really fooled by his lie.

"You never know. Sometimes winter arrives without warning. You're the one who says that all the time!" Arthur replied sensibly.

"It's true, I do say that. But usually in November!" she pointed out. "I also say that it's almost midnight and therefore time for you to go to bed. And I've also told you a hundred times that I don't want you in this room!"

"Why? There's nothing left in it now," Arthur replied sadly.

Grandma realized that she no longer had any real justification, but she insisted, on principle.

"True, there are no more objects—but the memories are always here and I don't want you to disturb them," she concluded. She walked over to the calendar on the wall and tore off the page for July 31, revealing the page for August 1. The torn-off page went into a small box which was labeled THE DAYS WITHOUT YOU in black marker. The pile was rather large.

"Go on! Off to bed!"

Arthur obeyed reluctantly, while Grandma locked the study door with the key, which she put back in its place on the post of her bed. She joined her grandson in his room as he finished putting on his pajamas.

Grandma turned down his covers. The boy slid in without saying a word.

"A short story, but no more than five minutes," said Grandma gently, trying to make amends.

"No, thanks. I'm tired," Arthur replied, closing his eyes.

Grandma was a little surprised, but did not argue. She smoothed down his hair, took the candle, and went out the door, leaving the room bathed in moonlight.

As soon as the door was shut, the boy jumped up and stretched.

"You can do it, Arthur!" he said to himself. He half opened the door and listened. He could hear the sound of the shower. Grandma was taking advantage of the last few gallons of hot water.

He slipped inside her bedroom. Steam was escaping through

the partially opened bathroom door. Arthur entered quietly, using his toe to test all of the floorboards that were likely to squeak.

He arrived at the bed and reached out his arm to get the key.

Prize in hand, his eyes fixed firmly on the bathroom, he crept backward to the door.

Suddenly, he bumped into something and let out a yelp of surprise. The something was in fact some*one*: his grandma— same family as her sly grandson, only with fifty more years of experience.

"You startled me!" Arthur cried. "I—I thought you were taking a shower."

"No, I was in the living room looking for my sleeping drops," she said, holding up the little bottle of herbal medicine. "And I advise you to go back to bed as fast as you can if you don't want me to make you drink the entire bottle!"

She pulled the key out of Arthur's hands, and he went dejectedly back to his room. Grandma sighed, replaced the key on its nail, and followed him. By candlelight, she discovered the boy in bed with the sheets pulled up to his chin.

"You have to sleep now, Arthur. It is almost midnight."

"I know," said Arthur, panicked by the fact that time was passing and there wasn't anything he could do.

"I'll close your door with a key. That will help you to avoid any temptation," Grandma said kindly.

Up close, one could hear Arthur gulp with alarm. But Grandma was too far away to hear. She smiled at him, went out, and locked the door behind her.

Arthur pulled off the covers and got up right away. His sheets and his covers were already attached to one another. All he had to do was open the window and throw them out.

He climbed onto the window ledge and slid down his makeshift ladder to the ground.

Grandma placed the candle on the little night table next to her bed. The weak light still made it possible to read the time on the old alarm clock.

It was twenty-five minutes to twelve.

The little flame also helped her count her drops: Three exactly, at the bottom of a large glass of water, which she drank in a single gulp. She then refilled the glass with water in case she needed it during the night.

She blew out the candle, placed her glasses on the little table and stretched out, letting sleep overtake her.

Arthur let himself drop from his cloth rope, which was too short to reach the ground. He got to his feet and ran as fast as he could to the front door.

Alfred jumped up when he saw Arthur arrive. He, who guarded the front door so proudly, was astonished to see Arthur outside. How had his master gotten past him?

Since the front door was locked, Arthur had to wriggle through the little flap door meant for the dog. For Alfred, it was one surprise after another. There was his master, walking on all fours and using *his* door!

Almost by reflex, Arthur slid in his socks across the living room floor. The large clock was ticking and indicated the time: twenty minutes to twelve.

Climbing the stairs was easy enough but he ran into problems at his grandmother's bedroom door: she had locked it.

"Oh, no!" Arthur had only a few minutes left to think.

He peered through the keyhole to be sure that the study key was still hanging on the bedpost. It was—the only bit of good news.

"Think of something, Arthur, think of something!" he said to himself.

He stepped back, turned around, and examined everything around him very carefully, searching for a plan to grab on to. In the window above the bedroom door, he noticed that one of the panes was broken.

Arthur had an idea.

He ran down to the garage, weaving his way inside by the beam from his flashlight. He climbed on the workbench and took down one of the fishing poles carefully arranged along the wall.

Alfred jumped up once more at the sight of his master passing by with a fishing pole in his hands. The dog gave him a look that clearly said *Who on earth goes fishing at this time of night?*

Arthur found a magnet on the door of one of the kitchen cabinets. He carefully slid his small, multipurpose Swiss army knife behind the magnet and lifted it up, then attached it to the end of his fishing pole.

Without a sound, but working as quickly as possible, Arthur piled chairs on the end table in the hall until they were high enough for him to reach Grandma's window with its broken corner. He climbed very cautiously up his makeshift scaffold and slipped the fishing pole through the small hole.

The dog watched him uncomprehendingly. There were fish in Grandma's bedroom?

Arthur carefully stretched out his pole, then lowered the line with the magnet toward the key on the bedpost.

Alfred had to investigate. He got up and trotted toward the piled-up chairs, causing one of the floorboards to creak.

Startled, Arthur was thrown off balance. He clung to the window ledge, wobbling precariously. The magnet swung back and forth in the room, knocking over the small vial on the night table, which began to drip into Grandma's glass of water.

"Arthur?" Grandma said, sitting up, half asleep.

Arthur stood still, not moving even an eyelash, and prayed that Alfred would do the same.

The dog obligingly froze, except for a very slight wag of his tail.

Grandma listened to the silence. A few crickets, one or two

frogs in the garden. Nothing alarming, but this silence was too good to be true.

She reached for her glasses, not noticing the herbal sleeping drops dripping into her water. She opened her bedroom door and looked to the left, toward the stairs and Arthur's room. All she could see was the dog, sitting alone in the middle of the hall, with his tail wagging, as always.

What she didn't see was Arthur, directly behind her, high up on the chairs, his fishing pole in his hand.

"It is time for you to go to bed, too!" Grandma ordered Alfred.

Alfred slipped down the stairs, his tail between his legs. This was an order he understood.

"Why is it that nobody wants to go to sleep tonight? Is it the full moon or something?" she muttered, going back in and closing the door.

Arthur could finally breathe. It was a miracle that he had not been discovered.

Grandma took off her glasses and placed them on the night table. She took the glass of water, into which the bottle of herbal sleeping drops had emptied itself, and drank it down in one gulp, making a face.

The effect was instantaneous. Grandma fell back on the bed asleep, without even having time to turn down the covers.

Arthur continued his precarious fishing expedition, while Grandma began to snore. The magnet slowly descended toward the key and attracted it. But the bedpost seemed to disagree, clinging to its prize. Arthur frowned and yanked on the line.

The dog quietly climbed up the stairs again, wanting to know how the fishing expedition was progressing. He advanced toward Arthur, who was struggling on top of his makeshift scaffold.

Alfred stepped again on the same creaking floorboard. The foot of the end table shifted. The pile of chairs lost its fragile balance.

"Oh, NO!" Arthur yelled.

Everything collapsed like a house of cards, making an awful din. The dog took off down the stairs at high speed, barking loudly.

Arthur's head poked through the middle of a chair. The gust caused by the catastrophe had been so violent that the bedroom door swung open. Grandma had forgotten to relock it!

Arthur disentangled himself and, peering into the room, realized that his grandmother was still stretched out on her bed, snoring contentedly.

"How could she possibly have slept through all that noise?" he wondered.

He entered the bedroom, walked toward the bed, and reassured himself that his Grandma was all right. *She must be alive if she's snoring like that*, he thought. Then he noticed the overturned bottle and understood what had happened.

He took the blanket and tucked in his dear grandma, whose

face looked thirty years younger thanks to the sleep she was finally getting.

"Sweet dreams, Grandmother!" he said, before picking up the key and disappearing out the door.

CHAPTER
7

Finally in the study, Arthur lit the candle again and turned back to the old
radiator.

"One quarter turn . . . to the left," he remembered.

He grabbed the tap and turned it. A noisy mechanism rum-
bled in the wall, detaching the radiator and pushing it to the
side. Another hiding place was revealed, much larger than the
previous one—big enough to contain a large leather trunk.

Arthur pulled the dusty trunk into the middle of the room.
Inside was a magnificent copper telescope in a beautiful red
velvet case. Also included was its large wooden tripod.

Arranged above the telescope in little compartments were
five small African statues, all lined up next to each other. Five
men in ceremonial dress—five Bogo-Matassalai.

Arthur looked at his treasure with amazement. He didn't
know where to begin.

The first thing he picked up was a small key, to which was
attached a label that read: ALWAYS KEEP THIS KEY WITH YOU.

Arthur placed it securely in his pocket. Then he unfolded a parchment tucked into the side of the trunk, which turned out to contain instructions and another map, rather simply laid out around the large oak in the garden.

Apparently the garden gnome covered a hole, in which the telescope had to be inserted, upside down. Then, a rug with five points (also in the trunk) had to be unfolded, and a statuette placed on each of the points.

All of this seemed simple enough. Arthur quickly memorized the directions, then took the telescope and its tripod in his arms and left the room.

As he was crossing the living room, the clock read eleven minutes to midnight.

Only eleven minutes to go.

Despite the beautiful full moon, Arthur realized he could not see very much outside, especially in the shadow of the great oak tree. "We need some light," he said to Alfred, who was following him everywhere.

Arthur put down the telescope and headed straight for the old Chevy. He climbed in behind the steering wheel, took the keys from their hiding place under the sun visor, and tried to remember how it worked.

"Why are you looking at me like that?" he asked the dog. "I've seen Grandma do this hundreds of times! How hard can it be?"

He turned the key in the ignition. The engine spit and

coughed and spit again, unaccustomed to being awakened in the middle of the night. Arthur turned on the headlights, but the truck was not in a good position to light up the old oak tree. He would have to move it. Arthur shifted into first gear and nervously stepped on the gas, but nothing happened.

"Oh—the emergency brake, silly!" he realized.

He pulled on the handle as hard as he could and released the brake. The truck took off with a jolt. Arthur yelled and tried his best to control it as it wove and bumped around the house. The steering wheel was absolutely enormous in his hands, plus he could barely see over the dashboard. He tried his best to avoid the trees but ended up swerving into the clothes-line, and pulling down the line with all its contents.

Imagine the scene: two luminous eyes under pale white sheets, charging across the lawn, shrieking like a ghost. Is it any wonder that Alfred ran off howling? And yet, despite all the racket and the headlights sweeping the countryside, Grandma continued to sleep soundly.

The pickup ended up rolling into the tree and lurching to a halt, but it was a very old tree and could take a few bumps. The good news was that now the light from the headlights was shining directly on the garden gnome.

Arthur hurried toward the little plaster figure and uprooted it from the ground.

"Sorry, old man," he said as he put the gnome to one side.

The gnome had done his job well. The hole he had been

hiding, which was not very wide around, seemed to go down into the earth forever. Arthur put down the tripod and placed the large end of the telescope into the hole, as indicated on the map.

He was still perplexed as to how this strange series of actions could open a door, but he was determined to see it through.

"You stay here and keep watch. I'm going to get the rest of the stuff," he said to his dog. Alfred gave the contraption a puzzled look as his master ran back to the house.

Arthur wrestled the heavy five-pointed rug out of the bottom of the trunk and threw it over his shoulder to drag it down the hallway. Then he slipped it through the guardrail on the stairs and picked it up in the living room.

The clock ticked steadily onward: four minutes to twelve. Arthur quickly dragged the rug outside and unfolded it so the five points were spread around the telescope, which poked through the hole in the center. He thought it must be a wonderful sight from above, this gigantic multicolored star spread out over the grass.

"Now the statues," said Arthur, returning to the house once more. He removed the five African figures from the trunk with great care and headed toward the stairs.

He descended slowly, one step at a time. *I had better not break any of them, because I bet they're at the heart of the spell*, Arthur thought.

The dog had remained outside, now used to the ghost,

whose yellow eyes were beginning to fade as the battery ran low.

But all of a sudden, shadows began to form on the ground.

Alfred pricked up his ears and shivered. The shadows slipped into the yellow light of the headlights. Enormous silhouettes . . . *worse* than ghosts.

Howling, the dog ran back to the house and shot through his small door. He tore through the living room and crashed headlong into Arthur, whose arms were filled with statuettes.

"No!" cried Arthur, but he could not stop himself from falling. The statuettes somersaulted for a moment in the air, almost in slow motion, before hurtling to the ground and smashing into a thousand pieces.

Arthur was desperate. The sight of the statues broken on the ground was unbearable.

The clock said one minute to midnight.

"I was so close. It's not fair!" he cried, his disappointment overwhelming him. He didn't even have the heart to yell at his dog, who was now hiding under the stairs.

He suddenly noticed a shadow moving across the grass outside. Arthur lifted his head and saw five enormous silhouettes bending their heads to come in the front door.

Arthur's jaw dropped open. He fumbled his small flashlight on and turned it in their direction.

The small light shone on a Bogo-Matassalai warrior in traditional dress. He wore a carefully tied tunic, decorated all over with jewels and charms. His hair was sprinkled with seashells, and he held a spear in one hand.

The man was sublime, towering—at least eight feet tall. His four colleagues were all as tall as he was.

Arthur was speechless. He felt even smaller than the garden gnome.

The warrior took a piece of paper from his pocket, unfolded it carefully, and read from it.

"Arthur?" the Bogo-Matassalai asked.

Still speechless, Arthur nodded his head. The chief smiled at him.

"There's not a moment to spare. Come!" the warrior said to him before turning around and heading out toward the garden.

Arthur, as if hypnotized, forgot his fears and followed him. The dog followed close behind, too terrified to remain alone under the stairs.

The five Africans assumed positions at the end of each point of the cloth—taking the places of the statuettes. Arthur stood near the telescope.

"Are you coming with me to the land of the Minimoys?" he asked nervously.

"Only one person can pass, and you are the one who must fight against M. the cursed," the chief replied.

"Maltazard?" asked the boy, remembering the drawing in the book.

The five warriors placed their fingers on their lips, shushing him.

"Once you are on the other side, never, never, *never* say his name. It is very bad luck."

"All right. No problem. Just M. the cursed!" Arthur repeated to himself, becoming more and more anxious.

"That is who your grandfather went to fight against. It is you who will have the honor of completing his battle," the warrior said solemnly.

Arthur gulped. The mission sounded impossible. If his grandfather had failed . . . how could he possibly succeed?

"Thank you for the honor but—perhaps it would be better if I gave my place to one of you. You are much stronger than I am!" he said humbly.

"Your strength comes from within, Arthur. Your heart is your most powerful weapon," the warrior replied.

"Oh?" Arthur said, unconvinced. "Perhaps, but . . . I am so small."

The Bogo-Matassalai chief smiled at him.

"Very soon you will be a hundred times smaller still, and your strength will only become more visible."

The clock chimed midnight.

"It is time, Arthur," the warrior said, handing him the instructions parchment.

Arthur read it with a trembling hand, as the clock continued to strike. There were three rings around the telescope.

Arthur grabbed the first.

"'The first circle, that of the body, turn three notches to the right,'" he read, trying to quell his uncertainty. He executed the move apprehensively.

Nothing happened, except that the clock chimed for the fourth time.

Arthur grabbed the second ring.

"'The second circle, that of the mind—three notches to the left!'"

He turned the second ring, which was harder to turn than the first.

The clock chimed for the eighth time. The African chief looked up at the moon and frowned at a small cloud that was rapidly approaching.

"Hurry, Arthur!" the warrior warned in a low voice.

Arthur seized hold of the third and last ring.

"'The third circle, that of the spirit . . . one complete turn.'"

Arthur breathed a deep breath and turned the ring as the clock was chiming for the eleventh time.

Unfortunately, the small cloud had reached its target, and little by little was covering the moon. The silvery light was disappearing. Arthur finished the turn and clicked the third ring into place just as the twelfth stroke of midnight pierced the silence.

Nothing happened. The Bogo-Matassalai were silent and immobile. Even the wind seemed to be holding its breath.

Arthur, worried, looked at the warriors, who were all staring up at the moon, now hidden by this little gray cloud that was unaware of the misfortune it had caused.

But all at once the wind came to their assistance and pushed away the cloud. The light from the moon began to grow stronger and stronger, and then, all of a sudden, a powerful ray blazed through the night, like a bolt of lightning linking the moon to the telescope. It lasted only a few seconds, but the shock was so great that Arthur was knocked to the ground.

Silence returned. Nothing seemed to have changed, except for the smiles on the faces of the warriors.

"The door of light is open!" the chief proudly announced. "You may now introduce yourself."

Arthur got up as best he could.

"Introduce myself?"

"Yes. And try to be convincing. The door remains open for only ten minutes!" the warrior added.

Arthur was immensely confused. He approached the telescope and looked through it. Of course, he couldn't see much— just a large, fuzzy brown mass.

Arthur grabbed the front of the telescope and turned it to sharpen the focus. Now he saw an opening in the ground, barely lit. The image quickly clarified until Arthur could see even the smallest bit of root.

All of a sudden, the top of a ladder appeared at the other end of the telescope.

Arthur could not believe his eyes. He looked away from the eyepiece and peered into the hole. No, he hadn't imagined it. There really was a ladder at the end of his telescope, a ladder that could not have been more than a few inches long.

He looked through the telescope once more. The ladder trembled a little, as if someone were climbing it.

Arthur held his breath. A small boy appeared at the end of the ladder and put his hands on the enormous telescope. It was a Minimoy!

Arthur was in a state of shock. Even in his wildest dreams, he would not have believed this possible.

The Minimoy cupped his hands as if he were trying to see something through the glass.

He had pointed ears, two eyes like black marbles, and freckles all over his face.

In a word, he was amazing.

CHAPTER
8

The Minimoy could finally make something out, although from his point of view it was simply an enormous eye.

"Archibald?" asked the little fellow with a slight gasp.

Arthur couldn't believe it. This creature spoke his language!

"Uh . . . no," he replied, dumbfounded.

"Introduce yourself!" the Bogo-Matassalai warrior reminded him. Arthur recovered his wits and remembered his mission.

"I—I'm Archibald's grandson. I must look a bit like him. My name is Arthur."

"I hope that you have a good reason for using the moon ray like that," warned the Minimoy. "The council strictly forbids its use, except in the case of an emergency."

"It is a very great emergency," the boy replied in as strong a voice as he could muster. "This garden is going to be destroyed, razed to the ground, wiped out! In less than three days, there will be no more garden, no more house, and, therefore . . . no more Minimoys."

"What are you saying? Are you a big joker, like your grandfather?" the Minimoy asked hopefully.

"This is no joke. There is a man who wants to bulldoze the land and build apartment houses!" Arthur explained to him.

"Apartment houses?!" the Mimimoy repeated, horrified. "What are apartment houses?"

"Large concrete buildings that will cover the whole garden," Arthur replied.

"But that's horrible!" cried the Minimoy, looking terror stricken.

"Yes, it is!" Arthur agreed. "And the only way to avoid it is if I can find the treasure that my grandfather hid in the garden. Then I can pay the man and none of this will happen."

The Minimoy nodded vigorously.

"Great! Perfect! That's a very good idea!" he said.

"But in order to find the treasure, I have to pass into your world! I need your help," Arthur specified, as the Minimoy did not seem to have made the connection.

"Oh! But that's impossible!" replied the little creature. "You can't just pass through like that! First we have to call a meeting of the council, and then it is necessary to explain the problem to them, and after they have deliberated maybe—"

Arthur cut him off. "We do not have time. This door is only open for ten minutes, and then it will close for another year. By then you will all be dead!"

The Minimoy froze. He had finally understood the importance of the situation.

Arthur glanced at the African chief to be sure that he had not been too harsh. The chief raised his thumb, a sign that he had done the right thing.

"What is your name?" Arthur asked, looking back through the telescope.

"Betameche," the Minimoy answered. "But you can call me Beta."

Arthur assumed a solemn voice. "Beta, the future of your people is in your hands."

The Minimoy began to squirm, terrified by so much responsibility.

"Yes, of course. In my hands. We must act," he repeated to himself in a low voice. He gesticulated so much that he nearly fell off the ladder. "We must warn the council! But the council is already meeting for the royal ceremony! I will be hanged if I disturb the royal ceremony!"

"Hurry up, Beta. Time is of the essence," Arthur reminded him.

"Yes. Of course. Time is of the essence," the Minimoy repeated, sounding increasingly more panicked.

Betameche had made himself dizzy from spinning around so much. He stopped for a second, then jumped down from the ladder and ran to a narrow passageway that resembled a mole's tunnel and was barely higher than he was.

"The king will be so proud of me! But I am going to ruin the ceremony!" Betameche kept repeating as he ran as fast as he could down the tunnel.

The chief of the Bogo-Matassalai approached Arthur and smiled at him.

"You did well."

"I hope it was enough to convince them!" Arthur replied in a worried voice.

Betameche was still running toward the end of his tunnel. Soon he came to a large hall built into a cave in the ground.

This was the Minimoy village: more than a hundred houses made of wood and leaves, tangled roots, hollowed-out mushrooms, and dried flowers. Here and there, braided roots served as small bridges connecting the houses. Betameche headed down a large avenue that, at this particular moment, was completely deserted.

Here the architecture was an incredible blanket of vegetation, a patchwork woven by beings who use what exists in nature. Some walls were made of dried earth, others of dandelion stems tied closely to each other, like fences. Dried leaves were generally used as roofing, but some Minimoys preferred wood shavings, arranged like tiles. Low walls, made from pinecone scales, separated some of the houses.

Betameche ran as fast as he could up the lovely avenue, which was lit by streetlamps made of flowers with luminous balls planted at regular intervals. The avenue ended at the council building, an enormous Roman-style amphitheater dug into the earth, forming a semicircular arena opposite the royal palace.

The entire population of the Minimoys was out in force, and Betameche now had to fight his way through them to reach the council. Using his elbows he pushed people aside, excusing himself as he went, until he finally reached the edge of the arena.

"Oh, no! Right in the middle of the ceremony! They are going to kill me!" he moaned in a low voice.

In the middle of the empty square stood the stone of the sages, in the center of which was planted a magic sword.

The weapon was magnificent. It was made of finely chiseled steel engraved with a thousand emblems. Only half of it was visible. The rest was buried deep in the stone, as if it had been welded there.

In front of the stone, a Minimoy was on one knee, head humbly bowed toward the sacred stone. The Minimoy's face could not be seen, but a few details of clothing indicated that it was a warrior. The legs were tied with laces from the feet up to the calves. On the belt were several cutlasses made from mouse teeth and small bags made from the skin of corn kernels.

"Oh, no. They are right at the important part!" Betameche fretted.

The door to the palace opened solemnly. It was a huge door

that took up a good portion of the front of the palace. It took four Minimoys to open it completely because it was so heavy and massive.

Two light bearers led the procession out of the palace. These were Minimoys in official dress—all bright colored and woven with golden threads. On their heads were hats resembling large transparent balls, each containing a glowworm. When they advanced, they lit up the way, like torchbearers.

They placed themselves on either side of the platform leading to the square, clearing a passage for the king.

His highness arrived with a slow and heavy tread. The king was rather large compared to the other Minimoys, like an adult looming over a child.

His arms were enormous and they reached down as far as his calves. He wore a thick white fur reminiscent of a polar bear and a large beard whose color blended in with the fur.

His face looked ageless, but he was at least two thousand years old. His head seemed surprisingly small in comparison with his body. And funnier, too, buried in his enormous hat with bells.

The king advanced to the end of the platform. He was followed by several dignitaries, comprising the rest of the council, who carefully positioned themselves along the sides.

Only one of them stayed close to the king. This was Miro, the mole. His costume would not have been out of place in Shakespeare's *Romeo and Juliet*. He wore small eyeglasses on the end of his nose and had a definitely worried air about him all the time.

The king raised his enormous arms and the crowd cheered him. "Dear citizens, notables, and dignitaries!" he began in a voice that was old but still strong. "The wars that our ancestors were forced to wage brought much unhappiness and destruc-tion." He paused for a moment as if to honor the memory of all those who had perished during that terrible time.

"Thus it was with great wisdom that the sages decided they would no longer wage war, and they buried the sword of power in the stone." He pointed, with a broad sweep of his arm, to the sword in the stone and the warrior, still on one knee.

"The sword was never to be used again, and we were left to resolve our problems . . . with peaceful methods."

The crowd seemed to share the king's sentiments. Except, perhaps, for Betameche, who was too anxious about his mis-sion.

The king continued his speech.

"The ancients wrote, on the bottom of the stone, the law that was to govern us: if one day our lands are threatened by an invader, then and only then, a pure heart, motivated by the spirit of justice, knowing neither hatred nor vengeance, may remove the sword of a thousand powers and lead a just battle."

The king let out a long sigh, full of sadness, before adding, "Unfortunately, that day has arrived."

The crowd began to stir as each murmured to his neighbor.

"Our spies have reported that M. the cursed is on the brink of sending a giant army to invade our lands." A wave of terror flew through the crowd. The first letter of his name was enough to frighten everyone.

"Let us debate!" cried the king, signaling the start of a joyful chaos in which everyone could express themselves without really discussing anything.

"Will this take much longer?" Betameche asked the nearest Minimoy.

The royal guard leaned toward him. "Oh, yes. Things have only just started!" said the officer. "We still have the royal summary, the speech of the sages, the warrior's promise, the ratification by the king, and then . . . the opening of the buffet!" he concluded, gleefully.

Betameche began to feel that all was lost. His hands were twisting in all directions, searching for courage.

"People! There is not a moment to spare!" shouted the king, restoring silence.

He is right, thought Betameche. *There is not a moment to spare!*

The king took a few steps toward the warrior, still solemnly bowed before the sword.

"The hour is grave. I suggest that we cut protocol short and immediately call upon the person who seems to me to have all of the qualities needed for this dangerous mission."

The king took a few steps more. An unexpected benevolence entered his voice.

"This person who, in a few short days, will officially replace me at the head of this kingdom . . ." A childlike smile suddenly made his face seem young. "I am of course speaking of the Princess Selenia, my daughter."

He tenderly reached out his arms in the direction of the kneeling warrior. The young girl stood up, revealing her angelic features. Her wild hair, with glints of mauve reflected in the light, was beautifully matched by the turquoise of her almond-shaped eyes.

She was proud and played at being a rebel and a warrior, but her grace betrayed her. She was a real princess, as pale as Snow White, as beautiful as Cinderella, as gracious as Sleeping Beauty, but as crafty as Robin Hood.

It was difficult for the king to hide his pride. The thought that this being was his daughter made him beam.

The crowd applauded wildly.

The king took one last step toward his daughter.

"Princess Selenia, may the spirit of the ancients guide you," her father said solemnly.

Selenia came forward, calmly reached for the sword, and was about to place her hand on the hilt when Betameche interrupted.

"Papa!" he cried, elbowing his way through the crowd. Selenia stopped dead in her tracks.

"Beta!" she growled impatiently. Only her little brother was capable of such silly antics at a time like this.

The king searched the crowd for his son.

"Here I am, Papa!" Betameche said, joining a furious Selenia.

"You did this on purpose, didn't you? Couldn't you wait ten seconds before acting up?" she snapped.

"I am on a very important mission," Betameche answered her, as serious as the pope.

"Really? Because my mission *isn't* important? I was about to draw the magic sword to battle against M. the cursed!"

Betameche shrugged. "You are much too proud and angry to be able to draw that sword, you know."

"Do tell, Mr. Know-It-All!" she replied. "Do I detect just a bit of jealousy in your words?"

"Not at all!" answered Betameche, lifting his nose skyward.

"All right! Stop squabbling, you two!" said the king, striding up between them. "Betameche! This is a very important ceremony. I hope that you have a really good reason for interrupting!"

"Yes, Father. The path from the lands above has opened," Betameche announced.

His words passed quickly through the crowd. An agitated murmur began building.

"Who dared?" cried the king in a terrible voice.

Betameche approached his enormous father.

"His name is Arthur," he explained timidly. "He is Archibald's grandson."

The crowd immediately was in an uproar. The name of Archibald resonated with everyone. The king was rattled.

"And what does this . . . Arthur want?" he asked.

"He wants to speak to the council. He says that a great misfortune is about to befall us and that only he can save us."

The audience was on the verge of panic and rioting. Selenia pushed her brother aside and took his place in front of the king.

"It's true, a great misfortune is coming—it is called M. the cursed and this Arthur has nothing to do with it! It is I, Princess Selenia of the royal family, who will take on the burden of protecting our people." Without hesitation, she turned and strode over to the sword. She placed her hand on the hilt and tried to pull it out with a graceful gesture.

But grace was apparently of no use, because the sword did not budge. So she tried force, using both her hands.

Nothing happened. The weapon remained one with the stone.

She then used her two hands, her two feet; she contorted herself, grimaced, pulled. . . .

Nothing happened. There was confusion in the crowd and also in the expression of the king, who seemed deeply disappointed and more than a little worried.

Selenia, exhausted, stopped for a second to catch her breath.

"You see: much too proud. I told you so!" Betameche said smugly.

"I'll show you proud!" replied Selenia, leaping down and advancing toward her brother, hands outstretched to strangle him.

"Selenia!" cried her father. "My dear daughter, I am so sorry," he said with affection. "We know how much you love your people but . . . your heart is clearly too full of vengeance for you to draw the sword."

"That's not true, Father!" she said passionately. "It's just—Betameche upset me! I am sure that if I calm myself down, in a minute I will be able to pull out the sword and everything will be back in order!"

The king studied her skeptically for a moment. How could he explain to her that her fury was blinding her without breaking her spirit?

"Selenia, answer me this. What would you do if you had M. the cursed right here in front of you?" the king asked her.

Selenia tried to contain her anger, which was demanding to be heard.

"I—I would treat him the way he deserves to be treated," she asserted.

"And that means?" pressed the king, knowing he was playing on her nerves.

"I . . . I—I would strangle that piece of vermin! For all of the crimes that he has committed and the misfortune he has brought upon us and also for—"

Selenia realized that she had fallen into his trap.

"I am sorry, my daughter, but you are not ready. The powers of the sword act only in hands motivated by justice, not by vengeance," her father explained to her.

"So what are we going to do? Are we going to allow that creep to invade us, to rob us, to strangle us and our children, too? Without saying a word? Without doing anything? Without trying anything?" she said, addressing the whole crowd.

The assembly was stirred. There was obviously some truth in what the young princess was saying.

"Who is going to save us?" she cried, in conclusion.

"Arthur!" Betameche answered with fervor. "He is our only hope."

Selenia rolled her eyes. The king reflected. The crowd wondered.

The council conferred among themselves, and then gave their sovereign a favorable sign. He nodded solemnly.

"Given the circumstances . . . and in memory of Archibald, the council agrees to hear what this young man has to say."

Betameche let out a yelp of joy. His sister scowled.

"Miro! Prepare the link!" said the king.

The little mole immediately launched into action. He jumped into his control center, which was a kind of circular counter filled with protruding handles and knobs of every shape and size.

Miro did some rapid calculations on his abacus, then pulled

handle number twenty-one. An enormous mirror, mounted on roots that served as its frame, emerged from the wall, like a rearview mirror on a car. A second mirror appeared shortly thereafter, catching the reflection from the first mirror. A third mirror descended from the ceiling and captured its reflection in turn.

Miro engaged the handles one by one and mirrors appeared from everywhere, transporting the same image throughout the town and through the long tunnel leading to where the enormous telescope lens was still planted in the ground.

When it was done, a total of fifty mirrors were lined up to capture the image from the lens.

Miro used two hands to activate a new handle. A plantlike device descended from the ceiling of the cave, opened like a flower, and released four luminous balls: one yellow, one red, one blue, and one green. These four colors lined themselves up to form a perfect white light, like a large projector ready to faithfully reproduce the image transported by the mirrors.

All that was missing was a screen. Miro pushed on a tab, the only one with a velvet top, and an enormous screen unrolled from the ceiling, filling the sky of the city.

Up close, it consisted of maple leaves that had been dried and then sewn to each other in a kind of magnificent patchwork. Miro pressed another button. One last mirror made it possible for the reflection to reach the projector, which would then send the image to the enormous screen.

A giant eye filled the screen—Arthur's.

The boy, still on his knees in his garden, couldn't believe it. He was in the middle of the Minimoys' council, face-to-face with the king. The latter was rather impressed by the size of Arthur's eye, which made it possible to imagine the size of the human being behind it.

Selenia turned her back to the screen and folded her arms as a sign of protest.

The king had regained some of his dignity and cleared his throat momentously.

"Hmm! Well, young Arthur, the council will hear you. Please be brief."

Arthur took a deep breath and announced, "A bad man is planning to destroy the garden that shelters you. I have only four more minutes left to pass into your world so I can help you. After that, there is nothing I can do and I'm afraid you will be totally annihilated."

The news ran through the crowd like a current of air.

The king seemed paralyzed.

"That—that *was* brief . . . and precise."

He turned to the council, who looked as lost as he felt. The king knew he was alone in making this decision.

"Your grandfather was a great and wise man. In his memory, we are going to trust you. Activate the transporter!" he thundered, raising his imposing arms.

Betameche whooped and ran off, bumping into his still-sulking sister as he passed.

Miro pulled a golden handle and an enormous red velvet curtain descended to cover the giant screen.

CHAPTER
9

Arthur turned toward the chief of the Bogo-Matassalai tribe. "I think it worked," he announced timidly.

The warriors did not look surprised.

Betameche bolted down the hall. He rushed up to a silk cocoon hanging from the ceiling.

"Gatekeeper! Gatekeeper! Wake up, it's urgent!" he cried, hammering on the cocoon. There was no reply. Betameche pulled out his multifunction knife and released a bizarre blade—obviously a cocoon cutter. He slit open the silk from one side to the other.

The gatekeeper, who had been sleeping peacefully with his head upside down, slipped through the silky walls and crashed to the ground.

"What in the name of a marshmallow!" the old Minimoy mumbled, rubbing his head. He untangled his long white beard from his legs and smoothed the hair on his ears. "Who dares to disturb me?"

The old imp recognized the young prince and his face lit up.

"Beta! You good-for-nothing! Can't you find any better way to amuse yourself?"

"My father sent me. We need a passage," explained the boy, stamping his feet with impatience.

"Again?" complained the gatekeeper. "Why does everyone want to pass at this very moment?"

"The last passage was four years ago!" Betameche pointed out.

"That's what I was saying! I was just about to fall asleep!" replied the gatekeeper, stretching.

"Hurry up! The king is impatient!" insisted the prince.

"The king, the king! All right, where is the royal seal?"

Betameche took it out of his pocket and handed it to the gatekeeper.

The gatekeeper took the royal object and inserted it into a box in the wall. "What about the moon? Is it full tonight? Let's see."

Muttering to himself, the gatekeeper opened a small trap-door in the wall, resembling the door to a garbage chute. A mirror was attached to it, reflecting the image of the moon above—imposing, shining, and, above all, full.

"It's beautiful," murmured the gatekeeper.

"Hurry up!" Betameche cried. "The beam is getting weaker."

"Yes, okay! It's okay!" he responded, grumbling.

The gatekeeper moved toward the three rings—the same

ones that Arthur had carefully lined up on the other end of the telescope. Except that on this side, for the Minimoys, they seemed enormous.

The gatekeeper seized the first ring.

"Three notches toward the right, for the body," said the old man, turning it carefully.

He moved to the second ring.

"Three notches to the left, for the mind."

The second ring turned slowly to the third notch.

The gatekeeper grabbed the third ring.

"And now, one complete turn . . . for the spirit."

The gatekeeper held the third ring tightly, like a child on a carousel, and turned it.

All at once, the beam that came from the moon changed and began to waver like the horizon line when it is very hot.

"Hold on," the Bogo-Matassalai chief said to Arthur.

"Hold on? To what?" replied the boy with astonishment.

He had barely asked the question when he began to shrink rapidly, faster than he could even speak.

By instinct, Arthur held on to the lens as he changed. He put his back up against the glass, all the while continuing to shrink.

"What is happening to me?" he asked, amazed.

"You are going to join our brothers, the Minimoys," the chief calmly replied. "But do not forget that you have only sixty hours to fulfill your mission. If you are not back by noon two days from tomorrow, the door will close . . . for a thousand days!" the chief declared firmly.

Arthur nodded his head, which was still shrinking. Behind him, the glass was now as big as the huge oak tree. Suddenly, the lens he was leaning against seemed to become soft, and Arthur sank into it. Then, quite suddenly, he passed right through the glass and fell into the telescope. There he rolled, bouncing like a puppet falling down a flight of stairs.

His fall came to a noisy end as he crashed against the last wall of glass at the end of the telescope, where it stuck into the hall. He rubbed his head as Betameche appeared on his ladder on the other side of the glass.

The two boys seemed equally surprised to see each other. Betameche smiled and made a "welcome" sign with his hand. Arthur, somewhat stupefied, did the same.

The Minimoy spoke to him and made broad gestures, but the thick glass muffled all conversation. Betameche exaggerated his gestures. He was obviously trying to make Arthur understand something.

"I can't hear you," Arthur cried, using his hands as a megaphone.

Betameche stood close to the glass and breathed on it to cover it with moisture. On it he drew the picture of a key.

"A key?" said Arthur, making the gesture of turning a key in a lock.

The Minimoy nodded his head. Suddenly Arthur remembered.

"Oh! The key! The one I am always supposed to keep with me!" He dug in his pockets and pulled out the old key, with its tag still attached.

Betameche congratulated him and pointed to a lock on the left wall.

Arthur hesitated, but Betameche gestured his encouragement. So Arthur put in the key and turned.

Immediately, an invisible mechanism was engaged and the ceiling began to descend at an impressive speed. Arthur looked up and saw the glass lens descending toward him.

He was caught in a trap. The ceiling was going to crush him. Arthur was overcome with panic. He banged against the glass and yelled for Beta to help him.

The Minimoy, all smiles, gave him two thumbs up.

Arthur was dumbfounded. He was sure the final seconds of his life were passing. He banged on the glass with all his strength, which did absolutely no good. "I don't want to die, Beta! Not now! Not like this!" the poor boy hollered helplessly. The ceiling was coming closer and would crush him in a few seconds. Arthur looked Betameche in the eyes, thinking that the last image he would see would be the joyful face of this evil elf.

The glass ceiling reached Arthur's head. He quickly flattened himself against the lens lengthwise.

But the pressure from the glass didn't crush him. Instead it pushed him into the softening glass, so Arthur was suspended like a spoon in a jar of honey. It was impossible to move in this dense and gelatinous substance. All you could do was wait until it spit you out on the other side.

Arthur fell from the lens and crashed to the ground at Betameche's feet, tangled up in hundreds of gelatinous threads, as if he had fallen through a vat of chewing gum.

"Welcome to the land of the Minimoys," announced the little prince with great joy, his arms wide open.

Arthur got up as best he could, trying to get rid of the threads that were clinging to him. He had not yet realized that he no longer looked like a regular human boy. He had become an authentic Minimoy.

"You frightened me, Beta! I couldn't hear anything, so I thought I was going to die and—" Arthur stopped in mid-sentence.

He had suddenly realized that his arm no longer resembled the one he was accustomed to. Was it possible . . . ?

He got rid of the sticky threads, little by little discovering his Minimoy body. Betameche took him by the shoulders and turned him around so that he could see his reflection in the lens.

Arthur was stunned. He touched his body, then his face, as if to verify that this was not a dream. "It's incredible," he finally said.

The gatekeeper looked up from mending his cocoon and smiled. "Good, you don't need me anymore. I am going back to bed." He climbed back into his cocoon, which he continued to mend from the inside.

Arthur was still hypnotized by his own reflection. "It's really incredible!"

"You can admire yourself later!" Betamache said, pulling him by the arm. "The council is waiting for you."

The chief of the Bogo-Matassalai tribe gently withdrew the telescope from its hole, while his brothers carefully folded the rug with the five points.

The chief looked down the hole one last time.

"Good luck, Arthur," he said with emotion.

He put the garden gnome back in its place and the little tribe disappeared into the night, as mysteriously as they had come.

The old Chevrolet's motor wheezed to a stop. The light from the headlights faded rapidly and finally went out.

The night once again took over and now the silence was complete . . .

Except for a slight, barely audible humming that came from one of the upstairs bedrooms.

This was most likely Grandma, snoring like a carefree loco-motive.

CHAPTER

10

The king was on his throne, pounding the ground with his scepter.

"Enter, Arthur!" he boomed in his powerful voice.

The two guards lifted up their swords and opened a way for Arthur, who now had to cross the square under everyone's watchful eyes.

The crowd welcomed him with cries of "ooh!" and "ah!" Arthur did his best to hide his embarrassment.

Selenia, her arms still crossed, studied this savior who had fallen from the sky. He looked more like a chick that had fallen from its nest, she thought. Betameche shot her a sideways glance and nudged her with his elbow.

"Cute, isn't he?" he asked the princess, who shrugged her shoulders.

"Common!" she replied, turning her back on him as Arthur passed right by her.

"Princess Selenia, my respects," Arthur managed to say, despite his shyness. He was so afraid that his heart would explode that he could barely look at her. He found her even more beautiful in person. He bowed slightly and continued on his path to the king.

Selenia would never admit it, but his politeness had just earned him several points.

The king was also charmed, but he did not wish to jump to conclusions too quickly. Only Miro the mole was not restrained by protocol. He approached Arthur and vigorously shook his hand.

"I was good friends with Archibald. I am very happy to meet his grandson!" he said, his voice filled with emotion.

Arthur was somewhat embarrassed to find his hand squeezed like a loaf of bread by a mole that he barely knew, but he smiled and nodded as courteously as he could.

"Miro! Leave him be!" said the king, always mindful of good manners.

The little mole pulled himself together and returned to his place. Arthur found himself standing in front of the king, and he bowed to him respectfully.

"Well, my boy, we are listening!" said the king, who was dying of curiosity.

Arthur gathered his courage and began. "In less than three days, men will come to tear down the house and the garden. This means that my world, and yours, will be destroyed and covered over with concrete."

A deathly silence ran through the crowd, like a disagreeable shiver.

"This is a misfortune even greater than that which we feared," murmured the king.

Selenia could stand it no longer. She turned around and poked Arthur with her finger. "And you, from your new height of half an inch, you came to save us—is that right?" she tossed out disdainfully.

"The only way to stop these men is to pay them. I think that is why my grandfather came to you four years ago. He was looking for a treasure he'd hidden in the garden that would help us to pay our debts. I came to complete his mission and to find this treasure," he explained. It must be said that the mission now seemed much more difficult than it had when he was dreaming in front of drawings, propped up with pillows on his bed.

"Your grandfather was a remarkable man," conceded the king, lost in his memories. "He taught us so many things! He was the one who taught Miro how to tame images and light."

Miro acknowledged this with a sigh full of nostalgia.

The king continued. "It is true, he came to us looking for his treasure, which was entrusted to us for safekeeping. Sadly, we failed him—the treasure was stolen from us some time ago, and we did not know where it was. And so your grandfather went in search of this famous treasure, and after traversing the seven lands that make up our world, he finally found where it was . . . in the midst of the forbidden lands, at the center of the kingdom of shadows—in the heart of the city of Necropolis."

The room shivered as everyone imagined this descent into darkness.

"Necropolis is controlled by a powerful army of fanatically devoted henchmen, all in the grip of their king, who rules as absolute master: the celebrated M. the cursed."

A few spectators fainted.

"No one has ever returned from the kingdom of shadows," concluded the king.

"Still ready for this great adventure?" asked Selenia provokingly.

Betameche had had enough, and he stepped in between Arthur and Selenia.

"Leave him alone! He's just learned that he has lost his grandfather. That's hard enough, isn't it?"

The phrase echoed inside of Arthur's head. He hadn't yet clearly understood what the king was saying. His eyes filled with tears. Betameche realized that he had made a mistake.

"Well—I meant to say—we haven't had any news and—no one has ever come back . . . so . . ."

Arthur held back his tears and filled his lungs with courage.

"My grandfather is not dead! I am sure of it!" he said.

The king approached him, uncertain how to deal with the boy's distress. "My dear Arthur, I am afraid that my son is right. If your grandfather fell into the hands of M. the cursed, or one of the awful henchmen that make up his army, there is little chance that we will ever see him again!"

"Exactly!" Arthur cried. "M. may be cursed but he is no idiot! What good would it do him to get rid of an old man? None. On the other hand, why not keep a man with such infinite knowledge, a genius capable of solving all kinds of problems?"

The king looked intrigued by this hypothesis.

Arthur continued, fired up with excitement. "I will go to the kingdom of shadows and I will find my grandfather along with the treasure! Even if I have to rescue him from the claws of this evil Maltazard!" he declared in a passion.

The crowd gasped with horror. Arthur had just said the name that was never supposed to be spoken—the name that brings misfortune. And, as everyone knows, misfortune usually comes quickly.

An alarm resounded throughout the city at that exact moment. A guard appeared at the palace door shouting, "Alert at the main gate!"

There was total panic among the Minimoys. They ran in all directions, they jostled each other, they lost their heads. The king left his throne and quickly headed for the central gate, the main entrance to the town.

Selenia pushed Arthur's shoulder. He was confused at having set off such an uproar.

"You really made an entrance!" the princess said to him

angrily. "Didn't anyone tell you that you must never say that name?"

Poor Arthur was wringing his hands. "Yes, but—"

"But the fine gentleman still does whatever he feels like doing—is that it?" She stormed off without giving him time to explain or even to apologize.

The entire Minimoy populace clustered around the central gate, and the guards had to use their nightsticks to clear a passage for the king and his two children. Miro pulled a handle and a little mirror appeared above them, a bit like a periscope. The mole looked up and observed what was happening on the other side of the gate.

A long pipe, like a giant avenue leading to the entrance, stretched before him, out to infinity. Everything seemed calm.

Miro turned the mirror slightly to check the sides of the pipe.

All at once, a hand appeared on the mirror. A cry of astonishment resounded through the crowd. Miro turned the wheel of the mirror to lower the image. Then they all saw a Minimoy, lying on the ground outside in very bad shape.

"It's Gandolo! The ferryman from the great river!" cried a guard in recognition. The king leaned toward the mirror to have a better view. "Incredible! We thought he was lost forever in the forbidden lands!" he said, amazed.

"I guess that proves that you *can* come back!" Selenia responded.

"Yes, but in what condition! Open the doors quickly!" the king ordered.

Arthur cast a worried glance toward the mirror as the guards slid back the large beams that blocked the door. Something had caught his eye—on the lower right side of the image. Something strange, like a corner becoming detached.

"Stop!" he cried.

Everyone froze in place.

The king turned toward the boy and gave him a questioning look.

"Sire, look! It looks like something out there is coming unglued."

The king looked for himself. "Why . . . yes, it does. But I'm sure it's nothing serious. We can glue it back later," he said, without understanding.

"Sir, you don't understand! That's a painted canvas! It's a trap! My grandfather used this method in Africa to protect himself from ferocious beasts!" Arthur explained.

"But we are not ferocious beasts!" Selenia remarked. "And we are certainly not going to let this poor unfortunate soldier die! Besides, if he has returned from the forbidden lands, he must have many things to tell us! Open the gates!" ordered the princess.

Outside, Gandolo was crawling along the ground, his hand outstretched in front of him. "Don't open the gate! It's a trap!" he rasped under his breath.

Of course, no one heard Gandolo's plea, and the guards began to open the heavy gate. However, they still hesitated to run to the rescue of the poor ferryman, out in the open, exposed pipe.

Only Selenia stepped forward, ready to brave the unknown danger.

"Be careful, my child," insisted her father, whose size was much larger than his courage.

"If any henchmen were waiting to attack, we would see them coming for miles!" replied the Princess with great courage.

At first glance, the enormous empty pipe did seem to extend infinitely into the clear distance. But only at first glance. Arthur was convinced that this was really a trap, into which his favorite princess was about to fall.

He couldn't stand it anymore. He grabbed a torch from one of the guards and threw it with all his might. The flaming torch flew over Selenia's head and crashed headlong into a painted canvas stretched across the pipe that, up to then, had been invisible.

The crowd was dumbfounded. Arthur was right! Selenia couldn't believe her eyes. The torch fell to the ground and immediately set fire to the gigantic canvas, which flared up like a piece of straw.

"Oh, no!" Selenia cried, watching the wall of flames consume the canvas. Arthur shot past at full speed and grabbed Gandolo by the legs.

"Selenia, come on! We have to get him out of here!" Arthur yelled over the noise of the flames. The princess woke from her state of shock and grabbed the injured man under the arms.

"Close the gates!" ordered the king in a frightened voice.

Arthur and Selenia ran as best they could, weighed down by poor Gandolo's body. The canvas was almost entirely consumed when the last large piece fell to the ground, revealing an army of M.'s horrible henchmen.

The fire was still too intense to cross, and the henchmen were impatiently lunging forward on the other side of the frame. There were about one hundred of these evil insects, each one uglier than the next. Each wore armor made from the shells of rotten walnuts.

M.'s henchmen carried all kinds of weapons, mainly swords. For battle, they had brought with them the famous "tears of death," drops of oil held together by braided cords and attached to the end of a sling. The cord was lit, the drop was tossed, and a tongue of fire would spread over everything in sight.

Each henchman had his own mount—mosquitoes, trained and harnessed for war.

The chief henchman saw the gates closing and decided to begin the assault despite the intensity of the fire. He lifted his sword in the air and let out an unearthly cry.

In chorus, one hundred henchmen joyously echoed him.

"Hurry up, Selenia," yelled Arthur, as the gates were fast closing and the first mosquitoes passed over his head. Selenia called on all her strength, and together the three of them tumbled inside.

The king threw himself against the door and, with powerful arms, finished the work of the guards.

Several mosquitoes crashed into the gate as the guards were bolting the safety bars. Unfortunately, a dozen henchmen on mosquitoes had managed to enter the city and were already circling in the air.

There was panic everywhere, as each Minimoy tried to reach his battle station.

The henchmen had raised their tears of death and were whirling them around over their heads. The mosquitoes swooped down like bombs and the balls of fire exploded on the ground, leaving an immense trail that consumed everything in its way.

"We have to fight, Arthur! Until the end!" Betameche proudly cried.

"I would like to, but with what?" Arthur called back.

"Here!" said Betameche, giving him his stick. "I'm going to look for another weapon!"

Betameche took off, leaving Arthur with his stick.

The henchmen did a dance of triumph in the air above, punctuating each step with a falling bomb.

Out of nowhere, a fierce ball of fire swooped down and hit

the king from behind. The Minimoy stumbled and fell to the ground—in two pieces!

Arthur let out a cry of horror before he realized the sovereign was unhurt. Selenia rolled her eyes and went to help her father up as Palmito, his faithful malbak, got up on his own.

Palmito was a large furry animal with a flat head, which was practical for attaching him to the king's throne. It was this creature who served as the body of the king in order to provide him with the strength and assurance required of royalty—because, in reality, the king was nothing but a little old man, even smaller than his daughter, who gently dusted him off.

"Are you okay?" the king asked his faithful companion.

Palmito nodded and smiled sheepishly, as if to apologize for falling over so easily.

"Go hide in the palace!" the king said to him. "Your big, beautiful fur is too much of a target for the tears of death!"

The malbak seemed hesitant to leave his master.

"Hurry up! Now!" the king ordered him.

Palmito disappeared into the palace.

The king looked up at the disaster that was overtaking the city and the mosquitoes' aerial ballet overhead.

"Organize the counterattack!" cried the king.

Everyone grabbed what they could to put out the fires that were blazing throughout the city. Mothers collected their children and slid them down safety hatches that were designed for that very purpose.

On the left flank, a dozen Minimoys mounted a kind of homemade catapult.

The chief of the operation put on his helmet and sat down in his shooting seat. He activated the viewfinder in front of him. A cartridge began releasing raisins one by one into a wooden spoon connected to a complex system of springs.

The chief tracked a mosquito in his viewfinder, then released the trigger. A raisin was launched into the air, but it missed its mark. Automatically, the cartridge released another raisin into the spoon.

The head marksman launched another raisin that, unfortunately, missed its target yet again. The henchman, annoyed at having been shot at like a pigeon, dove toward the catapult and fired a tear of death. Luckily he also missed his target, but the explosion sent Arthur flying. He landed heavily on a raisin that had just been released into the catapult.

The chief marksman did not see him, as he was too absorbed with targeting the mosquito in his viewfinder.

"No, wait!" yelled Arthur, suddenly aware of his dangerous position.

The chief activated his valve and the raisin shot into the sky, with Arthur aboard clinging on for dear life. The projectile shot through the air over the city, heading straight for one of the mosquitoes.

"Did you see that? It's Arthur! He's flying!" marveled the marksman.

"You're the one that shot him into the air, imbecile!" replied his superior.

The henchman saw the raisin hurtling toward him just in time to duck and narrowly avoid it. But then Arthur leaped onto the mosquito's back, throwing the creature off balance for a moment.

The henchman turned to check the damage and spotted Arthur behind him, holding on as best he could. Terrified and trying not to show it, the boy thrust his stick in front of him and assumed a wicked look.

The henchman smiled menacingly and took out a monstrous sword, made of steel. The warrior stood up on his mount and advanced toward Arthur with the clear intention of cutting him in two.

Arthur tried, as best he could, to stand up, too, but it wasn't easy on a mosquito that was zooming through the air like a rocket ship.

The warrior raised his arm and lunged at Arthur with all his might.

The boy ducked at the last minute, and the henchman's arm, pulled by the weight of the sword, twisted around his neck and half suffocated him. He teetered for a moment, then suddenly lost his balance and fell, to Arthur's great surprise.

Now Arthur was left to take command of the creature. He grabbed a rein in each hand and tried not to panic.

"Okay! This can't be any more complicated than Grandma's car!" he said to himself nervously. "To move to the left—probably all you have to do is pull to the left."

Arthur lightly pulled the left rein. The mosquito immediately flipped over and began to fly upside down.

Arthur let out a yell and caught hold of the ends of the reins just in time to avoid plummeting to the ground. The creature flew every which way, confused by the mixed signals it was getting. It took off in a mad frenzy, skimming the ground above the city.

"Watch out, Beta," Arthur screamed, a hairsbreadth away from knocking his friend out with his dangling legs. Betameche threw himself down on the ground, but Arthur and his mosquito were already climbing back into the air.

Almost immediately, another henchman began to give chase.

Miro saw it and turned his seat in the direction of the two mosquitoes as they flew into a tunnel. Arthur, still hanging from the ends of the reins, guided the creature as best he could. Behind him, the henchman had unsheathed his sword and was brandishing it over his head.

Miro identified their paths and pressed a button. A mirror sprang out suddenly from the wall of the tunnel, just as Arthur shot past. His pursuer was smacked in the face, and stopped dead in his tracks.

Another henchman, who saw what happened to his

colleague, flew up to the ceiling of the tunnel and began skimming along it.

"Pay attention to the walls," he screamed to his comrades in arms. "There are traps in the walls! Fly closer to the ceiling, it's saf—"

He didn't have time to complete his sentence. Miro released a mirror from the ceiling, the way a fighter releases an uppercut, and the henchman crashed headlong into it. The shock was so violent that he was thrown from his mount, which flew on without him.

Arthur hung from the ends of the reins, pursued by yet another henchman. The warrior had drawn his sword and was preparing to cut our hero into slices like a sausage.

The henchman approached, his sword swinging in the air. Arthur prepared himself for the end. The warrior struck with a mighty blow. Arthur lifted his legs out of the way, and the sword got caught in the reins.

"Sorry," called Arthur, who was always polite, regardless of the circumstances.

Furious, the henchman tried to untangle his sword by pulling upward. The mosquito interpreted this sudden movement as a change of direction and reared up angrily. The henchman, clinging to his sword, was torn off his mount.

Arthur lost his balance, let go of the reins, fell, and landed on the back of his pursuer's mosquito. Arthur's spirits rose as he grabbed the reins and rolled them around his stick.

"Good work, Arthur!" he reassured himself, plucking up his courage.

This time, he pulled very slowly on the leather strap, and the mosquito executed a magnificent wide turn to the left. The centrifugal force was impressive, but Arthur held on.

"Wow! That's it, I've got it! The battle is mine!" he cried fervently. Just then a raisin hit him right in the face. He lost control of his mosquito, momentarily stunned by the shot.

"I got him!" the marksman shouted triumphantly, leaning over the side of the catapult.

"That's Arthur you've unseated, idiot!" the chief retorted furiously.

Arthur and his uncontrollable monster were nose-diving into another henchman, who was brandishing a tear of death.

"Watch out!" Arthur cried to the henchman, who could not see the catastrophe that was about to befall him from above.

The two mounts smashed into each other, and the tear of death exploded on Arthur's mosquito.

Fortunately, Arthur had had the clever idea of jumping into the void before the collision. Given his new size, he felt like he was falling from a height of about a hundred feet.

Luckily, he once again landed on a mosquito without a rider.

He was saved, with only one small problem: he had landed sitting backward, so it was impossible to see where his new mount was taking him.

Meanwhile, his former mount had caught fire and was in

a nose-dive, headed directly toward the king. Selenia saw it coming.

"Watch out!" she cried, throwing herself at her father. The old man tripped under the weight of his daughter, who threw herself over him like a blanket.

The mosquito hit the ground and exploded in a long trail of fire.

"Are you all right, Father?" a worried Selenia immediately asked.

"I will be all right," replied the king, visibly weakened. "But for the moment I think I would prefer to remain here on the ground. There's a better view of the show from here," he joked, feeling himself incapable of getting up for the moment. Selenia smiled at him and remained at his side, prepared to defend him with her life.

After a series of complex acrobatics, Arthur managed to turn himself around so he was now facing forward. He grabbed the reins one more time and gave a couple of small tugs. The mosquito reacted better than a Ferrari and began to chase after a henchman.

The king spotted him flying overhead.

"Selenia! Look!" he said to his daughter.

The young princess searched the skies for a moment and noticed Arthur's pursuit. She was struck speechless, torn between jealousy and amazement.

Arthur managed to guide his mount directly above the

henchman's. He cleared his throat to attract the warrior's attention. The latter looked up and saw Arthur. He was also struck speechless.

"Need some ammunition?" the boy asked. Then he pulled on the cord that was holding back all of his mount's tears of death. The henchman tried as best he could to catch the first ones, but he was like a skier confronted by an avalanche. He quickly lost control of his mosquito, and together they smashed against the wall.

"Arthur!" cried Selenia, her hands over her face.

Arthur made a very tight turn in order to avoid the collision, just like a real fighter pilot, then triumphantly flew to safety.

CHAPTER

11

Selenia let out a sigh of relief. She turned toward her father and caught him smiling at her. He had figured out his daughter's true feelings for Arthur. Feeling exposed, she gave her father a very sharp look.

"What?" she snapped, as cold as ice.

"I didn't say anything!" replied the king innocently, lifting his arms above his head as if he had just been arrested.

From his control seat, Miro was also smiling as he watched Arthur landing safely.

"I really like this boy!" He chortled to himself.

Betameche ran over to stand beside Arthur.

"Are you okay? Nothing broken?" the Minimoy asked with concern.

"I don't know. I can't feel my behind anymore!"

Betameche giggled.

The sky above the city was now clear; most of the mosquitoes had been downed. But two still remained, and these swooped down to land at the king's feet.

Selenia instinctively placed herself in front of her father. The two henchmen dismounted and unsheathed their swords.

"Don't worry. It's not the king that we want—it's you!" the henchman sneered.

"You won't have either one of us!" the princess bravely replied, reaching for her dagger. The henchmen sneered some more, and then rushed toward her with a yell.

Charging and yelling are probably the only two things that a henchman knows how to do well. The battle was an unequal one. Selenia managed a few passes with her dagger, and was able to beat them back briefly, but a well-aimed blow sent her dagger spiraling through the air.

Then she was on the ground, at the mercy of the two sinister warriors.

"Go ahead, grab her!" said one of them.

"Hey!" yelled a voice from behind them. The two henchmen turned around and discovered Arthur, armed with his trusty stick.

"Pick on somebody your own size!" Arthur said, tightening his hands around his poor stick.

"Do you see someone our size around here?" one of the henchmen said, glancing around.

"No!" his colleague replied, giggling.

Arthur, offended, filled his lungs with air and charged at the henchmen, his stick leading the way.

The warrior severed Arthur's stick with his sword at lightning speed, so that the remnant was level with his hand. The boy stopped short.

"You finish him off. I'll take care of the girl," said the other henchman darkly.

Arthur fell back, avoiding, as best he could, the powerful blows of the sword.

Selenia stuck to her father's side, ready to sacrifice her life for him. But the henchman cared nothing about sacrifices. All he wanted was to capture the princess.

Arthur was furious, frustrated, and overwhelmed by all these injustices. Wasn't there any divine protection from evil? Why didn't adults do anything to help, with all their big talk about justice, good, and evil? he wondered.

He tripped on a large stone and his hand landed on the hilt of the magic sword. Was this a sign from above?

Arthur didn't know. The only thing he did know was that a sword would be much more useful in his hand than in the stone. Arthur grabbed the sword and pulled it out, as if sliding it out of butter.

The king couldn't believe his eyes. Selenia's jaw dropped.

"A miracle!" cried Miro in awe.

The two henchmen looked at Arthur with suspicion, wondering how he had managed this magic trick. But, since all thinking for a henchman leads back to violence, the two warriors resumed their attack.

Arthur lifted his sword and began to fight. To his great surprise, the sword seemed light to him. He fought with grace and lightness, as if he were in a dream.

Betameche approached Miro.

"Where did he learn to fight like that?" the little prince wondered.

"It is the sword that gives him this power," Miro replied. "It multiplies the strength of the just."

The two henchmen quickly exhausted all of their moves. Arthur pressed harder, and with each new exchange he cut a bit off the henchmen's swords. Very soon, the two warriors were left with nothing but hilts in their hands.

Arthur took advantage of the moment to catch his breath and to smile a victor's smile.

"Now, down on your knees!" he declared, threatening them with the point of his sword.

Selenia advanced slowly and stood in front of the two warriors, who knelt with their heads bowed.

"We're sorry . . ." said the first.

"Princess," finished the second.

Selenia lifted her chin, as only a princess can.

"Guards! Take the prisoners to the retraining center!" ordered the king. A few guards appeared and led off the two henchmen.

"What is a retraining center?" asked Arthur.

"It is a necessary evil," the old king answered. "I don't like to subject anyone to it, but it is for their own good. After the shock treatment they will go back to what they were before they became evil insects: simple, gentle Minimoys."

Arthur watched the prisoners go, his throat tightening at the thought of the ordeal that awaited them.

Betameche ran up to Arthur, his face alight with amazement.

"You fought like a chief! It was incredible!"

"It's this sword, not me. It's so light, everything seemed easy," Arthur modestly explained.

"Well, of course—it's a magic sword! It has been in the stone for years, and you are the only one who was able to draw it!" announced Betameche with great excitement.

"Really?" asked Arthur.

The king approached, a paternal smile on his lips.

"Yes, Arthur! You are a hero now. Arthur the hero!"

Wild with joy, Betameche began to yell. "Long live Arthur the hero!"

The Minimoys, who were slowly returning to the square, began to cheer as they chanted the name of their hero. Arthur raised his arms in a timid wave, embarrassed by his sudden popularity.

Selenia took advantage of the general euphoria to distract her father. "Now that the sword has been removed from the stone, there is not a moment to lose! I ask your permission to undertake my quest, Father."

The king gazed at the jubilant crowd. They were happy and carefree now, but he couldn't help but wonder how long this moment of peace could last. He gave his daughter a look of deep affection.

"Unfortunately, my daughter, I agree with you. This mission must be undertaken and you are the only one among us who will be able to lead it to a successful conclusion. However, I do have one condition," he added.

"What is it?" asked the princess.

"Arthur is brave and valorous. His heart is pure and his cause is just. He shall accompany you."

His tone was unmistakable. Any discussion would be useless and Selenia knew it. She lowered her eyes and accepted her father's decision without argument, which was fairly unusual, for her.

"I am proud of you, my daughter," her father exclaimed. "I am sure that you two will make an excellent team!"

Only an hour earlier, the princess would have considered this remark a horrible insult. But Arthur had fought bravely and he had saved her father. There was something else, too, although she would never admit it: a little door had opened inside her heart, and somehow Arthur had slipped through.

Arthur could feel that something had changed, but he would have to live a while longer before he'd be able to define it. He smiled shyly at Selenia, as if to apologize for imposing on her.

Selenia's eyes narrowed, like those of a cat when it purrs, and she gave him a radiant smile in return.

The central gate of the city creaked open slowly. A guard stuck his head out and slowly advanced. He shot a flaming arrow. The projectile landed on the ground, some distance away. There was no painted canvas this time.

"The route is clear," called the guard, turning toward the gate, which was now opened wide. All of the Minimoy people were there to bid one last good-bye to their princess and their new hero.

Arthur slid the sword into a magnificent leather sheath that the Minimoys had given him. Miro laid a gentle hand on his shoulder.

"I know that you are going to look for your grandfather, but—" Miro paused, fidgeted, and then continued hurriedly. "But if, during your search, you should encounter a little mole wearing glasses who answers to the name Milo . . . that's my son. He has been gone for three months . . . probably the henchmen . . ." Miro broke off and lowered his head, as if sadness had made it too heavy for him to bear.

"We will watch for him. You can count on me," Arthur said without hesitation.

The old mole smiled, amazed by the young hero's energy and good heart.

"Thank you, Arthur. You're a good boy," he replied.

A short distance away, Betameche was preparing to put on his backpack. Two guards lifted the enormous bag, while the prince slid his arms through the shoulder straps.

"Are you sure you haven't forgotten anything?" joked one of the guards.

"I'm sure. Okay, let it go!"

The two guards, already panting with exhaustion, let go of the pack. Betameche fell back under its weight, landing on the ground like a turtle on its back.

The two guards doubled over with laughter, as did the king. Selenia sighed heavily.

"Father, does Beta really have to come with us? I'm sure he is going to slow us down, and we have so little time as it is!"

"Even though he is still young, Beta is the prince of this kingdom, and one day it may be his turn to rule!" the king answered. "He also deserves this chance to prove his bravery and to learn from the experience."

Selenia scowled, proving that she was still her old self.

"Fine! We'd better get going," she said, turning on her heels and striding away without kissing her father good-bye. "Let's go!" she called to Arthur as she marched past him.

Arthur waved good-bye to Miro and caught up with Selenia. Betameche looked up from where he was removing objects from his pack and saw his sister leaving.

"Hey! Wait for me!" he cried, putting his backpack on again

without taking the time to close it. He ran to catch up with his comrades, leaving a trail of items clattering to the ground behind him.

Selenia was already in the immense tunnel that led out of the city. Betameche caught up to her, gasping.

"You could have waited for me!" he complained.

"Excuse us—we have a country of people to save!" the princess retorted acidly.

The three continued into the darkness of the tunnel. Only the torch that Arthur was carrying dimly lit the way, forming a small ball of light around the three heroes.

Behind them, the Minimoy people were waving their last good-byes as the guards closed the heavy gates with a muffled boom.

The king sighed.

"I hope they'll be able to avoid the henchmen!" he said to Miro in a low voice. "And speaking of henchmen, how are our prisoners?"

"They are stubborn, but we are making progress," the mole answered.

The two henchmen in question had had their armor removed and were soaking in a large bathtub filled with multicolored bubbles. Beautiful Minimoys were blowing bubbles in various shapes around the room, while others danced nearby to a rhythmic tune. The ambiance was warm, sweet, and intoxicating enough to soften even the two chunks of granite that were these henchmen's hearts.

Two charming Minimoys approached and offered them drinks.

"No!" they replied in unison.

The painful process of retraining had begun.

CHAPTER
12

The tunnel in which our three adventurers were walking now seemed colder, darkness, and more threatening. Everywhere the walls were oozing, and each drop that fell from the ceiling hit the ground noisily like bombs being dropped from the sky.

"Selenia, I'm a little scared!" said Betameche, sticking close to his sister.

"So stay home! We'll tell you all about it when we return!" she replied with her natural scornfulness. "Do you want to turn back, too?" she asked Arthur.

"Not for anything in the world!" he replied without hesitation. "I want to stay with you—I mean . . . to protect you!"

Selenia rolled her eyes, seized the sheath from his hands, and buckled it to her belt. "Don't worry about me. I can protect myself!" she said, adjusting the magic sword.

"But it's thanks to Arthur that that sword was released from the stone!" cried Betameche.

"So?" the princess replied nonchalantly.

"Well, the least you could do is thank him!"

"Thank you, Arthur, for releasing the *royal* sword which, as its name indicates, can be worn only by the *royal* family. You're not king yet, as far as I know."

"Um . . . no," a somewhat confused Arthur replied.

"So then I am the one who should carry it!" she said, speeding up. The two boys exchanged dismayed glances. It wouldn't be easy traveling with her attitude.

"We are going to the surface to take a transporter. It will save time!" the princess added. Selenia climbed onto a joint in the tunnel and pulled herself up through a small hole toward the surface.

The three emerged into a forest of tall grass, thick, immense, and almost impenetrable. Of course, to a human-sized person, it was just a small patch of grass, somewhere in the middle of the garden opposite the house.

The second-floor window was still open. A gentle spring breeze brushed across Grandma's cheek as she attempted to awaken from her deep sleep.

"I slept like a log!" she said in a hoarse voice, rubbing the back of her neck.

She put on her slippers and shuffled to Arthur's room. She did not remember that she had locked it only hours before as she turned the knob and peered through the doorway.

The shape of Arthur was bundled under the covers, curled up in the middle of the bed, completely hidden from view. She withdrew with a smile and gently closed the door.

Grandma opened the front door and brought in the two bottles of milk left on the steps—proof that Davido had not yet taken control of the dairy, at least.

This good sign encouraged her to look up and appreciate the beautiful day that had just begun. A blue sky paraded over the cheerful garden and the magnificent trees. Magnificent except for one, that is, which appeared to be in a rather sorry state—the one with the front of a Chevrolet wrapped around its trunk like a scarf.

Grandma started with horror. "What on earth? Did I forget the emergency brake again?" she wondered aloud.

Meanwhile our three heroes were advancing at a healthy pace. They had to be moving at least five hundred inches an hour.

Selenia followed the path as easily as if it were her own garden.

"Selenia? Could you slow down a little, please?" her brother pleaded.

"Absolutely not! It's your own fault—you didn't have to load yourself down like a gamoul!"

"I took a little bit of everything, just in case," Betameche replied breathlessly.

Arthur looked up and saw that Selenia was headed for a centipede who, given their size, was charging toward them like an enormous truck. The creature looked gigantic, with a thousand legs as big as bulldozers. But Selenia continued her route straight toward the monster as if she hadn't seen it.

"Beta—do you have something 'just in case' we come across a thing like that?" asked Arthur, who was pretty close to panicking.

"Don't worry!" Betameche answered, taking something out of his pocket. "I have my knife. It has three hundred functions! I got it for my birthday."

The little prince proudly exhibited his treasure, which looked vaguely like a Swiss army knife, and described its functions.

"See here: a rotating saw, double knife, multiheaded pliers. And there: soap bubbler, music box, and waffle iron. On this side: seed opener, eight-perfume injector, surface vanillier, and for when it is too hot—the fan!" Betameche pressed the button and a magnificent Japanese fan appeared. The little prince immediately began to fan himself, as if bothered by the heat.

"That's funny. For my birthday last year, I got the same thing—well, not exactly!" Arthur answered, keeping an eye on the centipede moving toward them. "So . . . do you have anything for centipedes?" he added anxiously.

"There are all the classics, too!" continued Betameche without really listening. "There's the tulipod, machete, fixomats, gulpers and grinders, hole pluggers, a welding nautilus, an acorn driver—"

Selenia, who had heard just about enough, cut him off. "Is there *anything* that can make you shut up?" she said, drawing the magic sword. Betameche shrugged as Selenia advanced toward the centipede and began to slice its legs as if she were harvesting wheat.

The creature reared up, almost choking on the grass it was nibbling. Our three heroes strolled underneath the centipede as if they were traveling down a supermarket aisle. The centipede took off in the opposite direction, and with all those feet it raised quite a cloud of dust.

Arthur stood still and watched the gigantic animal pass over his head like an airplane taking off. Betameche didn't even look up from his knife.

"Then here, on the last side, there are all the new functions, like the frilled puller, which is very practical for hunting the plumed badarou."

"What kind of bird is that, a badarou?" asked Arthur, his eyes riveted on the centipede's belly.

"It's a fish," Betameche replied. "I also have a white grape peeler, a raisin humidifier, a toad launcher, a kaflon protector, and a series of fist weapons: the para-abacus, the antigisette, a twelve-shot sifflon, the brand-new double-faced karkanon . . ."

The centipede disappeared, leaving a cloud of dust and a

relieved Arthur behind.

"And, last but not least!" concluded Betameche, "the final function, my favorite: the comb!" He pressed a button that released a small tortoiseshell comb. The prince combed the three hairs on his head with genuine delight.

"That's one I don't have," said Arthur with a grin.

The central station, a crossroads for all travelers, was built on ground that was pretty much clear of trees. From a distance, it looked like a flat stone placed on the ground. Closer up, one could see that in fact two stones had been placed one on top of the other.

There was also an enormous counter that could accommodate several dozen passengers at a time. But today, the counter was empty.

Selenia approached the large stone on which the following could be read:

EXPRESSO-TRANSPORTATION
OF ALL KINDS

"Is anyone here?" Selenia asked no one in particular.

There was no reply. But the gates were open and torches were lit inside the offices.

"So, not too many people travel here, in your country," Arthur noted as he looked around.

"Once you have taken one voyage, you will understand

why!" Betameche answered sarcastically.

Arthur didn't like the sound of that, but his attention was drawn to a half ball, placed on the counter. It very closely resembled the kind of bell found at hotel front desks, so Arthur decided to try pressing it.

The object turned out to be an animal, which immediately started shrieking. The creature extended its feet, revealing its babies sleeping under the shell. The mother scolded him in an unknown language, most likely cricket.

"I—I am so sorry! I thought you were a bell!" said an embarrassed Arthur.

The creature looked even more offended and began howling once again.

"No, no, I meant to say: I didn't know that you were alive!" Arthur was in even deeper trouble now. The mother harrumphed several times and moved off along the counter, followed by her brood.

"That won't do, knocking out the clientele like that!" said an old Minimoy who had just appeared behind the counter. His little overalls were made from cornflower petals, and his large mustache was as hairy as his ears.

"I am really sorry," said Arthur.

Selenia came up to the window, cutting the conversation short.

"Excuse me, but we have no time to waste. I am the Princess

Selenia!" she proclaimed.

The old employee closed an eye to squint at her.

"Ah! I see! And is that imbecile over there your brother?"

"Exactly!" Selenia replied before Betameche could open his mouth.

"And who is the third joker, the one assaulting my customers?" grumbled the Minimoy, obviously in a bad mood.

"My name is Arthur," the boy answered politely. "I am looking for my grandfather."

The employee seemed intrigued. He began to think.

"You know, I transported a grandfather a few years ago . . . what the devil was his name . . . ?"

"Archibald?" suggested Arthur.

"Archibald! Yes, that's it!"

"Do you know where he went?" asked Arthur, his eyes full of hope.

"Yes, I remember it well. The old eccentric demanded that I send him to Necropolis! Right into the midst of the henchmen! The poor fool!" he commented.

"That's great!" Arthur exclaimed. "That's exactly where we want to go!"

The agent stood still for a moment, shocked by this response. All at once he slammed his window with a bang, bringing down the gate.

"That's too bad. It's full!" he said.

Selenia didn't have time for this. She took out her sword and cut a hole in the counter. She pushed open the newly sawed-out door, which fell to the ground with a crash.

The employee stood frozen at the back of his office, his mustache vertical with fear.

"What time is the next departure for Necropolis?" demanded the princess.

Betameche had already taken a master schedule out of his pack. It was at least eight hundred pages long.

"The next train leaves in eight minutes!" he said, finding the page. "And it's an express!"

Selenia took out a little purse full of coins and threw it at the employee's feet.

"Three tickets for Necropolis! First class, please!" ordered the princess.

The agent leaned on a huge lever and a giant walnut shell rolled over their heads along a bamboo stick cut in two lengthwise—similar to those in Arthur's water pipeline.

The walnut thundered past and wound up wedged in a hole in an apparatus that looked so complex that it was impossible, at first glance, to understand what it was for.

The agent opened a door in the walnut, like you would in a cable car. Our three heroes ducked inside and Arthur saw that the walnut was hollow, except for a part that had been formed into a bench.

Selenia pulled on a membrane in the middle of the walnut and attached it around her like a seatbelt. Arthur watched her carefully and copied what she did rather than annoy her with the thousands of questions he was dying to ask.

"Bon voyage!" said the agent, slamming the door behind them.

CHAPTER 13

Another door, not too far away, opened slowly.

Grandma peeked into Arthur's room and saw that the boy was still sleeping, buried under the covers. All the better. She would be able to surprise him. She pushed the door open with her foot and entered carrying a magnificent pearly tray, which held a sumptuous breakfast.

She placed the tray down on the end of the bed.

"Breakfast is served!" Grandma announced with a satisfied smile. She tapped on the covers and opened the curtains. The bright morning light entered the room and illuminated the breakfast on the tray.

"Come on, you big good-for-nothing, it's time to get up!" she said, tugging back the covers.

Suddenly, she let out a shriek. Her grandson had been transformed into a dog!

Of course, it turned out to be just Alfred, who had slept in Arthur's bed. The dog wagged his tail, thrilled with his grand oke. Grandma, however, was less amused.

"ARTHUR!" she yelled.

The missing boy was in no danger of hearing her from inside his walnut. He was much too busy trying to figure out his seat belt.

Betameche pulled out a small white ball, as light as a dandelion. He shook it energetically and it lit up. Betameche released this pretty lamp and it floated in space, gently illuminating the cabin.

"I only have a white one. I'm sorry," he said.

Arthur didn't mind. He was fascinated by the magic of this adventure. Even in his wildest dreams, he would never have imagined all this.

The transport agent took up the operator's position, a job as complicated as running an ocean liner. He pushed the first lever. A small needle turned on a disk, which listed the names of the seven lands that make up the Minimoys' world. The needle descended toward the dark part of the disk and stopped on FORBIDDEN LANDS. The enormous machine began to shake and the walnut slowly wobbled into place.

Arthur tried to see what was going on through the cracks in the walnut.

"I still don't understand how we are going to travel," he said.

"Well—in the walnut," responded Betameche, as if it were obvious. "How else would we go?"

The little prince unfolded a map showing the seven lands.

"We are here. And we are going there!" Betameche pointed as if it were a trip to the suburbs.

Arthur bent over the map and tried to figure out, despite the scale, where they were. He noticed that Necropolis was located not far from the house.

"I recognize that!" the boy said suddenly. "Necropolis must be right under the garage and water tank."

"What's a water tank?" asked Selenia, suddenly uneasy.

"It's where we keep all the water the house needs—in an enormous tank, which it looks like is located here . . . just above Necropolis."

Grandma turned on the fluorescent light in the garage. It was hopelessly empty. No trace of Arthur.

"Where did he go?" she asked the dog. Even if Alfred could speak, he knew very well that Grandma would never believe him.

"How many gallons does your tank hold, exactly?" questioned Selenia, obviously on the track of something.

"Oh, thousands upon thousands!" Arthur answered.

The face of the princess darkened. "I think I'm starting to get a picture of his sinister plans," she said.

"Whose?" Arthur asked.

"The plans of M.," the princess replied, as if Arthur were thickheaded.

"Oh—Maltazard?" Arthur asked in a conspiratorial tone. Betameche and Selenia stiffened and he realized his mistake.

A muffled rumbling immediately arose from deep below them, signaling the approach of the kind of catastrophe that saying the name of M. always brought.

"In the name of a humpbacked gamoul!" screamed Selenia. "Weren't you ever taught to watch your language?"

"I—I'm so sorry," Arthur stammered.

The transport agent had his stethoscope placed against an enormous tunnel. He could feel the rumbling, and it was becoming louder.

"Departing for Necropolis in ten seconds," he called, putting on his safety goggles.

Betameche pulled out two red, cottonlike balls from his pack. "Do you want some mouf-moufs to put in your ears?" he asked Arthur.

"No, thanks," replied the boy, his attention focused on the ground, which had started to vibrate.

"Are you sure? You're making a big mistake. These are top quality mouf-moufs. They are completely new, never been used, and thanks to their self-cleaning fur, you can also—"

He was cut short mid-sentence by Selenia stuffing a mouf-mouf into his mouth.

The ground had been vibrating; now it was trembling furiously. Arthur had to hang on to keep from being flung all around.

The transport agent pushed a second lever. The needle turned once again around another disk. This one was the power indicator. The needle stopped in the red zone, where it read MAXIMUM.

Grandma was in a panic. She went through the house three times, and five times through the garden. She found not a trace of where Arthur might have gone. She stood one more time on top of the front steps and used her hands as a megaphone.

"ARTHUUUUR!"

Despite the noise and the shaking, Arthur perked up his ears. He could have sworn he'd heard a far-off voice calling his name. He leaned over to the tiny slit in the joint of the walnut and tried to locate the voice.

"Grandma?" he said.

"Blast off!" the conductor announced.

An umbrella opened automatically above the transport agent, while a veritable geyser shot out of the ground. Yes: the contraption holding the walnut was an automatic sprinkler. The force of the jet launched the walnut into the air and the trip was under way.

The nut hurtled through the air, crossing the garden at a height of several feet.

Through the slit, Arthur could see his grandma, who was turning to go back into the house.

"*Grandmaaaa!*" called the boy in one long shout.

Selenia was very sorry now that she had not put in her mouf-moufs.

Grandma turned around. Had she heard a small voice in the distance?

"Grandma! I'm here!" shouted Arthur, but his cry barely got through the walls of the walnut.

Grandma had neither seen nor heard anything. She stood watching the automatic sprinklers for a moment as they turned on, one after another.

Betameche finally managed to spit out his mouf-mouf.

"Selenia! Mouf-moufs are not meant to go in your mouth!" he yelped. "That was a terrible thing to do. Now I'm thirsty!"

"I have a feeling you'll be wet enough soon, don't worry!" answered Selenia, who was trying to observe the water jet from a hole in the walnut.

"How long does the flight last?" asked Arthur, hanging on to the bench.

"A few seconds—if everything goes well," the princess said in a concerned voice.

"What do you mean, if everything goes well?" said Arthur worriedly.

"If we don't have an unfortunate encounter with something!"

For once, Arthur felt that the princess was worried about nothing.

"What kind of unfortunate encounter could we have up

here, in the middle of the air?" he asked with a grin.

"One like this!" she cried, curling up on the bench.

All of a sudden, an enormous bumblebee surged out of the beating rain of the sprinkler and smashed into the walnut. The shock was violent, like two cars crashing into each other. The walnut was knocked completely off course, while the bumblebee, its wings damaged, whirled in a tailspin toward the ground.

Inside the walnut, there was total panic and chaos. It was worse than an earthquake. The walnut crash-landed in a patch of tall grass, where it rolled for a moment, then came to a standstill.

Each of the passengers slowly came to. Beta noticed that his backpack was empty, its contents scattered.

"Now I have to repack the whole bag!" He sighed.

"I've told you a hundred times—you should carry fewer things!" Selenia retorted, climbing to her feet.

Arthur was just happy to be alive and in one piece.

"Are trips around here always like that?" he asked.

"Long-distance trips like this are calmer than most of the ways we travel," Selenia answered.

"Oh?" said Arthur, trying to imagine a less calm form of travel.

Selenia looked through the crack again.

"Let's wait for the rain to stop before we leave. We'll be able to see more clearly then."

* * *

Grandma was still on the front steps when the automatic sprinklers shut off one by one. Silence was restored, magnifying her long sigh of desperation over her missing grandson.

She turned around, entered the empty house, and gently closed the door behind her.

"It's calmed down. We'll be able to go out now," Selenia announced.

Betameche finished replacing things in his pack while his sister tried to open the door, which had been crushed during the accident.

"That awful bumblebee dented the door! It's stuck!"

Arthur tried to help her, to no avail.

Outside, a monstrous earthworm was approaching the walnut. It was not the nut that interested it but the appetizing dandelion leaves that the walnut had crushed during its landing.

The worm paused by the walnut and inadvertently gave it a shove so the whole thing rocked precariously.

"What was that?" Arthur worried.

"I don't know," Selenia confessed. "But we'd better not stay here."

She unsheathed the magic sword and struck through the walnut shell with one swing. Unfortunately, she also pierced one of the segments of the earthworm outside, making it jump in surprise and kick the walnut hard. The shot was powerful and precise. The walnut flew through the air. Of course, Beta-meche's backpack was flung open once again. As our three heroes clung to the walls, the shell rolled and rolled and finally plopped into the stream, where it was carried off like a small boat.

Arthur climbed to his feet, feeling seasick.

"Everything will be fine once we stop moving," he managed nervously.

At that moment he noticed water starting to seep in through the joints in the shell and through the hole made by the sword. Selenia also saw what was happening and stared at the stream of water as if it were a poisonous snake.

"It's water! Arthur! We're taking in water!" she cried, start-ing to panic.

"It's terrible! We're doomed!" Betameche shrieked, clinging to his sister.

"Where are we? Arthur! Where are we?" demanded Selenia, now close to hysterics. Minimoys clearly reacted very badly to water.

"I don't know," Arthur replied, pulling the sword out of her hands. He brandished the weapon over his head and struck a powerful blow along the joint. The walnut broke in two and each half split off to float separately, leaving Selenia and Betameche in one half, Arthur on the other.

"Arthur, do something! Help us!"

Arthur felt that this was somewhat unfair, as he was the one being carried away on the sinking half. But chivalry has no limits.

"Don't worry, I'll save you!" called Arthur as the water climbed up to his waist. "I know this stream. There's a curve up ahead on the right! I'll catch you there."

"You call this a stream?" Selenia exclaimed, wondering whether Arthur was making fun of her.

"I'm coming!" Arthur called. He jumped into the water and tried, as best he could, to reach the bank.

"That boy is totally nuts!" Betameche observed, watching his friend swim.

Arthur managed to haul himself up onto the bank and immediately disappeared into the tall grass.

Selenia and her brother hugged each other in terror.

"I don't want to die!" Betameche cried in a trembling voice.

"Everything will be all right—calm down!" Selenia replied, holding him close.

"Do you think he will abandon us?" asked her brother.

Selenia thought for a moment. "I don't know human beings well enough to be sure, but based on the few that I've heard about—I'm afraid there's a good chance the answer is yes!"

"No!" cried the prince, devastated.

"Unless, of course . . . he's in love. I've heard humans will do almost anything when they're in love," Selenia added, her tone of voice indicating that she thought this was an unlikely hypothesis.

Arthur ran until he was out of breath, jumping over branches, bending blades of grass, dodging insects. No obstacle could stop him, not even the colony of ants that he encountered along the way.

Betameche clung to the princess.

"Dear gods, make Arthur be in love with my sister! Please!"

Arthur ran like a maniac, as if his life depended on it.

There was no question about it: this young man was in love. He dashed through the miniature jungle and bolted out on top of the bank.

The walnut shell and its occupants appeared around a bend in the stream.

Betameche spotted Arthur.

"Selenia! He *is* in love!" he cried joyously.

"Let's not get carried away," said the princess, a bit embarrassed.

Fortunately, Arthur heard none of this. He headed toward the stream, climbed on a tall stone, and leaped through the air. It was a world-class jump, worthy of a slow-motion replay on the evening news. As for the landing, it was not as smooth. Arthur smashed into the bottom of the walnut, knocking his friends over like bowling pins.

"You see! I didn't abandon you!" Arthur said proudly.

"Great! Instead of two of us dying, now it will be all three of us!" the princess retorted.

"No one is going to die, Selenia! You're not afraid of this

little stream, are you?" Arthur wondered.

"But it's not a little stream, Arthur! It's a raging river and there, at the end of it, are the Devil's Falls!" the princess cried.

Arthur looked downstream. It did sound rather as if the noise were coming from the depths of the earth. Water sprayed all around them as the shell was tossed and spun.

"I—I didn't know that was coming!" Arthur stammered.

The falls roared louder and louder as they came into view. They were monstrous, and well deserved their name. They were so powerful they made Niagara Falls seem like a trickle.

Arthur was paralyzed. The walnut, unfortunately, was not.

"Fabulous. Any bright ideas before we die?" Selenia asked, poking Arthur with her elbow.

Arthur gave a start. He looked around him thoughtfully and noticed a tree trunk that crossed the stream just before the falls.

"Do you have a rope in that three-hundred-function knife of yours?" he asked Betameche.

"Of course not! This is the small model," the prince responded.

Arthur turned to Selenia. "I have an idea! It's worth a try!" he said, jumping up. "Can I have your belt?"

"He really is nuts!" said Betameche in amazement.

"I need your belt to make a rope so we can climb onto that tree trunk. It's our only chance."

Selenia hesitated, then agreed. She removed her belt and

handed it to him. Arthur picked up the magic sword and quickly tied the belt around the hilt.

"Beta first, then Selenia! We must be quick—we only have a few seconds!" Arthur announced, brandishing the sword.

"Do you have any idea what you're doing?" Selenia asked, crossing her arms.

"Sure—it can't be any more difficult than throwing a dart!" he answered, eyeing the tree. Arthur took aim and threw the sword with all his might. The blade shot through the air like a rocket and the sword planted itself in the middle of the tree.

"Yes!" Arthur cheered, waving his arms. "Get ready, Beta!"

He had barely grabbed hold of the rope when Betameche was on his head, climbing like a monkey. Arthur balanced himself as best he could in the walnut as it tried to surge ahead down the river.

Betameche scaled the trunk and reached solid ground safely.

"Your turn, Selenia!" Arthur yelled over the deafening sound.

Selenia stared at the churning water below them in terror.

"Hurry up! I can't hold on much longer!" cried Arthur, who was using all his strength to hold her belt with two hands and the walnut with his feet. Selenia mustered her courage and clambered up the belt rope. At the top she stopped to catch her breath next to the sword, planted horizontally in the tree.

Arthur was nearly at the point of collapse. He let go of the walnut and it quickly floated away, leaving him hanging over the surging stream. The wind tossed him back and forth as he pulled himself painfully up the belt, hand over hand. The walnut shell flew over the edge and was swallowed up by the Devil's Falls, showing all too clearly what might have happened to Arthur and his companions.

Selenia climbed on the trunk and carefully descended to the ground. Arthur called on his last bit of energy and finally also reached the trunk of the tree.

Exhausted, he stayed there for a moment, kneeling, trying to catch his breath. Selenia had moved away. She was seated at the end of a branch, just above a small lake nearby, looking serene. Betameche was not far off, trying to squeeze out the bottom of his shirt. Arthur removed the sword from the tree and approached Selenia.

"Are you okay?" Arthur asked.

"I'd like my belt back," she replied.

Arthur turned the sword and began to untie the knot.

"As for me, I have never been so scared in all my life!" Betameche admitted, delighted to have his feet back on solid ground.

Selenia shrugged her shoulders, as if to brush aside the adventure.

"It was no big deal. After all, it was only water!" she said.

As if in punishment, the heavens decided at that moment to cause her little branch to break, and the princess fell into the lake. "Arthur! Help! I don't know how to swim," she shrieked, flapping her arms.

Arthur ran out onto the branch and executed a magnificent dive, smacking headfirst, as it turned out, into the shallow mud of the lake. He stood up, holding his head. The water was only knee-deep. The princess was still struggling.

"Selenia, look! You can stand!"

Little by little, Selenia calmed down and realized that her feet could touch the bottom. She hesitated a moment, then stood up. The water just reached her calves.

"Didn't you say something about . . . it's only water?" Betameche reminded her mischievously.

"Can I have my belt now?" Selenia insisted, as angry as a hornet. She pulled it out of Arthur's hands and turned away to put it on.

"That's twice he's saved your life on the same day!" said Betameche, always ready to add fuel to the fire.

"He did what any gentleman would do in his place," retorted the princess.

"Perhaps, but I think it's worth at least a brief word of thanks!" Betameche insisted.

Arthur signaled to him to let it drop. He wouldn't know how to react to a thank-you anyway. But Betameche loved to tease his sister about things that really annoyed her.

Selenia finished tying her belt and stalked up to a completely intimidated Arthur. She stopped in front of her savior and pulled the sword out of his hands.

"Thanks!" she said dryly, before passing in front of him and moving away.

Betameche smiled and shrugged. He could see that Arthur was more bewildered by the twists and turns of his sister's behavior than he had been in the waters of the raging river. Beta grinned and shook his head at him.

"It's like that with princesses!"

CHAPTER

14

Grandma opened the front door to two policemen in uniform, holding their hats politely in their hands.

"Thank you for coming. I wasn't sure if you would get the message I sent with the mailman. My husband disappeared four years ago and now my grandson . . . I can't take much more," Grandma told them, twisting her lace handkerchief in her hands.

"Don't worry, Mrs. S.," Martin the policeman said, as kind as always. "He has probably just run away. He must have been upset by everything that has been happening with Davido and the house and his parents—I'm sure he can't have gone too far." He glanced at the horizon thoughtfully, not realizing that all he really needed to do was look down at the lawn.

"We will look for him, and I am sure that we will find him. You can count on us!" said the other policeman. For a moment, the two of them resembled the patrollers that Arthur had invented to travel up and down the trenches, as proud and brave as the heroes of a television series.

Grandma sighed, only partly comforted.

"Thank you, officers."

The policemen went back to their car, replacing their hats on their heads.

Grandma waved good-bye as the police car left the garden. The vibration of the motor could be felt all through the ground and made the blades of grass tremble. At Minimoy level, this simple passage of a vehicle felt like an earthquake moving off into the distance.

"What was that?" asked Arthur in a worried voice.

"Humans," responded Selenia, who was used to it.

"Oh?" mumbled Arthur, feeling a little guilty. He had never imagined the destruction that a human being could cause during the course of simple daily acts.

Betameche had unfolded his map, which was by now completely wet and faded.

"We can't see anything! What are we going to do?" worried the little prince.

Arthur looked up toward the sky.

"Well, the sun is there, and the water tank is north. So we have to go in that direction!" he said, pointing to the road. "Trust me!" he added with a new confidence.

He pushed aside three blades of grass and walked straight into a giant hole. Fortunately, he caught hold of a root as he slid by, narrowly avoiding a bone-crushing fall. He crawled back along the root and climbed up over the edge of the crater.

"What on earth is that?" he asked, mesmerized by the gaping hole.

"The humans, again," Selenia replied sadly. "Since yesterday it seems that they have sworn to kill us. They made dozens of holes like that all over the place."

Aha—the holes dug by Arthur during his search for the treasure. He wanted to apologize, but he didn't quite have the courage to confess.

On the opposite side of the hole, an ant colony was building a road that descended to the bottom of the crater. Each ant carried a large sack of earth on its back.

"They have months of work ahead of them to repair and rebuild their system," said Selenia.

"If only we knew why these idiots were digging holes everywhere!" Betameche added with great annoyance.

Arthur's heart sunk to his boots. He wished he were brave enough to tell them that the idiot . . . was him.

"Don't be stupid, Beta! Humans don't know that we exist. So they can't possibly be aware of the damage they cause," Selenia explained patiently.

"They will know soon enough," Arthur interjected. "And this type of catastrophe will never happen again. You have my word."

"We'll see," Selenia replied with natural skepticism. "In the meantime, it is getting dark. We have to find a place to sleep."

The orange light at the end of the day made the country-side seem almost monochromatic. Only the sky, awaiting the night, had kept its deep blue color.

The little group headed toward a poppy, which waved proudly, very red and very alone. Betameche took out his multi-purpose knife.

"Where did they put the metaglue?" he wondered, triggering the mechanism. He pushed a button and an enormous fireball shot out of the object. Arthur had just enough time to duck before the flames passed directly over his head.

"Oops!" said Betameche by way of an apology.

Selenia grabbed the knife from his hands.

"Give me that, or you're going to end up hurting someone!"

"I haven't had it very long. I got it as a birthday present," explained the little prince to Arthur.

"How old are you?" Arthur asked.

"Three hundred forty-seven years old. In eighteen years, I will be an adult," explained Betameche happily.

Arthur took out a tangled-up abacus from Betameche's pack and tried to unravel this mystery.

Meanwhile, Selenia pushed the correct button and a spurt of metaglue attached itself to one of the poppy's petals. Spider-Man could not have done better.

She pulled a pick out from the knife and planted it in the ground. A small mechanism was released to wind the thread, pulling the petal down toward them and opening it, like the drawbridge of a fortress.

Arthur was still calculating.

"And . . . Selenia? How old is she?" he asked hesitantly.

"Pretty soon she'll be a thousand, the age of reason," Beta-meche replied with a touch of envy. "Her birthday is in two days."

Arthur was beyond confusion. And he had been so proud to be ten years old!

The petal was now completely open and sufficiently low-ered so that Selenia could climb into the flower. She took out her sword, caught the stamens, and cut them off at the base. Then she shook them until the little yellow balls fell off, form-ing a soft bed. Arthur watched her with awe.

Selenia threw away the stems of the stamens, now useless, and gestured to the two boys to climb into the flower. Betameche immediately threw himself down on the soft bed of yellow balls.

"I am dead tired! Good night!" he said, taking the time only to roll over before falling asleep.

Arthur was impressed. Here was somebody who didn't need Grandma's sleeping medicine.

"He falls asleep easily," he commented.

"He is young," Selenia explained.

"Three hundred and forty-seven years is still something!"

Selenia took the small luminous ball from her brother's backpack. She shook the ball to light it, and let it float inside the poppy.

"And you—will you really be a thousand in two days?"

"Yes," the princess replied simply, cutting the metaglue thread with one stroke of her sword.

The petal immediately folded up and surrounded them.

Inside, the ambiance was muffled and the light was soft. Selenia stretched out on the bed of yellow balls, like a cat relaxing on a carpet.

Arthur sat down beside her. Selenia was lost in her thoughts.

"In two days, I will succeed my father and rule over the Minimoy people until my own children are a thousand years old and succeed me in turn. That is how life is in the Seven Lands."

Arthur remained quiet for a few moments. He was thoughtful.

"But . . . in order to have children, surely you have to have . . . a husband?"

"I know. But that's all right, I still have two days to find one! Good night!" she said, turning around.

Arthur felt like an idiot, full of questions. He leaned over to check, but she was already snoring. The boy sighed and stretched out next to the princess. He slipped his hands behind his head and let a smile travel across his face as he fell asleep.

It was almost night. The first stars were shining. There was only this luminous poppy in the middle of a sleeping forest, like a lighthouse on an invisible coast.

Beta's knife lay near him, shining in the moonlight, waiting for the morning.

But a hand appeared over the edge of the poppy petals and seized the knife. A rough hand . . . a terrifying hand. The night closed in and covered the criminal's escape.

Grandma went out onto the front steps, a candlelit lantern in her hand.

She searched the dark with the aid of this weak light, but everything around her was quiet and she saw no sign of Arthur.

Resigned, she hung the lamp on a hook over the front door and went back into the house, very unhappy.

The night passed, and the first rays of sunlight appeared, outlining the black hills on the horizon.

CHAPTER
15

The sun was also rising on the land of the Minimoys, and one of its rays had just peeked through the top of the poppy. Selenia awoke and stretched like a tiger. Then she jumped up and kicked each of the two boys.

"Everybody up! We have a long way to go!" Her cry echoed around the flower.

The two boys got up very slowly, still sleepy. Arthur ached all over from the events of the past few days. He knew they still had a long way to go before they got to Necropolis . . . and that if they didn't get there and back in time, his whole mission would be a failure.

Selenia pushed a petal with her foot and light invaded the flower. The two boys shielded their eyes from the strong sunshine.

"Okay! We have a new plan!" the princess declared.

Betameche slid down a petal to the ground. Arthur followed him by jumping out. Selenia joined them, in turn, by sliding down the length of the petal, as if she were on a toboggan.

"Everyone to the showers!" she said, in her usual imperious voice.

Arthur stretched painfully.

"It's hard waking up in your country!" he complained. "Where I live, my grandma brings me breakfast in bed every day."

"Well, where we live, only the king is served in bed. And you're not king yet, as far as I know."

Arthur turned a telltale shade of red. To be king was his secret dream—but not for the power or luxuries like breakfast in bed, but simply for the happiness of being married to the woman who soon would be queen. It didn't matter to him that she was a thousand years old.

"Don't complain!" Betameche said. "She's been kicking *me* awake for the last two hundred years!"

Selenia stood under a dewdrop hanging at the tip of a blade of grass. She took one of her hairpins and pierced the drop neatly. A little stream of water spilled out. Selenia caught the water in her cupped hands and washed her face.

Arthur watched her do it with amusement. It was a change from his grandma's shower with its sticking curtain. He saw another drop, a bit larger, at the end of a leaf, and went over to stand underneath it.

"You shouldn't stand under that one," the princess advised him.

"Oh? Why not?" asked Arthur.

"It's ripe," she said, just as the drop detached itself and fell on Arthur. Instead of exploding, the drop absorbed him so he was trapped in the enormous mass like a fly in custard.

Betameche fell over laughing.

"You were fooled, just like a beginner!" he said.

"Help me, instead of laughing at me like a hyena! I'm trapped!" Arthur cried.

"I'm coming!" Betameche answered, bending his knees and jumping onto the drop, the way one would on a trampoline. Between bounces, he recited a little nursery rhyme that was very popular with the Minimoys:

> "A little drop of water, that fell early·in the day
> Rolled up to the road to drown its sorrow.
> No one heard it or helped along the way.
> So it left, saying 'See you all tomorrow!'"

Selenia let him recite only two lines before pulling out her sword and slicing into the drop, causing it to explode. Betameche sprawled onto Arthur. The two boys were drenched—all showered for the day.

"I'm really hungry, aren't you?" Betameche said, as if nothing had happened.

"We'll eat later!" Selenia snapped, adjusting her sword and beginning to carve out their route through the grass. Betameche got up and began searching in his backpack for his knife.

"My knife is gone!" he said in a worried voice. "Selenia, someone has stolen my knife!"

"Great news! That should keep you from hurting anyone!" his sister replied, already moving off into the undergrowth.

The little prince was angry, but he resigned himself to the loss and followed his companions.

Grandma appeared on the front steps of the house. The sun sent her its golden light, but no sign of Arthur.

The milk bottles weren't there, either. There was a note in their place. She picked it up and read.

> *Dear Madam,*
> *Your account is overdue. We cannot continue to*
> *make deliveries until you have paid in full.*
> *Thank you.*
>
> *Emile Johnson,*
> *director of the Davido Milk Corporation*

Grandma let out a brief laugh, as if this signature on the evil note came as no surprise. She took down the hurricane lamp with its burned-out candle and went back into the house.

Betameche was wolfing down strange little red balls he'd picked off the leaves. Arthur picked one himself and looked at it skeptically.

"It's my favorite food!" the little prince said with his mouth full.

Arthur sniffed the rather transparent ball and bit into it. It was somewhat sweet, with a tart skin. It melted in his mouth like an overlight marshmallow. Arthur was immediately entranced and took another bite of the ball.

"It's terrific!" he admitted. "What is it?"

"A dragonfly egg," said Betameche.

Arthur froze, choked, and spat out everything, totally disgusted. Betameche roared with laughter and helped himself to another.

"Come and see!" Selenia cried from a clearing farther up ahead. Arthur ran to join her, brushing himself off as best he could.

Selenia was at the edge of a large canyon, clearly created by human hands.

All along the canal, someone had planted, vertically and at regular intervals, monstrous pipes with red and white stripes.

Arthur was mesmerized by this all-too-familiar horror . . . that he had created. It was, of course, his bamboo pole, marked at intervals with straws. Never had he imagined that this work, seen from below, could be so ugly.

"How terrible!" Betameche exclaimed. "Humans are really horrible creatures!"

"Yes, seen from here, it's not very pretty," Arthur admitted.

"Does anyone know what it's for?" Selenia asked.

Arthur felt obliged to provide an explanation. "It's an irrigation system. It is used for transporting water."

"Water? Again?" exclaimed Betameche. "We're all going to end up drowning to death, aren't we?"

"I'm sorry. I didn't know," said Arthur, annoyed.

"Do you mean to say that *you* built this monstrosity?" asked the prince with a disgusted expression.

"Yes, I did, but it was meant to water the radishes!"

"Oh, you eat these disgusting things, too? Have I mentioned that humans are really mad?" Betameche said.

Selenia observed the construction analytically.

"Let us hope that your invention does not fall into the hands of M., because I can imagine how he might make use of it."

Arthur stiffened—because of what she said, but also because of what he saw behind Selenia's back.

"Too late," said Betameche, who had seen the same thing.

Selenia turned and saw a group of henchmen advancing from the bottom of the canyon. A few of them were riding mosquitoes; the others were on foot, cutting the straws to the ground with saws.

The cut straws fell to the ground and rolled toward the stream that had formed in the middle of the canyon. The straws then followed the path of the water, like enormous tree trunks traveling downriver.

Our heroes jumped into a bush and watched what was happening.

"I wonder what they are going to do with my straws," Arthur said.

"As long as they get rid of them for us, it's okay by me!" Betameche replied.

Selenia hit him in the head.

"Think before speaking such foolishness! They know that Minimoys can't stand water, except for washing. And now they have a way to transport water . . . wherever they wish." Her expression darkened, as if black thoughts were passing behind her eyes. "And where do you think they are going to reroute the water?" she asked, knowing the answer already.

A henchman cut another straw that fell with a horrible crash.

"Toward our village?" Betameche realized. "But that's horrible! We will all drown! All because of Arthur's invention?"

Arthur felt so guilty that he could hardly breathe. He felt a large knot fill his stomach. He jumped up, angrily brushing away tears.

"Where are you going?" Selenia hissed.

"I'm going to make up for my stupidity!" he said with dignity. "If what you say is true, the henchmen must be planning to send the straws straight to Necropolis—which means I'm going along with them!"

Arthur hurtled out of the grass and dashed into the end of the nearest freshly cut straw. Fortunately, the henchmen were too busy to notice him.

Arthur beckoned for his companions to accompany him.

"That boy is truly crazy!" Betameche announced.

"He's crazy, but he's right. The straws are going to end up in the forbidden city . . . and we will, too!" added Selenia before leaping out of her hiding place and throwing herself, in turn, inside the straw.

The henchmen had still seen nothing, but their work was bringing them steadily closer. Betameche sighed as he considered his choices.

"Okay, but they *could* ask me for *my* opinion now and then!" he remarked in an offended tone before running to join his comrades.

The henchmen reached the straw occupied by our runaways and kicked it down to the stream. The straw slid onto the water and began to float away. Inside, our three heroes were thrown in all directions.

"My back is aching all over!" Betameche complained.

"Stop whining and give me your mouf-moufs!" his sister ordered.

"If it's to put them in my mouth, no way!"

"Give them to me!" the princess cried with authority.

Betameche grumbled, but he took the mouf-moufs out of his pack and handed them to his sister.

"We are going to plug up the holes," Selenia explained, throwing a ball to each end. "Mints, quick!"

Beta grabbed his peashooter and inserted a small white candy. He blew the tube in the direction of the mouf-mouf, which inflated instantly, hardened, and turned violet.

He did the same thing on the other side, and now the straw was completely sealed on either end.

Selenia rubbed her hands happily.

"This way, we won't take on any water!"

"And we can travel calmly!" added Betameche, stretching himself out in the hollow of the straw.

The voyage did not remain calm for long, however. The little stream turned to merge with a stronger current of water that felt decidedly larger.

"Do you hear that muffled sound that keeps getting louder?" Betameche asked.

Selenia listened. There *was* a sound—a background noise that resembled a very low vibration.

"Hey, Mr. Know-It-All, do you know where this current is headed?" Selenia asked Arthur.

"Not exactly. But all the currents meet up with each other at some point, so they always end up at the same place, which is to say . . ."

Little by little, it dawned on Arthur what he was about to say.

"Devil's Falls!" our three heroes screamed in a single, panicked voice.

It was the end of the relaxed journey. The straws were rushing toward the fathomless waterfall.

"You always have such good ideas, don't you!" Selenia yelled at Arthur.

"I didn't think that—"

"Of course you didn't! Next time, *try* thinking before you act!" she screamed. "Betameche, find something. We have to get out of here!"

"I'm moving as fast as I can!" replied the little prince, who was once again emptying his backpack of useless objects.

"I'm sure it'll be fine," Arthur said. "The mouf-moufs are blocking the two ends. Nothing can happen to us! Besides, the falls are not that large—hardly three feet tall!"

The straw reached the edge of the monstrous waterfall, which was more like a thousand feet tall by Minimoy measurements. The straw tipped over gently and plunged into the void.

"AIIIIEEEEEEEEEEE!!!!" screamed our three heroes, but the deafening sound of the falls drowned out their voices.

After plunging for several seconds that seemed more like several hours, the straw landed with a splash among foaming whirlpools. The straw got stuck in a spin, came unstuck, rolled, and then, carried by the current, ended up heading toward a small, much calmer lake.

There was a pause.

"I really hate public transportation!" Betameche complained.

"We are past the falls. It will be calmer now!" Arthur assured them, untangling himself from Betameche's things.

The straws dispersed in the middle of the lake. It was almost too calm to be true.

Suddenly, a creature with jointed feet landed on top of their straw, like a car falling from the sky. Through the semitransparent wall of the straw, they could see its footprints. And, given their unfamiliar shape, there was cause for some concern.

"What is that?" asked Betameche, frozen with terror at the bottom of the straw.

"How should I know?" Selenia replied edgily.

"Quiet!" whispered Arthur. "If we are quiet it will surely continue on its way."

Arthur appeared to be right—for about three seconds. Then a monstrous saw sliced into the straw, a hairsbreadth away from Selenia, who screamed.

Horror reigned. Splinters flew everywhere and the noise was unbearable. The top of the straw was cut off, level with the small accordion section where a straw bends.

All three tried to scramble on all fours to the opposite end, but the creature leaped forward, blocking their way. Our heroes found themselves in the accordion section, on the water's edge, facing their doom.

The creature sawed again, even with the other end of the accordion. It detached the small, bulging section of straw hiding our three friends. This seemed to be the only part in which it was interested.

The three of them were terrified and clung to each other for comfort.

The creature was still standing on the striped accordion section. Only the bottom of its feet could be seen. But something must have caught its attention, because now the imprint of its knees, and then its hands, appeared. It was on all fours above them. Its head appeared, upside down, at the opening of the straw.

The creature had long braids, decorated with seashells, that hung loose in the air.

It was a Koolomassai. The creature lifted his safety goggles, observed our terrorized heroes for a moment, and smiled a wide smile, showing beautiful white teeth. Since his head was upside down, his smile was, too, and Arthur was not sure what to think.

"What are you doing in there?" asked the Koolomassai, laughing.

Selenia spotted a mosquito approaching in the distance.

"If the henchmen find us, we will not have the pleasure of telling you!" she snapped humorlessly.

The Koolomassai got the message and stood up.

"Is there a problem?" asked the henchman, landing his mosquito next to what remained of the straw. Arthur, Betameche, and Selenia held their breaths, huddled just out of the henchman's sight.

"No, nothing special. I was just checking to see if this was damaged," answered the Koolomassai employee nonchalantly.

"We are only interested in the tubes. This part doesn't interest us," said the henchman, pointing to the accordion section

"What luck! This is exactly the part that interests us! I gues we won't have anything to argue about, then!" added the worker cheerfully.

But the henchmen, as a general rule, did not appreciate humor.

"Hurry up. The master is waiting," barked the henchman, whose patience and intelligence seemed equally limited.

"No problem!" answered the Koolomassai. "Don't move," he whispered to Arthur and the others. "I'll come back for you!"

Then he disappeared, jumping from one straw to another.

"Hurry up, the master is waiting!" cried the Koolomassai to his comrades, who were dispersed among the other straws floating on the lake. The workers halfheartedly sped up, but with little enthusiasm. (It was a bit like those taxi drivers who deliberately slow down when you are in a hurry.)

The Koolomassai used a long stick to guide the straws toward another current of water. In passing, he separated the accordion sections and pushed them toward the shore. Our three friends followed the Koolomassai's advice and didn't move.

A kind of crane, built from wood and vines, caught the little piece of straw with our adventurers inside and tossed it into an enormous basket. The accordion section landed among a veritable harvest of twenty others.

The basket was attached to the back of an enormous insect— a gamoul, which is an extremely strong type of beetle that often served as a mule. The animal was also used in many popular expressions, such as "stubborn as a gamoul" or (and this was the case here) "loaded down like a gamoul."

"Where are we?" Arthur asked uncertainly.

"On the back of a gamoul. The Koolomassai is hiding us for the moment," Selenia said.

"He is hiding us so that he can betray us!" said Betameche.

"If he wanted to betray us, he would have done so already!" Selenia replied sensibly. "I'll bet we are going to a safe place now."

CHAPTER
16

A *metallic trapdoor rolled open in the side of the hill.* The gamoul raised up onto its legs and prepared to empty the contents of the basket into a black hole that bore a strange resemblance to a garbage chute.

"This is your safe place?" asked Betameche anxiously.

Dozens of accordion sections slid down into the black hole in an impressively chaotic manner, rolling to a standstill several inches below, on the dark ground. Arthur, Betameche, and Selenia managed to stay in their straw.

Nothing moved. Silence returned. The three heroes glanced at one another uncertainly.

"He said not to move. So we don't move until he comes to get us!" said Selenia authoritatively.

An automatic arm swooped up the accordion section and placed it vertically, standing on end, squishing the three of them into a heap at the bottom. The piece of straw began moving along a conveyor belt. The mechanical arm continued to do its work, aligning all of the accordion sections on the belt that carried them away.

A little farther down, another machine embedded a luminous ball in the center of each accordion, like an internal crown. Our heroes just managed to avoid getting "crowned" themselves.

The accordion section of the straw now had an orange light in its center, and they began to understand how these objects would be put to use.

A final machine caught the section of straws and attached them to a cable that stretched into space, a magnificent garland hung with evenly spaced striped Chinese lanterns. The lights continued around the edge of a circular dance floor. It was, in fact, an old record, placed on an antique record player that served as both bar and dance floor underground. The warm light from the lanterns created a muted ambiance for meeting people. There were also lots of small tables provided for this purpose. Toward the right side were the arm and stylus of the record player and the DJ. Toward the left, the enormous bar was buzzing with activity. Half the customers were obviously henchmen from the royal army of M.

Arthur and his friends observed this strange nightclub from above, still gripping the inside of their "Chinese lantern."

"I can't hold on much longer," said Arthur, exhausted.

"Do you really want to go down there?" asked Selenia, pointing with her nose toward a new group of henchmen that had just entered the bar.

After a moment's thought, Arthur replied, "I guess I can hold on a little longer!"

Just then they saw their Koolomassai friend arrive on the dance floor. He was followed by his boss, who was taller and broader.

Their Koolomassai looked up and examined the lanterns one by one, searching for the fugitives. Since the lanterns were translucent, they were rather easy to spot, especially since they were clinging to the sides in rather contorted positions.

"It's okay! You can jump down!" their Koolomassai called to them with a smile.

Arthur was so exhausted he immediately fell to the dance floor. He got up, somewhat embarrassed, and Selenia fell right into his arms, followed by Betameche, who fell into his sister's arms. Arthur remained like that for a moment, with these two parcels in his arms. Then his knees collapsed, and the three tumbled to the ground.

"These are the three that the henchmen are looking for everywhere?" the bigger guy asked, somewhat skeptically.

"I thought so—but I might have been a little excited from all the candyfruit," the Koolomassai confessed.

"You know, it's the root you're supposed to eat, not the entire tree!"

"Oh—really?" the employee replied.

"Yes!" said the boss. "Go on, get out of here. I'll take care of them."

Their Koolomassai moved away, looking dubious, while our three heroes got to their feet. All of a sudden, the boss's face changed, putting on a smile worthy of a used-car salesman.

"My friends!" he announced, with arms open wide and teeth showing. "Welcome to the Jaimabar Club!"

A rickety-looking mosquito put four glasses down on the table next to them.

"Would you all like some jack-fire? It's the special drink of the house for our guests who aren't old enough to have alcohol!" explained the boss.

"Oh, yes! cried Betameche enthusiastically.

"Jack?" the boss said, rapping on the mosquito's head. "Hit it!"

The mosquito sprayed the red liquid directly into the glasses. It foamed, smoked, and ended by bursting into flames.

The boss blew on the flame until it was just smoke.

"Long life to the Seven Lands!" he proclaimed, extending his glass for a toast.

The others each extinguished the flames in their drinks and lifted their glasses. The boss drank his down in one gulp, followed immediately by Selenia and Betameche. Arthur didn't move. Wisely, he first wanted to see the effect of the drink.

"That's great!" said Betameche.

"It's very thirst quenching," Selenia added.

"It is my children's favorite drink!" the boss said proudly.

The three faces turned toward Arthur, who still hadn't drunk any. It was almost humiliating.

"To the Seven Lands!" cried the boy, against his better judgment.

He raised his glass and drank it down in one gulp, which was a big mistake. He turned red as a beet. It was as if he had just consumed a raw jalapeño in chili sauce and maple syrup. It was as if he had swallowed a volcano. Arthur felt sure smoke must be coming out his ears, as if he had just spent twelve hours in a sauna.

"Yes . . . thirst quenching!" he squawked, with what little remained of his voice.

Betamache ran his finger around the bottom of the glass and licked it.

"It has a slight taste of apple!" said the young connoisseur.

"It's not the least bit like apple!" Arthur replied.

A group of henchmen appeared in the doorway, surveying the place, as if they were searching for something or someone. Selenia ducked her head to hide her face.

"Nothing to be afraid of!" the boss assured them. "Those are just recruiters. They take advantage of the weakness of certain customers to make them enlist in the royal army. As long as you are with me, you have nothing to worry about."

Our friends relaxed.

"How is it that the henchmen have not yet alienated or

oppressed your people, the way they have all the others who live in the Seven Lands?" Selenia asked suspiciously.

"Oh, that's simple!" said the boss. "We produce ninety percent of the candyfruit root they love so much. The army of henchmen wouldn't last a day without their root! Since we are the only ones that can prepare it, they leave us alone."

Selenia was a bit skeptical about this whole business.

"What plant do these roots come from?"

"That depends. Linden, chamomile, verbena—only what's natural!" he affirmed with a sly smile. "Would you like to try some?" he offered, like a snake suggesting an apple.

"No, thank you, Mr . . . ?"

"My friends call me Max," the boss replied with a smile showing all thirty-eight teeth. "And you? What is your name?"

"I am Selenia, daughter of King Sifrat de Matradoy, fifteenth of that name, ruler of the First Lands."

"Wow!" said the boss, acting impressed. "Your highness!" he added, bending over to kiss her hand. Selenia pulled it away to point to her companions.

"This is my brother, Saimono de Matradoy de Betameche. You can call him Beta."

Arthur had recovered enough to introduce himself.

"And I am Arthur! From the house of Arthur! Why have you cut all my straws?" he asked. The jack-fire was making his head spin and he was having trouble forming coherent thoughts.

"It's a business arrangement. The henchmen asked us to clean them and guide them to the black river, the one that leads directly to Necropolis."

At this piece of news, our three heroes sat up, full of hope.

"That is precisely where we need to go! Can you help us?" the princess asked.

"What? Slow down, Princess! Necropolis is a one-way trip! Why would you want to go to such a place?" inquired the boss.

"We have to destroy M. before he destroys us," Selenia answered.

"Oh, is that all?" Max said sarcastically.

"That is all," Selenia replied, as serious as ever.

Max looked worried. "Why does M. want to destroy you?" he asked.

"It's a long story," the princess assured him. "Let's just say that in one more day I have to choose a husband and succeed my father, and M. the cursed does not want this to happen. He knows that once I have assumed power, he may never be able to invade our land. It is written in the prophecy."

Max seemed very interested, especially by the part concerning the husband.

"Marriage, eh? What is the name of the lucky man?"

"I don't know. I haven't chosen him yet," replied the princess.

Max sensed an opportunity. "Before we continue, you deserve a little fun! Jack, bring us some more of that excellent drink! This one's on me again!" offered the boss, to Beta's great delight.

While Jack the mosquito busied himself with refilling the glasses, Max scurried over to the DJ, located next to the arm of the record player.

"Easylow! Spin this platter for me!" the boss told him hurriedly.

DJ Easylow leaned over to the back of the record player and woke up the two Koolomassai who were slumped there asleep on their hoards of candyfruit root.

"Get up, guys! Time to work!" Easylow told them.

The two sleepers slowly got up and stretched, as if they were made of marshmallow. They walked over to an enormous five-volt battery and rolled it up to the battery receptacle. As soon as the battery was engaged, the lights went on over the dance floor. The turntable began to move and Easylow pushed the stylus to the song of his choice.

Max leaned over to Selenia.

"May I have this dance?" he asked, with exaggerated politeness.

Selenia smiled. Arthur did not. "We have a long road to travel, Selenia! We should be going!" he said, very worried about this new competition.

"Five minutes of relaxation never hurt anyone!" Selenia replied, accepting Max's offer as much for the fun of dancing as for the opportunity to tease Arthur.

Max and Selenia stepped onto the dance floor and started to waltz.

"Beta! Do something!" Arthur cried.

Betameche, in response, drank down his jack-fire.

"What do you want me to do?" he asked. "She will be a thousand years old soon. She can make her own decisions!"

Arthur scowled. Betameche glanced from the dance floor to the bar and noticed a Koolomassai with a knife in his belt.

"Hey, that's my knife!" Betameche exclaimed. "I'm going to have a word or two with that thief!" The little prince got up, gulped down his sister's jack-fire, and headed toward the bar with a determined step.

Arthur was alone, desperate, at his wits' end. He grabbed his glass and gulped down its contents. Perhaps the magical jack-fire would make him so confused that things would start to make sense again.

CHAPTER

17

It was like a game: Max kept trying to get closer to Selenia, and she politely resisted, glancing over at Arthur whenever she could to see how he was reacting.

"You know, finding a husband in such a short time won't be easy!" Max observed. "But I can help you out, if you like."

"That's very nice of you, but I think I can manage," Selenia replied, amused.

"I like to be of service. It's my nature. Besides, you are in luck; things are rather calm at the moment. I have only five wives right now!"

"Five wives? That must be a lot of work, keeping them happy!" Selenia said with a smile.

"I'm a very hard worker!" Max assured her. "I can work day and night, seven days a week, without ever getting tired!"

Arthur was slumped on the table, his sad eyes following the sight of his beloved princess dancing with someone else.

"Anyway, she's too old for me!" he said to himself. "A

thousand years old, although she looks my age. I'm only ten!"

A henchman recruiter sat down opposite him, blocking his view of the princess.

"What's a handsome fellow like you doing in a place like this?" the henchman asked, with the smile of a hunter who has just smelled a pigeon.

Betameche reached the bar and shoved the knife thief, who splashed his drink all over himself.

"Hey! Watch it!" said the Koolomassai in an extremely annoyed tone of voice.

"That's my knife! You stole it from me!" Beta yelled, as belligerent as a pit bull. "It's *my* knife. I got it for my birthday!"

The Koolomassai reached out his arm and held the boy at a distance.

"What? Calm down, grumpy! What if it just so happens that I have the same knife as you do?"

"It's mine, I'm sure of it! I could pick it out of a thousand! Give it to me!" insisted Betameche.

A henchman approached the two of them with the confident stride of an officer.

"Is there a problem?" asked the soldier.

"No! Everything is fine!" the Koolomassai assured him in honeyed tones.

"No! Everything is *not* fine!" Betameche retorted. "He stole my knife!"

The thief began to smile, as if it were all a joke.

"He's just fooling around! I can explain everything, Captain!" As if by magic, the Koolomassai pulled out two slices of candy-fruit root with a smug air.

"Would you like a little root?" suggested the sly devil.

The henchman hesitated, but couldn't resist for long. He lifted up his visor and revealed his face. This was the first time Betameche had seen the face of a henchman, since they were usually helmeted, and he immediately realized he could have happily gone through life without it. The henchman's head was completely bare—of everything. No hair, no eyebrows, no ears, no lips. The face was almost round and smooth, like a stone polished by years of erosion. It was a multicolored insect face, eaten away by diseases. The two small red eyes were empty, like eyes that have seen too much war. In short, he was not pleasant to look at. The henchman took the root and put it in his mouth, which was barely a hole in his face. He chewed for a minute, then smiled a frightening smile.

Betameche was worried. Things did not seem to be going his way, to say the least. How did they get themselves into this mess?

Meanwhile, Max was still working on Selenia.

"So? What do you say?" he asked.

"Well, you're very nice, but marriage is an important choice that cannot be decided too quickly," Selenia replied, as playful as a cat with a mouse.

She cast a glance at Arthur, but he was not looking at her. He had his nose in a contract that he was moments away from signing. The henchman recruiter was handing him a pen and sliding the contract toward him.

Arthur bent over to sign, but Selenia's hand appeared and prevented him from doing so.

"Excuse me, officer, but I would like to dance with this boy one last time before he commits himself to something other than me!"

The henchman didn't like this, but Selenia was already dragging Arthur onto the dance floor.

"It's very nice of you to give me this dance!" Arthur said to her, with a happy smile.

"The jack-fire is really having a peculiar effect on you, you idiot. Do you know what you were about to sign?" Selenia asked him with immense irritation.

"No. Not really, but it's not important!" Arthur answered.

"Do you really think I will marry a guy who gets woozy after a little jack-fire and who dances with two left feet?"

It took Arthur a few seconds, but he got the message. He stood up straighter and attempted to control his feet better. Selenia smiled at the superhuman efforts of her companion, who was doing what he could to fight the effects of the magic jack-fire.

"That's better," she conceded.

* * *

Easylow watched the couple from a distance.

"Are you going to let that dwarf steal her away from you?" he asked Max, who was standing next to him, also watching them.

"A little competition never did anyone any harm!" Max said with a smile, not really worried.

Arthur was reviving a little. Dancing was clearing his head. "Do you—do you really think that . . . I might have a chance with you? Despite, you know . . . our age difference?"

Selenia started to laugh.

"In our country, we count years according to the flowering of the selenielle, the royal flower—that's where my name comes from, too."

"Oh! Well, then . . . in Minimoy years, how old am I?"

"About a thousand years. Like me," replied the princess, amused.

Arthur puffed out his chest a little, flattered by his sudden maturity. It made him want to ask a million questions.

"And were you ever a little girl like me? I mean—I'm a boy, of course—but were you . . . a little girl like the ones in my neighborhood? My size?"

"No. I was born a Minimoy," answered Selenia, who was somewhat disturbed by the question. "And I have never traveled beyond the Seven Lands."

There was regret in the voice of the princess, but she would never admit it.

"I would like to take you, one day . . . into my world," Arthur confided, already saddened by the idea of ever having to leave her, even if it was in a thousand years.

Selenia was increasingly ill at ease.

"Sure, why not!" she replied, somewhat disdainfully, as if to minimize the importance of their words. "But while we are waiting, may I remind you that we have a mission to complete. Remember Necropolis?"

The word resounded in Arthur's head and woke him up instantly.

The henchman recruiter knew he had lost his client and he returned to the bar, looking for a new victim. He passed by Betameche, still engaged in conversation with the thief and the officer. The Koolomassai thief was in fine form, talking his smoothest talk.

"And then, suddenly, I tripped on a knife stuck in the ground! First I thought it was a trap, you know?"

The henchman laughed, his mouth full of root. "That's a good one!" he guffawed, without knowing himself whether he was referring to the joke or to the candyfruit.

Betameche sighed in desperation. He did not seem destined to recover the knife that the henchman officer was now slowly turning in his hands.

The recruiting agent joyfully seized two new victims and dragged them off. Selenia watched them leave. It gave her an idea.

"I bet that we could follow those recruiting agents to Necropolis!"

Arthur agreed.

"You are right! We will get there! It is our mission!" he cried, carried away by a burst of excitement. "Once we are there, I will find my grandfather, I will discover the treasure, and I will give that cursed Maltazard a thrashing that he will never forget!"

The whole world came to a halt. Easylow grabbed the edge of the disk and stopped the music. Twenty henchmen turned to see what joker had had the bright idea of pronouncing this forbidden name.

"Oops!" said Arthur timidly, realizing his mistake.

"I don't know if you would make a good prince, but in the meantime, you are truly the king of blunderers!" Selenia said reproachfully.

Max began to grin. "Things are picking up here," he rejoiced. "Showtime!"

He signaled to Easylow, who released the disk and kicked the stylus. The music started up again.

The henchmen were closing in on the retreating couple. Things were looking very, very bad.

"Arthur? You have three seconds to clear your head of the jack-fire!" Selenia barked.

"What? Okay! But . . . what can I do to get clear in three seconds?"

Selenia smacked him right in the face—the kind of slap you don't want to get very often. Arthur shook his head. His teeth felt like they were floating.

"Thanks. I'm better now!"

"You should be!" she said, drawing the magic sword.

"And what am I supposed to fight with?" worried Arthur.

"You figure it out!"

Selenia was on her guard, as the disk, which continued to turn, brought them near Max and his DJ.

"Hey, kid!"

The boss had pulled out a sword and he threw it to Arthur.

"Thank you, sir!" replied the boy, amazed by this chivalry.

"Go ahead! Make them all dance for me!" said Max to his DJ, who pushed the stylus into a new groove. Arthur took his position alongside Selenia, while the henchmen deployed themselves in a circle around the pair.

Betameche had followed the henchman officer who was holding his knife and helpfully advised him. "If you press number seventy-five, you will have a laser saber. It's a classic but always effective."

"Oh? Really? Thanks, kid!" the henchman replied, still on a woozy sugar high from the candyfruit root. He pressed number seventy-five and immediately a monstrous flame set fire to his helmet and everything inside it. The henchman's body had not moved, but his head was now in ashes.

Betameche recovered his knife from the henchman's hands.

"A thousand pardons. My mistake. Maybe it's the opposite? Fifty-seven?"

Betameche pressed button fifty-seven and the knife released a laser saber, blue like steel.

"That's better!"

The three heroes were united once again, but things did not look good. They stood back-to-back, swords in front of them, forming a dangerous triangle.

All at once, the henchmen let out their famous battle cry, and the fighting began.

Easylow put on his cutoff gloves, grabbed the edge of the disk, and began to scratch to give the battle some rhythm.

Selenia executed pass after pass, demonstrating her skill and agility. She had the grace and power of a true knight.

Betameche had an easier weapon and caused plenty of damage, sweeping his saber in wide arcs and knocking over henchmen as if he were bowling.

Arthur had less experience, but he was lively enough to fend off blows. He swung out his sword to repel an assault, but the attacker smashed his weapon to smithereens.

Max pretended to be disappointed. "Oh, poor boy! Who could have given him such a poor-quality sword?" he said with false compassion. Easylow looked at him, and the two merce-naries began to laugh like hyenas.

Arthur ran around the dance floor, dodging the blows rain-ing down from every side. He took refuge on the other side of the stylus. The henchmen scrambled to get to him but wound up crashing into the rapidly moving needle, causing it to skip and scratch out the music like they do in the best dance clubs.

"That kid has rhythm in his blood!" observed Max with a professional grin.

Three henchmen stood in front of Betameche, all also armed with laser sabers.

"Three against one?" Betameche scoffed. "Have you no shame? Very well, I triple the power!"

Betameche pressed a button that made his laser disappear and replaced it with a bouquet of flowers.

"Um . . . beautiful, aren't they?" he joked, embarrassed by his mistake.

The henchmen yelled and charged toward the little prince, who took off running. He threw himself under a table, where he found Arthur already hiding.

"My weapon isn't working anymore!" exclaimed Betameche, searching for the right button.

"Mine isn't, either!" Arthur replied, showing him the broken-off blade.

A henchman approached the table and sliced it in half with a single blow from his laser saber. The two friends rolled to either side.

"On the other hand, his works very well!" cried Arthur with great alarm.

Betameche starting punching buttons at random on his

knife and ended up finally releasing a weapon of sorts: a minuscule pipe that shoots out one hundred soap bubbles per second. A cloud quickly formed around them—not really dangerous to anyone but very practical for hiding.

The henchmen rapidly lost track of their targets. This made them extremely angry, and they beat the air with their swords, succeeding only in bursting several pretty, multicolored soap bubbles.

Selenia eliminated one henchman, then ducked to her knees, sword over her head, to block the assault of another warrior. She unsheathed the backup knife that the henchman had strapped to his ankle and planted it in his foot. The henchman was paralyzed with pain.

"Hey, careful over there! Don't damage my floor!" the boss called angrily.

Arthur crawled out from under the cloud of bubbles and tripped over Beta's backpack. He found himself sprawled on the feet of a henchman. The warrior slowly raised his sword, savoring the evil moment.

Arthur was doomed. He tried to scramble away and felt his hand close over some mysterious pellets that had fallen out of the backpack. With a yell, he threw them at the henchman's feet, without the slightest idea of what might happen. It could save him or blow him up before the henchman got to him. Either way, he had nothing to lose.

The little glass balls scattered around the feet of the

henchman, who stopped to peer at them, too stupid not to be curious.

A magnificent bouquet of exotic flowers suddenly bloomed from the floor, as if by magic. It was bigger than the henchman!

"Flowers! Isn't that nice!" said the henchman. He stepped around the bouquet and approached Arthur menacingly. "I'll place them on your grave!" the warrior snarled, brandishing his sword.

He was blinded by his own evil, and so he failed to see, behind him, the gigantic flower opening its vast, carnivorous mouth. The beautiful plant clamped the henchman in its jaws, then took the time to chew him very carefully. Arthur watched, stupefied, as the monstrous flower opened its mouth and emitted a loud burp.

"Excuse *you!*" said Arthur, a bit disgusted.

Betameche pushed another button on his knife. This *had* to be the right one. There were three henchmen around him who did not look in the mood for games.

A three-beamed laser appeared from the knife.

Betameche grinned and proudly flourished his weapon. The three henchmen looked at one another, then each one of them pressed a button on his laser, releasing a new saber with six rotating blades. Betameche was petrified.

"Wow—is that a new model?" he asked, trying to distract them.

The henchman facing him nodded with an evil grimace,

then struck the prince such a violent blow that his knife was sent flying. The lasers retracted and the knife slid across the ground to where a foot reached out and stopped it. A foot wearing a warrior henchman's boot, size forty-eight . . . covered with blood.

Easylow grabbed the disk and stopped the music. The dance floor froze. The fighting paused. Silence greeted the leader of the henchmen: Darkos, Prince of Shadows—son of Maltazard.

Our three heroes came together, gasping with exhaustion.

Darkos had the appearance of a henchman, but his build was more imposing and his armor more frightening. He was better armed than a fighter plane; in all the Seven Lands, there did not exist a weapon that he did not possess. Except, perhaps, for this little knife that he had blocked with his foot. He bent down slowly and picked up the object.

"So, Max—having a party and not inviting your friends?" he said ominously, turning the knife over in his hands.

"Nothing official!" Max assured him, smiling to hide his unease. "This was just a small, improvised party to welcome the new clientele!"

"New clientele?" Darkos mused. "Show me."

The warriors parted to each side of the dance floor, revealing our three heroes standing together.

As he approached them, Darkos saw the princess, and a big smile of recognition spread across his face.

"Princess Selenia? What a pleasant surprise!" he said, stopping directly in front of her. "What is someone of your rank doing in a place like this at such a late hour?"

"We came for a little dancing," she replied defiantly. Darkos took the bait.

"Very well—then let's dance!" he said, snapping his fingers.

A henchman hit the record player arm, landing the needle on a slow dance. Darkos bowed slightly and offered the princess his arm.

"I would rather die than dance with you, Darkos," Selenia snapped.

The atmosphere felt as if a button had just been pushed to launch an atomic bomb. The henchmen edged away worriedly. Violence and destruction always resulted when Darkos was insulted, especially in front of everyone. He stood up slowly from his bow, and smiled a sinister smile.

"Your wish is my command!" he said, unsheathing his enormous sword. "You will dance alone for eternity!"

Darkos raised his weapon, ready to cut Selenia into pieces.

"What about your father?" the princess said calmly. The creature stopped his arm in midair. "That's right, Darkos—what will your father, M. the cursed, say when you tell him that you have killed the princess he's been searching for? The only person who can bring him the ultimate power that he so dreams of having?"

Selenia had hit the right note. Junior was clearly thinking carefully now.

"Do you think he'll congratulate you? Or that he'll have you burned with the tears of death, like he burned all his other sons?"

There was uneasiness in the ranks. Selenia had mastered her subject and Darkos slowly lowered his weapon.

"You are right, Princess. I thank you for your clairvoyance," he said, replacing his sword in its sheath. "It is true that dead, you have no value. But alive . . . !" He smiled the smile of someone who has had a very wicked idea.

But Max had read his thoughts. "Easylow—it's closing time!"

The DJ winked and headed toward the back of the room.

"Take them away!" Darkos cried, and thirty henchmen rushed toward our heroes.

Arthur watched the attackers approach, like a surfer watching a tidal wave.

"We're going to need a miracle!" said Arthur.

"Death is nothing if the cause is just!" cried Selenia, ready to die nobly, as befits a princess. She brandished her sword in front of her and screamed a battle cry to give herself courage.

At that exact moment, the lights went out. Whether it was Selenia's scream, or DJ Easylow cutting off the power in the back, it was now completely dark, and there was total panic. Sounds of iron, boots, blades, and chattering teeth rang out.

"Gotcha!"

"There they are!"

"I have one!"

LUC BESSON ✱ 215

"Let me go, you imbecile!"

"Sorry, boss!"

"Ouch! Who bit me?"

This is just a sample of the sounds rising from the shambles once they were plunged into darkness.

Finally, a match flared, illuminating Max's laughing face. He lit a lamp and surveyed the amusing spectacle. Darkos came and stood in the circle of light. He was mad with fury and the red light did nothing to help his looks.

"What is going on here?" he spluttered with rage.

"It's ten o'clock. Closing time," Max responded cheerfully.

"You close at ten o'clock now?" growled Darkos.

"I am only implementing your instructions, my lord," Max replied, with all the fake devotion of a henchman.

Darkos, still seething, was at a loss for words.

"We'll make an exception for tonight! A special reopening!" he yelled, loud enough to break even the strongest eardrums.

Max took a slow look around.

"Okay," he said calmly.

Easylow reconnected the battery and the lights came back on, revealing a pile of henchmen in the middle of the dance floor. It resembled a rugby match riot that had ended badly.

Darkos advanced. "Now at last I have you, Selenia. Your little quest is over."

The pile began to sort itself out as best it could. The last henchmen to emerge were somewhat ragged, but they were proudly carrying their three prisoners, trussed from head to foot.

Darkos looked at the prisoners. His face darkened with fury. They had accidentally tied up three of the henchmen.

Our heroes were gone.

"That blasted little princess!" Darkos looked as if he might explode.

"FIND THEM!" he roared.

CHAPTER
18

Darkos's voice echoed down into the basement, where our three heroes were hiding.

"Did you hear that?" Betameche shuddered. "He sounds monstrous!"

"I hope that Max and his friends won't be punished because of us," said the princess.

"You don't have to worry about them," said Arthur. "I'm sure Max can talk his way out of anything!"

Selenia sighed. She didn't like running away, but she knew Arthur was right.

"Come on! Time is passing and we have a mission!" Arthur said, taking her arm. Selenia let herself be pulled, and our three heroes took off into the darkness.

For quite some time they followed the oozing, dull, blue-green edge that bordered an interminable concrete wall. Finally they arrived at a sort of gigantic plaque on the ground, made of cast iron. Selenia knelt beside a hole in the center of it.

It was not very big—hardly big enough to pass through. The walls were muddy and looked as if they descended forever.

"There. It's there," said Selenia.

"What's there?" replied Arthur, hoping she wasn't saying what he thought she was saying.

"The direct route, one way, to Necropolis," Selenia explained, staring into the bottomless hole. "This is where the unknown really begins. No Minimoy has ever returned safely from that nightmare city. So you should both think very carefully before following me," the princess said gravely.

The three friends looked at one another in silence. Each was thinking about the amazing adventures they had already experienced and wondering how much worse it could get.

Arthur met Selenia's eyes and she forced a brave smile.

He slowly extended his hand over the hole.

"My future is tied to yours, Selenia. And so my future is at your side."

She put her hand in Arthur's.

Betameche placed his hand on top of theirs.

Our three heroes thus sealed their pact. They would go to the end together, for better or worse.

"By the grace of the gods!" said the princess solemnly.

"By the grace of the gods!" the two boys echoed in unison.

Selenia took a deep breath and leaped into the hole. Betameche held his nose and followed his sister, without pausing to think. The hole swallowed him up in turn.

Arthur was still for a moment, thinking that this well swallowed bodies like quicksand. Then he took a deep breath and jumped feet first into the hole.

"It's you and me, Maltazard!" he cried before disappearing into the night and the mud.

Once again he had pronounced the cursed name.

Let us hope that this time, it will bring him better luck.

TO BE CONTINUED . . .

BOOK TWO:

ARTHUR and the FORBIDDEN CITY

CHAPTER

1

As the sun sank slowly over the peaceful valley, Alfred the dog opened one eye. A slight breeze signaled that the temperature might finally be bearable. He got up slowly, stretched his legs, emerged from the shadow of the windmill where he had been hiding, and trotted across the grass.

From the tall chimney of the house by the river, a young sparrow hawk followed the dog with its piercing eyes, but only for a few seconds. That prey was too large. The bird turned its head slowly, looking for another victim. Suddenly it let out a hoarse, powerful cry that awakened Grandma, who was stretched out on the couch in the living room.

Grandma sat upright. "How could I doze off like that?" she asked herself, rubbing her eyes. The events of the last few days came back to her. Arthur, her adored only grandson, had disappeared—just as her husband had done four years earlier, in the garden by the oak tree in search of a treasure.

She had searched the garden from one end to the other,

torn the house apart, and called for him from all the neighboring hills, without finding a trace of her grandson.

She imagined so many different explanations . . . perhaps extraterrestrials, for one. She imagined large green men coming down from the sky in their UFO and kidnapping Arthur. She was almost sure of it.

She missed his little blond head, tousled hair, and two large brown eyes, always with their look of wonder. She missed his voice, as sweet and fragile as a soap bubble. A tear made its lonely way down her cheek.

She looked at the sky for a moment through the window. It was uniformly blue and desperately empty. No trace of extraterrestrials. She let out a long sigh and looked around her at the silent house.

It was lucky that the sparrow hawk had woken her up. The coolness of the room and the hypnotic tick-tock of the clock had made it impossible to resist taking a nap.

The young bird of prey cried again.

Grandma perked up her ears. She was ready to interpret anything as a sign, a mark of hope. She was convinced that the sparrow hawk had seen or heard something, and she wasn't entirely wrong. The bird was indeed declaring that he had heard something even before it was visible on the horizon.

That something was a car, accompanied by a cloud of dust that glistened in the sunlight. The sparrow hawk scrutinized the car from the chimney top as if he were equipped with radar.

Grandma listened carefully. She could hear a faint rumbling in the distance.

The sparrow hawk let out two small cries, as if to indicate the number of passengers inside the car.

Grandma turned her head slightly, the way you would turn an antenna in order to capture a signal. The engine noise could suddenly be heard everywhere, and the trees began to stir, echoing its horrible sound.

The sparrow hawk decided it was time to leave, which was not a good sign. Perhaps he could sense the series of events that was about to take place.

Grandma jumped to her feet. There was no doubt about it—the sparrow hawk had sent her a signal. Grandma composed herself, straightened her dress over her considerable frame, and searched frantically for her slippers.

The noise of the engine invaded the living room. Grandma stopped her search and headed toward the door wearing only one slipper, limping like an old pirate with a wooden leg.

The engine stopped. The door of the car squealed as it opened, and two worn leather shoes emerged, stepping onto the gravel. Grandma reached the door and struggled with the key.

"Why on earth did I lock the door?" she grumbled to herself,

her head down. She did not notice the two silhouettes outlined by the sun behind the door.

The key rattled a little but finally turned in the lock.
Grandma was so surprised by what she saw as the door
swung open that she could not help letting out a little cry of
horror.

There was nothing particularly horrible about the smiling
couple standing on the landing, except perhaps their bad taste.
The lady was wearing a dress with large purple flowers, the
man a plaid jacket of greenish yellow. It was hard on the eyes
but nothing to scream about.

Grandma stifled her cry and tried to convert it into a welcoming noise.

"Surprise!" chanted the couple, in perfect unison.

Grandma spread her arms and tried as best she could to
assume a natural-looking smile. Her mouth said Hello while her
eyes said Help.

"What a surprise," she ended up blurting out. Arthur's parents were standing in front of her, as real as a nightmare.

Grandma continued to smile, blocking the front door like a
soccer goalie.

Since Grandma was not moving, not speaking, but only
stood there with her strange smile, Arthur's father was forced
to ask the question that she feared the most.

"Is Arthur here?" he asked jovially, without a moment's

doubt about what the answer would be.

Grandma smiled some more, as if hoping to suggest a positive answer without actually lying. But Arthur's father was
waiting for a reply. So Grandma took a breath and said, "Did
you have a good trip?"

This was not really the answer that Arthur's father was waiting for, but he was a good driver, so he launched into a detailed
account. "We took the shortcut to the west," he explained. "The
roads are narrow there, but according to my calculations we
saved about twenty-five miles. Which means, given the price
of a gallon of gas, that we—"

"That we had to turn every three seconds for two hours,"
complained Arthur's mother. "The trip was a horror and I am
grateful that Arthur did not have to suffer such punishment."
Then she added, "So where is he?"

"Who?" asked Grandma, as if she were hearing voices.

"Arthur. My son," the younger woman answered, somewhat
concerned—not for her son but for the mental state of her
mother. Could it be the heat? she wondered.

"Aaah! . . . He is going to be so happy to see you," Grandma
offered as a reply.

Arthur's parents looked at each other, wondering if perhaps
the old lady had finally gone deaf.

"Arthur. Where is he?" Arthur's father repeated slowly,
making his words very distinct.

Grandma smiled once more and nodded.

This answer convinced no one, and she finally had to say something. "He is . . . with the dog," she said. This was just at the edge of lying, but the answer seemed to satisfy the couple.

At that exact moment, Alfred decided to make an appearance, wagging his tail and instantly destroying this perfect alibi.

Grandma's smile crumbled.

"All right, Mom. Where is he?" Arthur's mother asked in a much firmer tone of voice.

Grandma would have gladly strangled Alfred, but she contented herself with giving him a sharp look. "So, are you and Arthur playing hide-and-seek?" she asked Alfred a little too sweetly.

Alfred seemed to understand what Grandma was saying. His tail gradually slowed down. He knew that he had probably done something stupid and was already pleading guilty.

"They love to play hide-and-seek, those two," Grandma explained. "They could play for days! Arthur hides and—"

"And the dog counts to a hundred?" Arthur's father replied, wondering whether he was the victim of a huge practical joke.

"Yes, that's it! Alfred counts up to one hundred and then he looks for Arthur!"

The parents looked at each other with great concern. Had

Grandma finally gone off her rocker?

"And . . . do you have an idea where Arthur might be hiding?" Arthur's father asked gently.

Grandma nodded her head energetically. "Yes! In the garden!"

Never had a lie been so close to the truth.

CHAPTER
2

Deep in the garden, sliding along immense blades of grass where the roots of trees were born, was the bottom of an old wall built by the hand of man.

In this wall, eaten away by time, was a small crevice that ran between the stones. When you are barely half an inch tall, this is an impressive chasm, a very deep hole, which our heroes were rapidly approaching.

Princess Selenia was in the lead, as usual. She had lost none of her strength, and their mission seemed to occupy all her thoughts. She walked along the path as if she were strolling down Main Street, totally unaware of the absolute void that bordered the route on either side.

Behind her, always staying close, was Arthur. He was still fascinated by everything that was happening to him. Arthur, who, a day or so earlier, had felt bad about being less than five feet tall, was now proud of his half-inch stature. And he thanked his lucky stars every moment for this adventure.

He breathed deeply, as if to take better advantage of his luck. At this point, it should be mentioned that Arthur's eyes were not so much on the chasm as on Selenia.

It should also be mentioned that Selenia was very pretty. Even from behind you could tell she was a princess. In any event, that's what could be seen in Arthur's look, as he followed her like Alfred the dog. Back when he was a normal height and on the other side of the garden, he had seen a picture of her in one of his grandfather's books. He still couldn't believe he was having a real adventure with her.

Betameche, Selenia's brother, lagged behind. He still had his backpack, filled with thousands of things, all of which were useless except in weighing him down so he wouldn't fly away.

"Beta, come on! Time is wasting," his sister called out in the grumpy way she always spoke to him.

Betameche let out a huge sigh. "I'm tired of carrying everything," he complained.

"No one asked you to bring half the village," the princess replied acidly.

"We could each take a turn carrying, couldn't we? That way I could rest a little, and we could move faster," Betameche offered.

Selenia came to a sudden stop and looked at her brother. "You're right. We'll save time. Give it to me!"

Betameche took off his backpack and handed it to his sister who, in one swift movement, threw it into the abyss.

"There! Now you will be less tired and we will travel faster," the princess announced. "Let's go!"

Betameche watched in horror as his backpack disappeared into the bottomless void. He couldn't believe his eyes.

Arthur had no intention of involving himself in this family quarrel. He suddenly became very interested in the crystals covering the wall.

Betameche was seething.

"You are nothing but—but a little *pest!*" he cried.

Selenia just smiled. "The 'little pest' has a mission to accomplish that cannot be delayed. If the pace is too much for you, you can go home! There you can tell all your stories and be fussed over by the king!"

"At least our father has a heart," Betameche retorted.

"Yes, he does, and you had better take advantage of it, because the next king will not have one!"

"Who is the next king?" asked Arthur timidly.

"The next king . . . is me," said Selenia proudly, lifting her chin.

Arthur was beginning to understand, but some things still confused him. "Is that why you absolutely must get married in the next two days?" he asked.

"Yes. The prince must be chosen *before* I assume my duties as sovereign. That's the way it is. That's the rule," answered Selenia, speaking faster in order to avoid more questions.

Arthur let out a sigh. If only he had more time. He needed time to know whether this warmth that he was feeling inside his chest, and which often rose to his cheeks, could be considered a sign of love.

Now he understood why Martin, the police officer back home, would get so tongue-tied whenever he flirted with Grandma. In the human world, Arthur was only ten, but by Minimoy standards he was hundreds of years old—old enough, he thought, to be in love and to marry Selenia.

But he needed more time to really understand the word "love." It was a word that was much too big for him.

He loved his grandmother, his dog, their pickup truck . . . but he did not dare to say that he loved Selenia. Besides, all he had to do was think about it, and he started blushing.

"What's wrong with you?" asked the princess, amused.

"Nothing," murmured Arthur, blushing even more. "It's just the heat. It is so hot here!"

Selenia smiled at this lie. She snapped off one of the small stalactites hanging from the wall and handed the piece of ice to Arthur. "Here—rub this on your forehead and you'll feel better."

Arthur thanked her and held the piece of ice to his forehead.

Selenia knew that what he was feeling had nothing to do with the temperature, as it was around freezing in this endless chasm.

The stick of ice melted and Arthur was suddenly overcome

by a burst of courage. "May I ask you a personal question, Selenia?"

"You may always ask. I will decide whether to answer," the princess answered, as shrewd as ever.

"You have to choose a husband in two days but . . . in nearly a thousand years, you haven't found anyone who suited you?" asked Arthur.

"A princess deserves an exceptional being: intelligent, courageous, recklessly brave, a good cook, one who loves children—" she began, as she always did.

"Who knows how to do the housekeeping and the laundry while her ladyship takes a nap," Beta interrupted.

"An exceptional individual, one who understands his wife and protects her, even against the stupidity of certain members of her family," Selenia shot back, fixing an angry look on her brother. And then she began to dream out loud . . .

"A handsome guy, of course, but also true, loyal, with a sense of duty and responsibility. An infallible being, generous and luminous!"

Her eyes met Arthur's. He was beginning to feel a bit ill. Each adjective sounded like the blow of a hammer to his head.

"Not one of those weaklings who can't even handle a little jack-fire," added the princess.

"Of course," Arthur replied, crushed under the weight of unhappiness. How could he have imagined for even a second that he had a chance? Arthur had none of those qualities. He was neither infallible nor luminous, and if he had to describe himself, he would more likely use the words "small," "stupid," and "ugly."

"Choosing a fiancé is the most important thing for a princess. And the first kiss is a crucial moment," Selenia said. "Not because of one's feelings! Here, the act is much more than symbolic, because it is during this first kiss that the princess shares all her powers with the prince. Immense powers that will make it possible for him to rule in her absence if necessary. All the peoples of the Seven Lands will owe him allegiance."

Arthur had not actually suspected the importance of this first kiss, and now he understood better why Selenia had to be careful to choose well. "And that's why M. wants to marry you—is that it? For your powers?" he asked.

"No! It's for her great personality!" Betameche joked.

Selenia shrugged. Arthur gave her a long look, ready to forgive her all her faults in exchange for a smile. Anything else seemed impossible. She was too beautiful, too brave, too intelligent, and too much of a princess to be interested in an ordinary boy like him.

"He will never be my husband," Selenia declared like a clap of thunder in a cloudless sky. For a moment, Arthur thought she meant him. He bowed his head, crushed. Selenia glanced at him mischievously.

"I was referring to M. the cursed, obviously," she said.

Arthur felt better, but he wished he could ask her the thousand and one questions that were burning inside him. Despite his efforts to keep them in, one of them ended up escaping.

"When you have to choose your . . . husband, how will you be able to tell the difference between those that are there for your powers and those who really . . . love you?"

There was so much sincerity in the voice of this little boy that even a beautiful, pretentious princess could not be insensitive to it. Perhaps for the first time, she really looked at him, and smiled.

"It is very easy to distinguish between the true and the false, to know which suitor is sincere and which is only there for wealth and power. In fact, I have a test for it." She had let down the bait and she watched Arthur swim around it.

"What—what kind of test?" he asked.

"A test of trust. The one who claims to love me must be able to have complete trust in me. The kind of blind trust that he has in himself. This is generally very difficult for a man," Selenia explained. Her little fish had his mouth open and was ready to bite.

"I trust you, Selenia," Arthur replied, taking the bait—hook, line, and sinker.

Selenia smiled. The little fish was on her line. She stopped and looked at him for a moment. "Really?" she asked, her almond eyes fixed on him, as formidable as those of a serpent.

"Really," Arthur replied.

Selenia's smile widened.

"Is this a marriage proposal?" she asked. It was like a cat sticking its paw into a goldfish bowl.

Arthur turned bright red. "All right . . . I know I'm still a little young . . ." he murmured, "but I did save your life a few times and—"

Selenia interrupted him. "Love is not about protecting someone you do not want to lose! Love is giving everything to the other person—even your life—without hesitating, without even thinking about it!"

Arthur was disturbed. He saw love as something big and powerful, but still undefined. Love for him was a feeling that made him lose his balance. He had not understood how high the stakes were and that, sometimes, it could cost you your life.

"Are you ready to give your life? Out of love for me?" Selenia asked, still mischievous.

Arthur was somewhat lost. There was no way out of this fishbowl—only a slippery wall that let him swim around in circles. "Okay . . . if that is the only way to prove my love . . . yes," he conceded, feeling a bit nervous.

Selenia approached him and walked around him, like a mouse around a piece of cheese. "Good. Let us see if you are telling the truth," she said. "Step back!"

Arthur took one step back, thankful to have passed this first test.

"Step back again," Selenia commanded. Arthur glanced at Betameche, who rolled his eyes and sighed. His sister's games had never amused him.

Arthur hesitated a moment, then took a good step back.

"Step back again," Selenia commanded.

Arthur glanced over his shoulder. There was the cliff edge, the one they had been walking along for hours. It bordered space so deep that it disappeared into absolute darkness.

Arthur now had a better understanding of the test. This was far from a traditional game of Simon Says. But he had set out to prove his courage, so he stepped back again until his heels touched the edge.

Selenia put on a beautiful, satisfied smile. *This little fish is very docile,* she seemed to be thinking, but the test was not over.

"Arthur, I asked you to step back. Why are you stopping? Don't you trust me anymore?"

Arthur was confused. He could not understand the connection between love and trust, the step back, and the chasm that was awaiting him. He suddenly regretted all the times he had slept through math class. Perhaps if he had paid attention, he would now be able to solve this equation.

"Don't you trust me?" insisted Selenia.

"Of course," replied Arthur, "I trust you."

"So why have you stopped?" the princess asked provokingly.

Arthur thought a moment and found his answer. He slowly straightened up, threw out his small chest, and looked Selenia right in the eyes. "I stopped . . . to say good-bye," he said solemnly.

A glimmer of panic appeared in her eyes.

Betameche understood immediately. The poor boy, too honest to play his sister's games, was about to do the unthinkable. "Don't do it, Arthur," Beta stammered, too worried to make the slightest movement toward Arthur.

"Farewell," said Arthur melodramatically.

Selenia's smile collapsed like a house of cards. Her game was turning into a nightmare.

Arthur took a big step back.

"No!" Selenia yelled. She covered her face with her hands.

Arthur disappeared, swallowed up by the endless chasm.

Selenia cried out in despair. She turned away from the chasm and fell to her knees, her face buried in her hands. She could barely understand what had happened.

"With a test like *that* you will never get married,"

said Betameche angrily.

Just then, Arthur appeared in the air behind Selenia, as if he had bounced off something. He did not seem in control of his movements, but he was able to put his fingers to his lips, signaling to Betameche to keep quiet. Astonished, the little Minimoy nodded before Arthur disappeared again.

Selenia, too preoccupied with her unhappiness, had seen nothing.

"You know, when you play with fire, you get burned," said Betameche.

His sister agreed sadly.

Betameche was delighted. Now that he had the chance to punish his sister a bit, he had to rub salt into the wound. "How can you call yourself a princess when you let your most ardent suitor die?"

"How could I do that?" cried Selenia, moved to sincerity. "How could I be so stupid and so mean at the same time? I thought I was a princess and then I behaved like the most selfish girl in the world! I don't deserve my name or my rank! No punishment will ever make up for my guilt!"

"Yes, I can't think of anything that would," agreed Betameche, as Arthur appeared again, in an even stranger position.

"Oh, I am proud and cruel," the princess sobbed. "I believed that he was not worthy of me, when it was I who was not worthy of him. My head sacrificed him but my heart chose him."

"Really?" said Betameche.

"From the first moment I saw him," confessed Selenia between sobs. "He was so cute, with his big brown eyes and his lost expression. Gentleness and beauty lit up his face, while his posture breathed nobility. His step was graceful, light—"

Arthur bounced back again in the most shocking contortion yet, calling to mind a disjointed puppet.

"He was kind, brilliant, daring—" said the princess.

"Charming?" asked Arthur, mid-somersault.

"Yes, the most charming of all the princes that the Seven Lands have ever known. He was charming, brave—" She stopped cold. Where had that question come from? She whirled around and saw Arthur bounce into view, upside down.

"Charming, brave, what else?" he asked, delighted with so many compliments.

Anger appeared instantly on Selenia's face. She looked like a teakettle ready to whistle. "And—a real smooth talker!" she cried in a voice so loud it flipped him right side up.

Arthur disappeared again as Selenia approached the edge to find out the secret of his survival.

Arthur was bouncing off a giant spiderweb that was

woven from one side of the precipice to the other. His fall had been without danger and his exit purely theatrical. But Selenia did not appreciate the drama. He wouldn't get away with this treachery. She unsheathed her sword and waited for Arthur's return.

"You are the most manipulative person I know," she yelled, as he twisted aside to avoid being struck by her sword. "You'll see there is a price to pay when you play with the feelings of a princess!"

"Selenia, if everyone who loves you has to kill himself in order to prove it, you will never find a husband," Arthur replied sensibly.

"He is right," added Betameche, always ready to throw a little more oil on the fire.

Selenia turned around and, with a single swing of her sword, sliced off the three rebellious hairs on top of Betameche's head.

"You've been his accomplice right from the start! You are a terrible brother!" Selenia snapped. And the two began to squabble, to the amusement of Arthur who had finally figured out how to control his bouncing.

The spiderweb was sturdy enough to hold him, but on the far side there was a thread that shook slightly with each rebound. These small, regular vibrations ran the length of the thread and were carried through a cavern.

The thread then disappeared into the darkness. It was a darkness much more dense than that inside the void, and also more disturbing.

But curiosity being stronger than fear, we cannot stop from entering this cave or following this thread into the darkness. Where we will soon find two shapes—two eyes. Red. Filled with blood.

Arthur was laughing now, unaware of the danger. "Come on, Selenia! Forgive me," he called on another of his rebounds. "Yes, I knew that there was a spiderweb, but I still listened to you, didn't I? I'm just lucky this web was here!"

Selenia was not interested in games or even in words. She was thinking more along the lines of a good spanking for this impudent knave.

But the punishment she was imagining would come on its own. All at once, Arthur's acrobatics came to a sudden stop. He had gotten his leg caught between the threads of the web.

This changed the nature of the vibration, a change that communicated itself along the thread and into the cave. The two red eyes that lived there seemed to appreciate the news, and the spider began to advance.

When you are less than an inch tall, you see life from a different perspective. What seemed to a human to be a gentle little spider, now appeared to be a veritable tank with eight legs, as furry as a woolly mammoth's. She stretched her face full of stingers and slobbered a little. In spider language, this was what passed for a smile.

The large mandibles began to move along the thread as the creature stalked toward its web.

CHAPTER
3

"What do you mean 'disappeared'?" Arthur's mother exclaimed, sinking down on the sofa. Arthur's father sat down next to his wife and put his arm around her shoulders.

Grandma was making knots with her fingers, like a schoolgirl with a bad report card. "I don't know where to begin," murmured the old lady.

"Perhaps you should start at the beginning," Arthur's father suggested.

Grandma cleared her throat. She wasn't feeling very comfortable in front of this audience. "Well, the day Arthur got here, the weather was very nice. The water in the river was particularly warm and Arthur wanted to go fishing. So we took his grandfather's fishing poles and left on an adventure which, in reality, went no farther than the garden's edge."

The audience of two did not move, and there were only two explanations for that: either they were captivated by Arthur's fishing adventure, or they were dismayed to see Grandma so shamelessly trying to buy time.

"You cannot imagine how many fish that little guy can catch in one hour! Come on, guess," Grandma demanded with enthusiasm.

Arthur's parents looked at each other, not wondering about the number of fish their charming son was able to catch but rather how much longer Grandma would try to stall.

"Would you please get to the details of our son's disappearance?" asked Arthur's father.

The old woman sighed.

Her grandson had disappeared. They had to accept this painful reality.

She sat on the edge of an armchair, as if not to disturb it. "Every night I tell Arthur about Africa, using his grandfather's books and travel journals. They are of course very informative, but Archibald was a poet so his books are also full of tales and legends. Arthur especially liked the story of the Bogo-Matassalai and their little friends, the miniature Minimoys," Grandma said with a tremor in her voice. Speaking about her missing husband was always difficult. It had been four years since he disappeared, and it still seemed like yesterday.

"What does that have to do with Arthur's disappearance?" her son-in-law asked drily, bringing Grandma back from her reverie.

"Well . . . Arthur became convinced that not only do the

Minimoys exist but that they live in the garden," Grandma concluded.

Arthur's parents looked at her with disbelief. "In the garden?" repeated Arthur's father, who needed a confirmation of this rubbish.

Grandma nodded.

Arthur's father collected his thoughts, which took only a moment. "All right. Let's imagine there are Minimoys in the garden. What does that have to do with Arthur's disappearance?" he asked.

"Well, unfortunately, Mr. Davido arrived while we were having birthday cake. You know how quick Arthur is at understanding things," Grandma said.

"Who is this Davido? And what was he doing with the cake?" asked Arthur's father, feeling that the conversation was getting away from him.

"Mr. Ernest Davido is the landlord. Arthur quickly realized that we are having some money problems. In fact, if I don't pay Mr. Davido the money we owe very soon, the house and land will belong to him. Arthur decided that he had to find the treasure that his grandpa hid, to help me," the old woman explained.

"What treasure?" asked Arthur's father, suddenly taking a real interest in the story.

"Rubies, I think. They were a gift from the Bogo-Matassalai, and Archibald buried them somewhere in the garden."

"In the garden?" Arthur's father repeated again. He seemed able to retain only what interested him.

"Yes, but the garden is quite big. That's why Arthur wanted to find the Minimoys, so they could guide him to the treasure," concluded Grandma. It all seemed perfectly logical to her.

Arthur's father paused for a moment, like a dog in front of a rabbit hole. "Do you have a shovel?" he asked, with a gleam in his eye.

It was almost nightfall. Magnificent streaks of navy blue crossed the sky. The headlights of the parents' car were two points of yellow light illuminating the garden. From time to time, a shovel would poke out of a hole and throw its contents aside.

Occasionally, another shovel, slower and less full, would also appear.

Grandma sat on the steps opposite the garden that was no longer a garden. It looked like a battlefield. There were holes everywhere, as if a giant mole had gone mad. And there was the mole now, sticking its head out with a yelp. It had just broken its shovel.

In fact, it was Arthur's father, who was barely recognizable with his face covered in dirt. "How are we supposed to do this with such rotten equipment?" he exclaimed, angrily tossing the shovel handle aside.

His wife emerged from the neighboring hole. "Dear, calm

down. There is no use in getting angry," she said soothingly.

"Give me your shovel," Arthur's father said grumpily. He practically grabbed the tool from her hands, dove into his hole, and began working even harder.

Grandma was sorry, as sorry as her garden was now. Despite her usual good humor, she was beginning to feel depressed.

"What's the use of finding the treasure if Arthur is not here to take advantage of it?" she asked.

Arthur's father reappeared. "Don't worry, Grandma. He's probably just lost, that's all. But I know my son. He can manage. I am sure that he will find his way home. Since he's always hungry, he will most likely be back by dinnertime," he added, thinking he was being reassuring.

"It's ten o'clock at night," Grandma said, looking at her watch.

Arthur's father looked up and noticed that it was already well into the night.

"What? Oh, yes, that's true," he said, amazed at how fast time flies when you are looking for buried treasure. "No problem, then he'll go directly to bed. That way we can save on one meal," he joked.

"Francis," Arthur's mother said angrily. Her vocabulary sometimes seemed limited to this word, which she always used with the same tone of annoyance.

"Oh, it's all right. I was just joking," Arthur's father said. "As a matter of fact, though . . . I am a little bit hungry myself right now."

"All I have is what's left of Arthur's birthday cake," Grandma offered. "We'll have to eat it by candlelight, since our electricity was turned off when we couldn't pay our bill."

"Perfect," said Arthur's father, thinking more of the cake than of the electric bill. "Since we weren't there when it was served, we can have it now!"

"*Francis*," complained Arthur's mother, following them inside.

CHAPTER

4

Arthur was having a hard time freeing himself from his trap. The threads were covered with a slightly sticky substance that did not help matters, and he became increasingly more entangled.

"You've got to help me, Selenia!" he called, loud enough to be heard on the path above.

"Why?" Selenia replied, secretly pleased at his predicament. She figured no real harm would come to him and thought that it might teach him a lesson. "This will give you time to think about what you've done!"

"I haven't *done* anything!" Arthur shouted. "I just did what you asked and had a little bit of luck. That's all. Don't be angry with me for that. And, besides, everything you said about me was very nice!"

"I didn't mean any of it!" replied the princess.

Betameche spoke up. "Oh, really? Then why did you say it? Now you just say things that you don't mean?"

"No, I always mean what I say," murmured Selenia, "but

this time, it was different. I was motivated by remorse and guilt. I would have said anything to soothe my conscience."

"So you lied?" insisted Beta.

"No, I never lie," Selenia snapped back, feeling more and more as if she were in a trap. "Both of you get on my nerves. Okay! I'm not perfect. Are you happy now?"

"Yes, I am," replied Betameche, delighted by this confession.

"I'm not," said Arthur, who had just noticed the spider. Even though she was impressive, it was not her size or her appearance that frightened Arthur—it was the direction she was taking. The creature was heading straight for him and most certainly not to say hello. More likely, it would be good-bye!

"Now what are you complaining about?" Selenia asked as she leaned toward Arthur. "Perhaps you think *you're* perfect?"

"Not at all! Quite the contrary. I think I am small, stuck, and completely powerless! And I am really in need of help," answered Arthur, beginning to panic.

"That's a nice confession. A little late, of course, but good to hear," the princess added.

The spider continued along her route, following the thread that was leading directly to Arthur.

"Selenia, help! A giant spider is heading straight for me," cried Arthur.

Princess Selenia glanced at the spider. "This spider is a perfectly normal size! Must you always exaggerate?" commented the princess, completely unimpressed.

"Selenia, she is going to eat me!" screamed the young man, completely panicked.

Selenia knelt on the ground and leaned over the edge a little, as if to make their conversation more intimate.

"I would have preferred that you die of shame, but ... eaten by a spider is not too bad, either!" she said with a note of humor that only she seemed to find funny.

She got up with a big smile.

"Farewell," she said lightly, and disappeared.

Arthur was at the mercy of the monster. Abandoned, petrified, liquefied. In a word, already dead. The spider would have licked her chops, if she had any.

"Selenia, I will never make fun of you again. I swear it on the Seven Lands and on my life!" begged Arthur, but his pleas went nowhere. The edge of the chasm where Selenia had been was now desperately empty. She was gone.

Arthur was crushed. For having toyed with the feelings of a princess, he was going to die, eaten by this creature with eight hairy legs. He struggled, but to no avail. Every movement only made him more stuck and more entangled, and he was rapidly losing strength. He was tied up like a piece of meat, ready to be put into the oven.

"Selenia, I beg of you, I will do anything you want," he cried in a last burst of hope.

The head of the princess appeared, like a jack-in-the-box springing out. She was right above him, on the other side. "You promise never to make fun of Her Royal Highness again?" she asked slyly.

Arthur was at his wit's end and in no position to negotiate. "Yes, I promise! Now, quick, untangle me!" Arthur pleaded.

Selenia did not seem in much of a hurry.

"Yes who?" she asked.

"Yes, Your Highness," said Arthur anxiously.

"Your what Highness?" she insisted.

"Yes, Your Royal Highness!" Arthur cried.

Selenia hesitated for a moment. "Deal," she said, holding up her chin as only princesses know how.

The spider was on them, her large mouth open wide.

Arthur would have liked to scream, but he was paralyzed with fear and no sound would come out.

Selenia stood up, turned around, and slugged the spider. The creature stopped dead in her tracks, groggy. The beast waved her head from side to side and realized that her jaw was now making a strange sound. The little princess had struck hard, and it was now sounding like a machine that had lost its nuts and bolts.

It wasn't only the spider that was speechless. Arthur's mouth was wide open. He couldn't believe his eyes. Selenia had just punched a spider in the nose! A few hours earlier, this vision would have seemed totally crazy to him—something that would make his mother send him to bed with two aspirins.

Selenia snapped her fingers in the direction of Betameche, who was perched on a small rock nearby, watching.

"Beta—lollipop, please!" ordered the princess.

Betameche rummaged through his pockets and took out a small, perfectly round lollipop wrapped in beautiful rose petals. He threw the lollipop to his sister, who caught it with one hand. With the other, she removed the wrapper, and the lollipop immediately blew up to an enormous size, like an air bag.

"Here, this will make you feel better," promised Selenia, stuffing the large pink bubble into the spider's mouth.

The creature froze and squinted at the stick coming out of her mouth as if she did not know quite what to do.

"Go on. It's grape," Selenia said.

At this, the spider stopped hesitating and began to lick it. Her blood-red eyes gradually turned a deeper color, the color of grapes, and became almond-shaped.

Selenia smiled at her. "Good girl," she told her, before returning to Arthur, still tangled up in the web. She took out her sword and cut the threads to free him.

"You saved my life and now I've saved yours. We are even," said Selenia as if she were announcing the results of a contest.

"You saved nothing," said Arthur rebelliously. "You knew from the beginning that I was in no danger. You left me hanging so that I would make you promises!"

"You knew that you weren't in danger, too! You looked behind you and saw that there was a spiderweb that would break your fall! But you wanted to mess with me and so you were caught in your own trap!" replied Selenia, whose voice had gone up a note.

"This from her ladyship, who plays at being an iron princess and who cries like a fountain when she loses her good-for-nothing friend!" Arthur retorted, getting a little annoyed.

"You know, you two make quite a couple," Betameche said with a laugh. "At least you will never get bored with each other!"

"Mind your own business!" Selenia and Arthur replied in unison.

"You claimed you would die for me and all you did was make fun of me. You are nothing but a dirty liar!" the princess continued to Arthur.

"Oh yeah? Well, *you* are nothing but a—"

Selenia stopped him in mid-sentence. "Have you already forgotten the promise that you just made to me?"

Arthur grimaced. How did he keep falling into these traps? "I made that promise under the threats of danger and fear," he defended himself.

"It's still a promise, isn't it?"

"Yes," Arthur conceded, somewhat reluctantly.

"Yes, who?" Selenia asked.

Arthur let out a big sigh.

"Yes, Your Royal Highness," he answered, looking down at his shoes.

"At last," she rejoiced. She ran lightly over and climbed up the front leg of the spider, mounting her as if she were a horse. "Let's go," she called.

Betameche jumped from rock to rock and clambered up the length of the creature's leg. He sat behind his sister, very happy that they were finally using a good vehicle. The creature's thick fur made it possible to settle in quite comfortably.

"Well, are you coming?" Betameche called to Arthur, who was so astonished that he still hadn't moved. In less than five minutes, he had gone from nearly being eaten by a giant spider to riding her like a camel!

All it took was a princess with a quick right hook and an inflatable lollipop to make the creature more docile than a little puppy. Even Alice, sometime resident of Wonderland, might already have had a nervous breakdown at this.

"Come on, hurry up! We have lost a lot of time!" Selenia called. "Or would you perhaps prefer running behind, like a faithful miloo?"

Arthur didn't know what a miloo looked like, but he could imagine what kind of domestic animal could easily run alongside a car. He summoned all his courage and grasped the front leg and hair of the spider. He climbed the length of this post, grabbed the fur, and nestled himself in behind Betameche's back.

"Let's go, my beauty!" Selenia cried, pressing her heels into the animal's sides. The spider promptly began to move along the edge of the precipice, just like a faithful donkey in the Grand Canyon.

CHAPTER
5

The spider's rhythmic motion had awakened the young prince's stomach. "I am starving to death!" exclaimed Betameche for the fifth time in as many minutes.

"Just tell us when you are *not* hungry, Betameche. That will be more helpful," his sister answered.

"It's not a crime to be hungry, is it? We haven't eaten for ages!" grumbled the young prince, who was holding on to his stomach as if it were going to run off and join another, more understanding, body. "And since I'm a growing boy, that means I have to eat a lot, doesn't it?"

"You can grow up later, when we're back home," said Selenia, cutting the conversation short.

In the middle of the rocky tunnel, right in front of them, was a gaping hole. The stone around it was disintegrating, as if some prehistoric monster had bitten it in anger. The hole opened onto a chasm. It was so deep that drops of water fell down it without making a sound.

260 * ARTHUR AND THE FORBIDDEN CITY

Selenia slid down the spider's front leg and stopped in front of a wooden sign next to the hole. It was marked: NO ENTRY. To be sure that this instruction would be clear even to those who couldn't read very well, a skull and crossbones was drawn above the words.

"It's here," said the princess.

Betameche swallowed nervously. Arthur got down from the spider and approached the hole to look down.

There was nothing to see. Nothing.

"Isn't there another entrance—maybe something a bit more welcoming?" Betameche asked.

"This is the main entrance," the princess answered, not at all fazed by the gaping hole. If this terrifying hole was the main entrance, Arthur could only imagine what the back entrance was like.

Arthur was beginning to think that he had lived through so many magical adventures in the last twenty-four hours that one more seemed routine. He had definitely decided not to ask any more questions. Besides, the one thing in the world that he had been most afraid of was confessing his love to the princess. Now that he had gotten that over with, he was no longer afraid of anyone or anything, not because this confession had given him wings but simply because all the rest, from now on, could not possibly be as terrifying as that one action.

The princess grabbed the spider and led it toward the

gaping hole. "Go on, big girl! Spin us a beautiful thread that will take us down to the bottom," the princess urged gently, scratching her under the chin. The spider half closed her large almond eyes as if she were about to purr. A long silvery thread came out of her and spiraled down into the opening.

Betameche did not find this flimsy ladder reassuring.

"If they wrote 'no entry' and took the trouble of adding a skull and crossbones to it, that should certainly tell us something, shouldn't it?"

"It's a standard greeting here," replied the princess maliciously.

"A standard greeting! They must not have many visitors!" Betameche retorted.

Selenia was becoming annoyed. She was fed up with his little nasal voice making comments at every step. "Would you have preferred: 'Welcome to Necropolis, its palace, its army, and its private prison'?"

At this response, the prince clamped his mouth shut.

"Yes, that sign means 'welcome to the city of death.' Follow me only if you have enough courage to fight," Selenia concluded, before catching the thread between her knees and slipping down into the darkness.

Very quickly, the woosh of her leggings against the thread faded and finally disappeared.

Betameche peered over the edge, but his sister's silhouette was no longer visible. "Perhaps I will stay and guard the spider. I am afraid she might leave if she's left alone," he said nervously.

"As you wish," said Arthur, seizing the thread. He crossed his legs around the cord, as he had learned in school, and prepared to descend.

"That way," Betameche said, as if to cover his cowardice, "when you come back we can make the return trip on her and we will be home sooner!"

"If we come back!" Arthur noted.

"Yes, of course, if you come back!" added Betameche with a wan smile. The idea of returning alone did not seem to enchant him either.

Arthur began to slide down the thread spun by the spider. In a few seconds his silhouette also disappeared into the impenetrable darkness.

A shiver ran through Betameche. No way in the world was he going to slide down that thread. He stood up and sighed with relief, believing he had escaped the worst.

Except that the atmosphere around him was not any more reassuring. There were traces of moisture on the walls. These magnified the echo of far-off cries, distorted by distance . . . endless cries of pain.

Betameche turned around to see what was behind him. He thought he saw something on the far wall. Despite the fear that was gripping his stomach, he moved a few steps closer to see what it might be.

There were images carved into the wall that were shining, thanks to the water that was dripping down them. They were skulls and crossbones, sometimes accompanied by the appropriate skeleton.

Betameche took a few steps back and stepped on a bone, which made a loud cracking sound. The young prince finally noticed that he was in the middle of hundreds of bones, like an open-air cemetery. He let out a cry of horror that went on to mix with the echoes in the back of the cave.

Beta turned to face the spider. "Listen, I really like you, but I shouldn't leave the other two all alone. They will get into trouble without me," he explained.

Betameche grabbed the thread and did not even take the time to cross his legs around it. All he wanted now was to make a fast escape from this unhappy place.

"Anything has to be better than this," he told himself, and leaped out into this black hole that swallowed all light.

Arthur's father was still in his own hole. Overcome with fatigue, he'd fallen asleep on his shovel.

The rhythm of the shovel's movement had slowed way down. Now you would need an appointment to spot a shovel, half full, coming out of the hole to be emptied. This treasure was not ready to be found, it seemed. And Alfred the dog wasn't exactly helping—he'd gone back and was now systematically filling in all the holes.

This was not really done out of a sense of solidarity but rather to prevent anyone from discovering *his* treasure: a dozen marrow bones he had patiently put aside, being the thrifty dog that he is.

Arthur's mother came out of the house with a tray in her hand. She had prepared a pitcher full of ice water and a small place setting on which she had carefully arranged peeled orange sections.

"Darling," she sang as she advanced carefully over this mined territory.

Even with the moon to guide her, the poor woman could not see much. She should have put on her glasses, but her natural vanity often prevented her from wearing them in public. This vanity would cost her dearly, since she did not see the dog's tail, or the impending catastrophe that went along with it. She stepped directly on Alfred's tail, which immediately set him howling.

Arthur's mother shrieked and lost her balance. She teetered forward one step, then one step back, and then fell into the very hole her husband was sleeping in.

The pitcher slid on the tray and, with surprising reflexes, she managed to grab it by the handle. She saved the pitcher, but not its contents. Her husband caught the ice water right in the face. He, in turn, howled inhumanly and began to fight off the ice cubes which were flying everywhere, primarily down his shirt.

Alfred grimaced. He did not like water either, especially not when it was as cold as this was.

"How could you be so clumsy?" Arthur's father shouted. "Can't you pay attention?"

Arthur's mother did not know how to apologize. She collected the ice cubes, now covered with dirt, and put them back into the pitcher, as if that would do any good.

Grandma appeared on the front steps, another tray in her hands. "I brought you some hot coffee!" she offered.

Arthur's father waved his arms frantically. After the ice cubes, he was not at all thrilled about the prospect of receiving a cup of hot coffee in his face.

"Don't move," he cried, as if Grandma were about to step on a snake. "Put it down there and I'll come and get it a little later," he added.

Grandma did not know what to think. She knew that her daughter had married an eccentric, but here she must have missed a chapter. She shrugged, put the tray down on the steps, and went back into the house without saying a word.

Arthur's mother tried to sponge off her husband with her delicate little silk handkerchief. It was like trying to empty a bathtub with a straw. Grumbling, he climbed out of the hole and headed for the house. His wife followed him, with Alfred the dog right behind.

Arthur's father reached the steps and sighed a deep sigh. His shirt was already beginning to dry. And, after all, it was only water. He tried to smile at his wife as she came up to join him, still a little clumsy without her glasses. She really was very endearing, he thought.

"I'm sorry, dear. I spoke harshly to you because I was startled," he said sincerely.

"Oh, no, it was my fault. Sometimes I am so clumsy," she confessed.

"No, no!" replied Arthur's father, who had been thinking the same thing. "Would you like some coffee?"

"I would love some," she answered, pleased by this little gesture of love.

Arthur's father took a cup, put in two lumps of sugar, and added a cloud of milk. While he did this, his wife was looking for her glasses in the various pockets of her dress. So she did not see the spider that was descending along a thread a few inches away from her face.

Arthur's father turned toward his wife, cup in one hand, coffeepot in the other, and began to pour the coffee delicately.

"A good cup of coffee will wake us up!" he commented.

He did not know how right he was. His wife had finally found her glasses and put them on. The first thing she saw was a monstrous spider, rubbing its hairy legs together, one inch from her nose.

She immediately let out a wild shriek. It sounded like a baboon having a fingernail ripped out. Her husband jumped back, tripped on the tray, and fell flat on the porch. The coffeepot flew out of his hands and emptied itself all over him. His cry, compared with hers, sounded more like a mammoth having a tooth pulled . . . so, whatever else you might think of them, at least the couple was harmonious in their pain.

CHAPTER

6

Their unworldly cry, times two, echoed to the ends of the Seven Lands and even beyond, as far as Necropolis.

Selenia looked up as if she could see the cry that had just passed, distorted, bouncing from wall to wall. Arthur finished sliding down the long spider thread and landed behind Selenia. He had also heard the sound, but he was light-years away from imagining that it could have come from his parents.

"Welcome to Necropolis," said the princess with a little smile.

"So far it is not as terrible as the welcome message was!" noted Arthur, who was already covered with cold sweat.

"Here, the word for welcome is the same as the word for death!" Selenia explained. "We have to stay together," she said just as Betameche arrived, knocking them down like bowling pins. The group scattered with a great deal of noise.

"Boy, you never miss an opportunity, do you?" groaned Selenia, climbing to her feet.

"I'm sorry," replied Betameche, beaming. He was delighted to be with them again.

Arthur got up and brushed himself off. He noticed with astonishment that the spider's thread was being pulled back up the hole. Selenia had seen it, too, but didn't seem worried.

"How will we get back if the spider isn't there?" asked Arthur.

"Who ever said we *would* get back?" replied the princess cynically. "We are on a mission here. Once it is done, then we'll have time to think about our return." With that, she started down another tunnel with a determined step, chin forward, as if she feared nothing and no one. Arthur and Beta followed without arguing.

The road they were taking soon led to another, this one as wide as a main street.

Our three heroes tried to be as inconspicuous and silent as possible, since this street, carved in the stone, was far from being deserted. There were peasants from all of the Seven Lands, there to sell their goods. There were gamouls loaded with carefully cut metal plaques and selenielle vendors who had come to dispose of their harvest.

Selenia slipped into the crowd headed toward the great market of Necropolis.

Arthur was amazed to see so many people and so many colors. He would never have suspected the existence of all this life only a few yards underground his grandmother's garden.

There was no comparison to the little village where he lived and its supermarket that he loved to visit.

This market was huge and full of life. It was the center of all commerce, all traffic. It was not the sort of place one went to unarmed, and Selenia kept her hand on the hilt of her sword. Mercenaries of all kinds strolled through the market, ready to sell their services. Street hawkers grabbed the last remaining free spaces. A few suspicious-looking types set up gambling tables in the middle of the road, where you could bet on anything, from a couple of raisins to a couple of camels. Impossible to know what you would win, but you could certainly lose your health.

Arthur was a little frightened by all this. He was certainly impressed by the mixture of happy commerce and disreputable behavior. It was an amazing coexistence that actually seemed to work. The reason was simple: the henchmen.

Above each street corner, at a reasonable height, was a sentry box with a henchman, surveying the joyous chaos. Surveillance was total and permanent. Calm reigned because M. the cursed ruled with the iron fist of terror.

The Necropolis market was the first thing that Maltazard created when he came to power. The prince of darkness became rich by filling the Seven Lands with hordes of henchmen that he had trained to pillage and steal on his behalf. But pillaging and stealing were not enough. He knew that much wealth remained hidden, buried, and even swallowed

As soon as a henchmen attack was rumored, the villagers made their best treasures disappear. Not all of it, of course, since not finding anything would have angered the master, but enough that he could tell more was hidden away somewhere.

Maltazard killed very few citizens, but not because he was good-hearted. His mercy was purely commercial. "A person who dies is one less worker to build my palace," he loved to say.

The best way to extract the riches he could not steal was to encourage his people to spend them. The lure of gain, of wealth, the desire to possess . . . so Maltazard built, right into the rock, hundreds of galleries, where he offered stands at a good price. Maltazard, by all accounts, had a good head for business. This was how the Necropolis market began. Now it was enormous and it made a fortune for Maltazard, who received a commission on every item bought or sold, no matter how small.

Our friends advanced through the chaos with prudence and curiosity—prudence because of the henchmen standing above their heads at every crossroads, and curiosity, as they saw creatures of all kinds. Arthur had never even dreamed of beings this strange . . . like this odd group of animals with protruding eyes who were holding up their ears in order not to step on them.

"Who are they?" asked Arthur, very intrigued.

"The Balong-Botos. They are from the Third Land. They come here to be barbered," Betameche explained.

"Barbered?" Arthur said.

"Their fur is very highly valued, so they come to sell it in the market," Betameche explained. "It grows long enough to be shaved twice a year. That is how they make a living. The rest of the time, all they do is sleep."

"And why do they have such big ears?" Arthur wondered.

"The Balong-Botos do not kill animals, so they do not have fur coats from animal skins to protect themselves from the severe winters of their region. Instead, parents pull on the ears of their children, beginning when they are very young, so that they can lengthen enough for each Balong-Boto to roll itself up in them during the winter. That has been their tradition for thousands of years."

Arthur couldn't believe it. Like all kids his age, he hated having his ears pulled. It had never occurred to him that they could end up keeping him warm in winter.

Distracted by a baby Balong that was having its ears pulled, Arthur walked straight into a post. Two posts, to be exact. Arthur looked up and discovered that these two posts were legs attached to a rangy creature. It resembled a beanpole mounted on the legs of a pink flamingo.

"It's an Asparguetto," Beta noted in a low voice. "They are very big and very sensitive!"

"Do not take the trouble to excuse yourself, young man,"

said the animal, bending toward Arthur. On its face it had green plates for glasses, the color of candy, which looked almost like a mask. Underneath them, you could barely see its small blue eyes.

"I'm sorry! I didn't see you!" Arthur said politely.

"I am not transparent, you know!" the Asparguetto replied in a calm voice. "Not only do I have to bend all day to be able to move in this place that is so not designed for people my size, but then I have to suffer these constant insults to my person."

"I completely understand," said Arthur gently. "I used to be tall! I know what it's like!"

The Asparguetto looked at him blankly. "So it's not enough to bump into me—now you have decided to make fun of me?" asked the sensitive creature.

"No, no, not at all! I just meant that I used to be almost five feet tall and now I am only half an inch." Arthur knew he was digging himself in deeper. "I wanted to say that . . . it is not easy to be tall in the world of the small, but . . . it also not easy to be small in the world of the tall."

The creature did not know what to think about this. He peered down at the strange little short-legged fellow for a moment.

"You are excused," the Asparguetto finally said, closing the discussion. It went striding off over a few more stands on his way to another street.

"I warned you," said Betameche. "They are supersensitive!"

Arthur watched the Asparguetto disappear in a few long strides. Too amazed to respond, he turned back to Beta and encountered another rather strange group of animals in front of them. These were large, furry creatures, as round as balloons, with small weasel faces and a dozen legs in constant motion.

"Those are the Boulaguiris. They live in the forest of the Fifth Land," Betameche noted. "Their specialty is polishing pearls. If you bring them a pearl in bad condition, they will eat it and six months later, they will bring it back to you, more beautiful than ever."

Betameche had barely finished his description when a Boulaguiri proved his words. The creature approached a small stand carved into the stone. A Cachflot greeted him. The Cachflots were the only individuals authorized to run businesses in Necropolis. Whether buying or selling, all transactions passed through their hands. It was Maltazard himself who granted the privilege to this tribe from the far-off Sixth Land. Legend had it that their chief, named Cacarante, had saved the life of M. the cursed by lending him money so that he could have his face redone. The sovereign was not ungrateful, and he rewarded him in this way. The Cachflots had been growing rich in Necropolis for many years.

The Boulaguiri extended one of his paws to the vendor, who shook it civilly but without great enthusiasm. Politeness, here as elsewhere, is necessary for commerce.

After exchanging a few words that neither Arthur nor Betameche could hear, the Boulaguiri began to contort himself, as if he had been overcome with terrible stomach pains. Arthur grimaced in sympathy as if his own stomach felt just as bad.

The face of the Boulaguiri changed colors several times before shifting to the most sickening pale green color. Then he emitted a loud burp and a magnificent pearl popped out of his mouth. It fell into a box lined with black cotton that the Cachflot was holding. The dealer caught the pearl with a pair of tweezers, while the Boulaguiri slowly returned to his normal color.

The Cachflot examined the pearl. It was sublime, glowing with a thousand points of light. The buyer accepted the deal with a small nod of his head. The Boulaguiri gave him a beautiful smile, revealing that the creature did not have teeth. He began to contort himself for another delivery.

Arthur was amazed at this sight, even though such marvels were common in the streets leading to Necropolis. But a cry of joy awakened him from his reverie. Betameche had just found a seller of bellicornes. The boy was jumping for joy and began a little dance of thanks.

"What on earth is wrong with you?" asked Arthur.

Betameche grabbed his comrade by the shoulders. "These are bellicornes in syrup!" he shouted. "There is nothing better in all of the Seven Lands than bellicornes in syrup!"

"And what exactly are these bellicornes?" Arthur asked, wary of the culinary tastes of his friend.

"Dough made of sentinelle, soaked in gamoul's milk, then mixed with eggs to hold it together, sprinkled with chopped nuts, and covered with a delicious rosewater syrup." Betameche recited the recipe, savoring every word.

Arthur was delighted—there didn't appear to be anything weird about these cookies. They actually sounded a bit like gazelle horns, cookies his grandmother made from time to time using a recipe that she had brought back from Africa.

Betameche took a coin out of his pocket and threw it to the Cachflot, who caught it in midair.

"Serve yourself, my lord," he said, the perfect merchant.

Betameche took a bellicorne and bit into it. He let out a small sigh of satisfaction, then began to chew very slowly to make the pleasure last. Arthur could resist no longer. He took a bellicorne and bit off the end, shiny with syrup. He waited a few seconds, in case there were secondary effects, like there had been with the jack-fire, but nothing happened. The syrup melted in his mouth, while the lightly sweetened dough reminded him of almond paste. Arthur continued to eat.

"Isn't it the best thing that you have ever eaten in your entire life?" Betameche asked as he finished off his fourth bellicorne.

Arthur had to admit that it was really good.

"Are my bellicornes really fresh?" asked the merchant, with

the smile of someone who already knows the answer.

The two friends nodded energetically, their mouths full of syrup.

"The rosewater came from this morning's roses and I picked the eggs myself barely an hour ago," he declared, a good baker proud of his product.

Arthur stopped dead in his tracks, his mouth wide open. One detail worried him. In his world, eggs were laid, they were collected, they were found, they were even stolen, but they were never "picked."

"Excuse me . . . what kind of eggs are they?" Arthur asked politely, making a face as if already expecting the worst. The vendor laughed at his client's naïveté.

"There is only one kind of egg suitable for making real bellicornes, of course. Caterpillar eggs, taken from underneath the mother," said the merchant. He proudly pointed to his official plaque, naming him one of the best bellicorne bakers of the year.

In response, Arthur spit out the contents of his mouth right into the man's face.

The vendor stood still for a moment, shocked by the insult that the young Arthur had accidentally made.

"I'm so sorry—I can't handle caterpillar or dragonfly eggs!" explained Arthur.

This was going to end badly, Beta could tell. He took advantage of the last few seconds of surprise to swallow a dozen cakes at a speed approaching the world record.

The Cachflot had regained his composure. He took a deep breath and began to shout: "Guards! Over here!"

At these simple words, there was panic in the street.

CHAPTER
7

Everyone ran around, yelling in various languages. Suddenly, a hand grabbed Arthur by the shoulder and pulled him violently back. "This way!" whispered Selenia as she dragged Arthur behind her. Betameche grabbed a few more bellicornes and joined his comrades, scattering cakes every which way.

The three heroes elbowed their way through the general panic, and ducked into a shop to avoid the patrol of henchmen that was rushing up the street.

Arthur caught his breath.

"We said to stay together, didn't we?" Selenia lectured them, annoyed at having to supervise two irresponsible boys.

"I know, but there were so many interesting people all of a sudden!" Arthur said.

"The more people you talk to, the more likely we are to be noticed. We have to be discreet!" Selenia insisted.

Another Cachflot, all smiles, appeared behind them. "Can't one be discreet and *elegant*, too?" he said in honeyed tones. "Come and take a look at my new collection. It's a feast for the eyes!"

As the merchant had guessed, no princess in the world could refuse this type of invitation.

Meanwhile, a little farther away, the bellicorne merchant was describing, with big, unflattering gestures, the two professional thieves who had assaulted him. The chief of the henchmen listened attentively. It did not take him long to realize that these must be the same runaways who had escaped from Darkos at the Jaimabar Club.

This type of news spreads quickly in Necropolis, because it is rare that inhabitants of the First Land come to visit the forbidden zones and even more rare for one of them to insult Prince Darkos.

The chief of the henchmen turned to his men.

"Search all the stores. They can't be far," he ordered.

Fortunately for our three heroes, the troops went off in the wrong direction.

The chief grabbed the last soldier by the neck. "You, go warn the palace." The soldier froze, and then took off like a rabbit.

Selenia saw him pass by their shop, faster than lightning.

"At least now we know the direction of the palace!" commented the princess. She threw a coin to the merchant, then buried her face in the hood of her new Balong-boto fur coat. Arthur and Betameche did the same. They looked like three penguins, disguised as Eskimos.

"My pleasure!" the smiling merchant called after them as they left.

The camouflage seemed effective—no one noticed them in their multicolored furs.

"You could have chosen something lighter. I am dying of the heat!" Betameche complained, buried in a fur that was too big for him. "We have to stop for something to drink," he added.

"You're hot, you're hungry, you're thirsty! When are you going to stop complaining all the time?" Selenia asked in utter exasperation.

Betameche scowled and began to grumble quietly to himself.

Selenia picked up the pace, afraid of losing track of the henchman. The street became slightly wider, then opened onto an enormous square, located in a cave whose roof was so high it could not be seen from the ground.

Selenia stopped at the edge of this monumental arena, where thousands of onlookers were milling around.

"The Necropolis market," whispered Selenia, awed by the size of the place. She had heard it described many times, but everything that she had imagined was smaller than this. The square was filled with people, and the crowds moved like the surface of an agitated sea. Things were bought, sold, exchanged, discussed, argued over, stolen. . . .

Arthur was speechless before this spectacle. One pair of eyes was not enough to take in the multitude of sights. It reminded him of his grandpa's enormous bait bucket, filled with hundreds of worms. The vision before him was just as colorful and certainly noisier.

They could hardly hear over the roar and babble, and Selenia had to yell to be heard. "I've lost sight of him," she shouted, annoyed. It was not surprising that the henchman had disappeared, given the chaos in the market.

"Why don't we just ask the way to the palace? People here must know where it is, right?" asked Arthur naively.

"You don't understand. Everything is sold here, and it is information that sells the best. Ask for the palace and you will be handed over to the guards in a minute!" said Selenia.

Arthur looked around him and noticed that no one looked very trustworthy at all. They all had bulging eyes, jaws full of teeth, furs that were too long, and legs that were too numerous. He had never seen such a variety of weapons as those hanging from every belt. It was like a real western.

Our three heroes craned their heads in all directions, searching the crowd for a sign that might put them on the path to the palace.

On the other side of the square was a monumental façade, sculpted with all kinds of strange faces. It looked more like

the entrance to a horror museum than a palace but, knowing
the personality of M. the cursed, Selenia felt she was on the
right path.

Working their way through this crowd, which was thicker
than the thickest pea soup, took them about twenty minutes.
Finally they arrived at the foot of the façade.

"Do you think this is it?" whispered Betameche. "It seems
kind of scary for a palace!"

"Given the number of guards in front of the door, I'm guess-
ing it's not the entrance to a kindergarten!" Selenia replied.

Actually, in front of the imposing door, which was locked
three times, were two full rows of menacing henchmen, each of
whom looked ready to slice up anyone who dared to approach,
even to ask for directions.

"Maybe there's a back entrance," Selenia suggested.

"Good idea," her two followers replied in unison, not really
in the mood to take on two rows of henchmen.

Suddenly, the crowd behind them opened up to let a procession pass.

"Room! Room," cried a potbellied henchman. He was leading a convoy consisting of a dozen wagons piled high with
fruit, grilled insects, and other equally delicious dishes. They
were all pulled by gamouls, who were somewhat jumpy in the
midst of such a large crowd.

Selenia approached to watch the convoy pass. "What's going

on?" she casually asked a stranger with bulging eyes.

"It's the master's meal. The fifth of the day!" noted the stranger, who was as thin as a rail.

"And how many does he have like this?" asked Betameche, slightly envious.

"Eight meals a day, like the fingers of his hands," answered the old man with the hungry face, watching the convoy pass by.

"And he's going to eat all that?" wondered Arthur.

"What do you think? He barely touches it. All he eats is a grilled insect or two. When I think that one of these meals could nourish my people for six moons!" the old man confessed. He sighed with despair and moved on, disgusted by this opulence.

"Why doesn't M. give away the food that he doesn't eat rather than throwing it out?" said Arthur.

"M. the cursed is evil personified. He takes pleasure in the suffering he inflicts on others. Nothing gives him more pleasure than a starving people crying for their survival," explained Selenia through clenched teeth.

"But he was one of you once, wasn't he?" Arthur asked.

"Who told you that?" asked the princess, visibly disturbed by the question.

"Beta told me that he was chased from your land a long time ago," the boy replied.

Selenia gave her brother an angry look that he carefully

avoided by looking elsewhere. "It's crazy, all these little details on the palace façade, isn't it?" Beta said, trying to change the subject.

"What happened? Why was he chased away?" asked Arthur. He'd forgotten his decision not to ask any more questions—he was dying to know a little bit more about the Minimoys and this terrible enemy.

"It's a long story that I'll tell you later. Perhaps! In the meantime, we have better things to do. Follow me!" Selenia elbowed through the hungry crowd and started walking along next to the convoy.

A little creature called a sylo was watching the food pass, his eight big eyes wide open. Hungrily, he reached out toward a piece of fruit. A violent crack of the whip hit his hand and he yelped.

The parents of the little sylo immediately hid him in their thick fur. A henchman stopped in front of the father sylo, his whip in his hands.

"We do not touch the master's food," the henchman reminded them.

The sylo bared its teeth, forty-eight razor-sharp blades. One more move against his child would probably have been very dangerous.

The henchman swallowed upon seeing this chain saw.

"All right, we'll let it go—this time," the henchman conceded.

Next to the enormous palace entrance, there was a cave cut into the rock wall. At the back of the cave was another, smaller heavy door, modestly decorated. As the convoy approached, this swung open automatically. The procession entered slowly, wagon after wagon rolling into the heart of the rock.

The crowd stood back from this entrance. No one dared to go any closer. No one, that is, except for our three heroes. Selenia had hidden herself behind a large rock nearby and was watching for the last wagon to pass through. She threw off her fur coat and prepared to jump.

"This is where our paths separate, Arthur," said the princess.

"No way!" replied the valiant Arthur. "I'm coming with you!"

But Selenia unsheathed her sword, faster than lightning, and pointed it at his throat to keep him away.

"This is something I have to do myself," said Selenia gravely.

"And me? What do I do?" asked the boy.

"You find the treasure and save your home. I will find M. the cursed and try to save mine," Selenia said in a low, determined voice. "If I succeed, we will meet back here in an hour," she added solemnly.

"And if you fail?" asked Arthur, sadness gripping him.

Selenia let out a long sigh. She had considered this possibility many times. She knew that her chances were very slim against M. the cursed and his infinite powers.

She had perhaps one chance in a thousand to succeed, but she was a real princess of the blood, daughter of King Sifrat de Matradoy, fifteenth of that name. There was no question that she would fight to the finish, no matter what.

She looked into Arthur's eyes and approached him, without lowering her sword.

"If I fail . . . be a good king," she said simply, as if a little door had just opened in her soldier's heart. She put her hand on his shoulder and placed a gentle kiss on his mouth.

Time stood still. Bees drew hearts with honey in a sky where carnations rained down. The clouds held hands around them, and an orchestra of thousands of birds drowned the sky with beautiful melody.

Never had Arthur felt so happy. He felt like he was sliding on a silk toboggan through the air. Selenia's breath was warmer than summer, her skin softer than springtime. He wouldn't have minded staying there for centuries, if the gods of love had let him.

Selenia stepped back and broke the charm.

The kiss had lasted only a second.

Selenia smiled at him. Her look had a new sweetness. "Now that you have all my powers . . . make good use of them." She turned and leaped for the door, darting through the gap just before it clanged shut.

"But—wait . . . we must . . ." murmured Arthur, starting after her. But even though Arthur was only half an inch tall, there was no way for him to slip in. The door was shut. Selenia was gone.

Arthur was overwhelmed. He had barely had time to understand what was happening to him and already he had to understand that it might never happen again. The young man touched his lips, as if to reassure himself that he had not been dreaming, but the princess's perfume was still there, all around his face.

Betameche came out from his hiding place, applauding. "Bravo! That was wonderful!" He grabbed Arthur's hands and shook them vigorously. "Congratulations! That was one of the most beautiful weddings I have ever attended!"

"What are you talking about?" asked Arthur, somewhat lost.

"Why, about your marriage, idiot! She kissed you. So you are married, for better or for worse, until the next dynasty. That's how it is with us!" Beta explained simply.

"You mean to tell me that—that kiss, that was marriage?" questioned Arthur, somewhat surprised by this bizarre custom.

"Of course!" confirmed Betameche. "A very moving cere-mony! Clear! Concise! Superb!"

"A little *too* concise, wasn't it?" asked Arthur, disoriented by the speed of events.

"Of course not! You have the main parts: her hand and her heart. What more could you want?" Betameche retorted with a logic belonging only to the Minimoys.

"Where I live, adults take a little more time. They get to know each other, they go out with each other, spend time together. Then they discuss it, and it is usually the man who makes the proposal. Then the kiss comes at the end, after they say 'I do!' in front of a minister and a whole lot of people," Arthur explained, thinking of his parents' marriage.

"Oh, my! What a waste of time! You must have a lot of time to spare if you spend so much of it on little details. It's only the head that needs all of this artifice. The heart understands the truth of things, and a kiss is the best way to say it," said Betameche.

Everything was moving much too fast for Arthur. After a kiss like that, he needed a good night's sleep and some aspirin.

"What more did you want?" his friend asked, seeing his crestfallen expression.

"Well . . . I don't know. A little celebration, perhaps?" said Arthur.

"That sounds like an excellent idea to me," said a voice too deep to be Beta's.

Our two friends turned around and found themselves face-to-face with twenty henchmen. They were all grouped behind their chief, the horrible Darkos, only son of the equally horrible M. the cursed.

Each time Darkos smiled, he looked as if he were going

to kill someone, his smile was so unfriendly. Even if he'd brushed his brown teeth fifteen times a day, it would change nothing.

Darkos approached Arthur with the slow step of a conqueror. "I will personally take care of preparing a small celebration," he said. The message was so clear that even the henchmen understood it and laughed stupidly.

Arthur also understood. This was going to be much less pleasant than his birthday party a few short days ago.

Arthur's mother was sitting at the kitchen table. She fingered the ten little candles that no longer had a cake or Arthur to shine for.

Ten little candles, for ten short years that had seen Arthur shoot up like a young wild animal. Arthur's poor mother could not stop remembering those ten birthdays, all of them different.

The first, when the light of the candles dancing in front of him had enchanted Arthur. The second, when he tried, in vain, to catch the little flames that slipped between his hands. The third birthday, when his still small breath required three tries to blow out all the candles. The fourth cake when he blew the candles out all together for the first time. The fifth, when he cut the cake himself, under the vigilant eye of his father, helping him handle a knife that was too big for his hand. The sixth birthday, the most important in Arthur's eyes, because on this occasion his grandfather had given him his own knife with which he proudly cut his own cake. It was also the last birthday his grandfather was there for.

The poor woman could not prevent a tear from rolling down her cheek. There had been so much happiness and unhappiness in only ten years. Next to these ten years that had flashed by like a shooting star, the ten hours that had passed since she found out about Arthur's disappearance seemed like an eternity.

Arthur's mother looked around for something to comfort her, something that would give her a bit of hope. All she saw was her husband, stretched out on the couch, overcome by fatigue. He didn't have the strength to snore or even to close his mouth, which was open to the four winds.

Under other circumstances, this picture would have made her smile, but today, it made her want to cry even more.

Grandma sat down next to her with a box of tissues.

"That's my last box," she said with sad humor.

The daughter looked at her mother and sighed a small sigh.

In difficult moments, the old woman had always been able to keep her sense of humor. She got that from her husband, Archibald, who elevated humor and poetry to the rank of basic values.

"Humor is to life what cathedrals are to religion—it is the best that we have invented," he liked to joke.

If only Archibald were here, Grandma thought. He would bring a bit of light into their now dark lives. He would know how to give them that little touch of optimism that never left him and that enabled him to make it through the war, the way a matador escapes the horns of a bull.

The old woman gently grasped her daughter's hands and shook them with affection. "You know, my dear daughter . . . what I am going to say probably makes no sense, but . . . your son is an exceptional little boy. Wherever he is, even if he finds himself in a bad situation, I have a feeling he will be able to get out of it."

Arthur's mother seemed somewhat reassured by these words, and the two women held each other's hands as if preparing to pray.

They would have to hope that Grandma was right because, for the moment, Arthur was in prison. His two little hands held the iron bars, and he watched the marketplace full of people, where there was not a single kind soul to come to his aid.

"Forget it! No one would risk helping a prisoner of M. the cursed," said Beta, huddling in a corner in the prison.

"Watch what you say, Beta! Selenia said we had to be careful," Arthur reminded him.

"Careful? Everyone already knows we are in prison!" sighed the little prince, completely depressed. "We have fallen into the hands of this monster. Our future is already clear! Only Selenia can save our lives . . . provided, of course, that she can save her own!"

Arthur looked at him and was forced to agree. Selenia was their only hope.

CHAPTER
8

Our little princess was advancing through the maze of unwelcoming halls in the royal palace, her hands firmly gripping her sword. She lost sight of the food convoy but managed to orient herself by the tracks left on the ground by the wooden wheels. She moved quietly from hiding place to hiding place, regularly allowing patrols of henchmen, which were as numerous as frogs in a pond, to pass.

Soon, the corridors dug into the rock became increasingly more ornate and the walls were covered with black marble. Flames from the torches were reflected in the smooth surface, making the hall appear endless.

Selenia's heart was beating regularly, but her hands were a little damp. This icy underground world was not exactly her favorite place to be. She preferred forests of tall grass, autumn leaves that made it possible to surf the hills of her village, fields of poppies in which it was so comfortable to sleep. A wave of homesickness swept over her. It is often only when we are experiencing unhappiness that we realize how valuable little day-to-day things really are: a great stretch upon waking, a ray of sunlight on your face, someone you love smiling at you. It's as if unhappiness is simply a way to measure happiness.

A patrol of henchmen brought Selenia back from her reverie, making her jump into a nearby doorway to hide from them.

She could not think of home now; she had to focus on her mission. She was still inside this palace of death, a black cathedral, as cold as ice. The floor was also marble, and of such a deep black that it created the illusion of falling. The tracks of the wagons were no longer visible. This stone was too hard to have any trace left on it.

Selenia arrived at a crossroads and had to make a decision. She stood there for a moment, relying on her instincts to guide her. Was there a force watching over these Seven Lands that would lend a hand, or would she have to face this test on her own?

Selenia waited a little, but no divine sign appeared. Not even a slight breeze to indicate the road to choose. She sighed and once again examined the two tunnels. There was a vague light in the one on the right and what sounded like distant music. A normal person would have immediately sensed danger and fled in the other direction. But Selenia was not a normal person. She was a princess devoted to her cause and ready to take any risk to accomplish her mission. She grasped the sword in her hand harder and entered the passageway on the right.

Soon she came to a corner and found herself in an enormous room. Dark slabs of glowing marble covered the ground, while thousands of stalactites hung from the ceiling, drops of water frozen in their descent.

Selenia took a few steps on the marble, as smooth as a lake, which seemed to absorb all sound. At the back of the room, she saw the wagons left by the slaves. Fruits of all kinds were overflowing the cart, the only traces of color in this universe of gray and black.

In front of the cart was a silhouette, its back turned to Selenia. She could see it was wearing a long cape, ragged at the ends, placed over asymmetrical shoulders. It was difficult, from this distance, to say whether the man wore a hat or whether his head was just a lot bigger than his body. It didn't matter— this emaciated silhouette was monstrous and seemed to come straight out of our worst nightmares.

This man with his back turned, nibbling bits of fruit from the ends of his clawlike fingers, could be no one but M. the cursed.

Selenia swallowed, grasped her sword to give herself courage, and advanced with slow, muffled steps.

Her vengeance was within reach. It was her own personal revenge but also that of all her people and all the peoples of the Seven Lands who, at one time or another, had been subject to the warlike arm of this conquering emperor.

Selenia's arm would correct all that and cleanse the memory

of the ancestors, soiled by years of slavery and dishonor. Her eyes riveted on her enemy, she advanced slowly, her breath short, her heart pounding. She raised her arm slowly in the air.

Unfortunately, the sword was long and the stalactites here were much lower than the others. As she lifted it, the blade struck the stone with a small, shrill sound.

The silhouette, holding a piece of fruit, froze in place. Selenia did likewise. She was as immobile as the rocks hanging from the ceiling.

The man set the fruit down carefully and let out a long, calm sigh. He still had his back to Selenia. He lifted his head, as if overwhelmed but not surprised by her presence.

"I once spent entire days polishing that sword, so that its blade would be perfect. I would recognize the sound it makes among a thousand others." The man's voice was cavernous. The walls of his throat must have been badly damaged because the air that passed through blew strangely, as if it were in contact with a cheese grater.

"It was not you," the man mused. "So who, then, was able to pull this sword from the stone, Selenia?" he asked, before slowly turning around.

Maltazard finally showed his face and it was a walking horror. Deformed, half eaten away, wrinkled by time, his face was nothing more than a devastated field. Crusts had formed here and there around still-weeping wounds. The pain must be constant and it showed in his worn-out expression.

You might have expected to see nothing there but fire and hatred. Quite the contrary; his eyes had the sadness of animals on the path to extinction, the melancholy of fallen princes, and the humility of survivors.

But Selenia did not gaze too deeply into the eyes of Maltazard. She knew they were the most formidable of his weapons. How many had fallen into the trap of his harmless look and ended up being toasted like almonds?

She held her sword in front of her, prepared for an evil blow, observing Maltazard and the rest of his body. It did not seem like much. Half Minimoy, half insect, it seemed to be decomposing. Some coarse stitching held most of him together and his long cape hid the rest as best it could.

His jaws opened slightly. This might have been a smile, or at least an attempt at one.

"I am very happy to see you, princess," he said in a softer voice. "I missed you," he added, apparently sincere.

Selenia stood straight and lifted her chin, like the courageous young woman she had become.

"I didn't miss you," she replied. "And I am here to destroy you!"

Clint Eastwood could not have done better. She fixed her gaze on Maltazard, ready for a duel, as if totally unaware of the impressive size of her adversary. It was David against Goliath, Mowgli against Shere Khan.

"Why so much hatred?" asked Maltazard, smiling even more at the idea of combat.

"You betrayed your people and massacred or enslaved all the others. You are a monster!"

"Don't speak of monsters," said Maltazard, whose face had turned green. "Don't speak of things you don't understand," he added, calming himself down. "If you knew how painful it is to live in this mutilated body, you would not say such things."

"Your body was in perfect condition when you betrayed us. It was the gods that inflicted this punishment on you!" retorted the princess, determined not to give in on any point.

Maltazard let out a thunderous roar, like a cannon spitting out a cannonball.

"My poor child—if only history could be that simple, or if only I had been able to forget . . ." he admitted with a sigh. "At one time I was known as Maltazard the good, Maltazard the warrior! He who watches and protects," he added with tears in his voice as he went on to tell his story.

Once Maltazard had been a handsome Minimoy, strong and smiling. He stood three heads taller than anyone else, which resulted in teasing by his comrades. "His parents must have given him too much gamoul's milk!" they amused themselves by saying. It made him smile. He did not have much of a sense of humor, but he knew that these little jokes were compliments in disguise. Everyone admired his strength and his courage.

After the death of his parents, casualties in the war with the Sauterelles—a war that pitted the two peoples against each other for many moons—no one dared to utter even the mildest of jokes about him anymore.

Maltazard became an adult without the pain of his parents' loss ever leaving his heart. True to the principles that his parents had taught him, he was courageous and obliging. His sense of honor and country were deeply developed.

When the terrible drought began that would last almost a thousand Minimoy years, an expedition was sent out to search for water. Even though the Minimoys do not like to get wet, water was necessary for agriculture and for the survival of the Minimoy people.

It was natural that Maltazard would ask permission to lead the expedition. The king, still young at the time, gave him the command with great pleasure. Maltazard was like the son he wanted to have—the kind of son that the king hoped Betameche would become one day. But in the meantime, the little prince was only a few weeks old, and the king placed all his hopes in Maltazard.

Selenia fought like a tigress, since she believed she should be in charge of this important mission. Even though she was still young, and no taller than a raisin, she said that only a princess of the blood was worthy of this mission. The king had a very difficult time calming her down and had to promise her that she would one day get her turn to serve her people.

So, one fine morning Maltazard set out, as proud as a conqueror, his chest filled with ardor and courage. He left the village to the sound of applause and cries of encouragement. Several young women could not stop their tears when they saw their national hero pass by, on the road to glory.

After a few days, the expedition took a turn for the worse. The drought had reached all the lands. The survivors had organized themselves into bands, and they protected their goods fiercely. Maltazard and his men were attacked by looters both day and night, falling from the trees, emerging from the mud or even the air.

After only one month of travel, only half of the wagons were left, and only a third of the men were alive to drive them.

The deeper they went into the interior of the lands, the more they encountered hostile territories, populated by ferocious beasts that until then had been unknown to them. The forests were filled with bloody hordes that were only interested in drinking and plundering, usually at the same time.

Each stream or natural well that they discovered was already desperately dry. They had to push on, farther and farther. The expedition traveled through carnivorous forests; lakes of dried mud; then barren, contaminated plateaus that civilization seemed to have abandoned.

Maltazard experienced all this suffering, all this humiliation, without batting an eye. He would never fail in his mission, and when, in the middle of a mountain, almost impenetrable, he finally found a small freshwater stream, he was not surprised.

Unfortunately, all that remained of the glorious expedition were four soldiers and one wagon to protect it. Maltazard and his men filled the water tank to the brim and started on their way back.

The return trip was a horror.

No more beautiful principles, rules of art, chivalry. Maltazard protected the water for his people the way a starving dog protects its bone. Each day he became more monstrous, not hesitating to cut in half anyone who represented a threat, and he passed from the art of defense to the art of attack.

It was, he said, the best way to anticipate problems. A good attack, rapid and bloody, would avoid any discussion and save the trouble of mounting a defense afterward.

Maltazard became, without realizing it, an enraged animal without any limits, blinded by his mission. His last soldiers died in bloody combat, and he finished the voyage alone, pulling with his bare hands the cistern that contained the precious liquid.

He arrived at the village at sunrise. He was welcomed with incredible acclaim—a welcome that is reserved only for true heroes, those who walk on the Moon or save entire countries with shots of vaccine.

As a savior, Maltazard was carried through the village on the shoulders of the people.

When he arrived before the king, he had just enough energy to tell him that the mission was accomplished, before collapsing, unconscious, worn out.

Selenia watched Maltazard as he told his story. She was interested but did not let any emotion show on her face. She knew the powers of this magician who could manipulate words as well as weapons.

"A few months later, the illness and evil spells contracted during the trip began to change my body," Maltazard continued in a voice full of emotion. "The rest of the story is the most tragic and the most painful to tell.

"Little by little, fear invaded the village. It was the fear of being contaminated. People moved away when I passed. No one spoke to me, or spoke very little. Smiles were polite but forced. The more my body deteriorated, the more people tried to avoid me. I ended up alone in my hut, cut off from the rest of the world, alone with my pain that no one wanted to share. I, Maltazard the hero, savior of the village, I had become, in just a few months, Maltazard . . . the cursed! Until the day they decided not even to pronounce my name and to call me by a letter: M. . . . the cursed!"

The fallen hero stopped, as if overwhelmed by so many painful memories.

Selenia waited several seconds. It was not her way to make

fun of the suffering of others, but it was her intention, calmly, to tell the truth.

"The version in the history book is somewhat different," she finally said.

Maltazard perked up, intrigued. He clearly did not know that his little story was included in the great Minimoy history book.

"And . . . what does the official version say?" Maltazard asked curiously.

The princess assumed her most neutral voice and recited what she had learned at school. At the time, her professor of history had been Miro the mole. Who, better than he, at fifteen thousand years of age, could recite the Great History? Selenia adored the classes when Miro got carried away, reliving the great battles, shedding a tear at the memory of marriages and coronations that he had had the honor of organizing. Each time he told about the great invasions, he could not stop himself from climbing on the tables, enacting the stories of heroes attacked from all sides, fighting alone against the enemy.

He always ended his classes exhausted and left immediately for a good nap. He knew the story of Maltazard by heart, and it was probably the only one that he told calmly, with much respect.

It was true Maltazard had left as a hero, with the king's blessing. The expedition lasted several months and was really terrible. The great warrior, who had learned to fight with honor and respect, very quickly had had to learn new ways to stay alive.

The external world, weakened by drought, had become an inferno in which, in order to survive, it was necessary to do evil things. Stories from far-off lands were carried back by traveling peddlers or lost travelers, and the Minimoy people were able to follow from a distance the fall of their hero who, tired of the constant attacks, began to plunder in turn. He may have fought for a noble cause and the survival of his people, but he looted and massacred to achieve his ends.

This made everyone back home uneasy. The great council met and debated for ten moons. When they finished, exhausted, they had a new text, which was called *The Great Book of Ideas*.

The Great Book of Ideas served as the basis for a major reorganization of the Minimoy world. The king wanted a more just society, based on respect for people and all things.

In a few weeks, the village was transformed. Nothing was cut down or torn without careful thought. Nothing was thrown away. Everyone joined together to learn how to recover and reuse everything. This was the third commandment. It was an idea that Archibald the benevolent had expressed years before and that they had never forgotten.

"Nothing is ever lost, nothing is ever created, everything is transformed." He admitted that the idea was not his originally, but that was of no importance.

The second commandment was taken from a book that Archibald also often spoke of, but that had a title no one could remember. "Love and respect your neighbor as yourself." This commandment was highly valued and everyone kept it well. People smiled more; they greeted each other; and they invited each other to share meals, even when the drought made it difficult.

The first commandment was by far the most important and had been inspired by Maltazard's misadventure: "Nothing justifies the death of an innocent." The council had adopted this idea without discussion and unanimously chose it to be the first commandment.

There were three hundred sixty-five commandments in all, treasured by those worthy to call themselves Minimoys.

While Maltazard had cruelly changed during his trip, Minimoy society had also followed a difficult path. When Maltazard returned to his village—not alone, as he claimed, but with his wagon pulled by a dozen slaves that he had captured en route—he received a mixed welcome.

Of course, the king thanked him for the lifesaving water, but there was no great celebration, as he had hoped.

First the slaves were freed and given food to last for several days as they journeyed back to their homes. Then there were many prayers for the Minimoys who had not returned from the expedition. Maltazard was the only survivor. He was the only one who could tell how his troops had been decimated, and many Minimoys had doubts about the exact details of these deaths.

But Maltazard did not notice their suspicions, and he took great pleasure in narrating his exploits. He described his journey in great detail, emphasizing his bravery and his courage, which got bigger and more impressive each time he told the story.

People listened politely, according to the eighth commandment that gives each individual the right to express himself and commandment number two hundred forty-seven, which states that it is impolite to cut somebody off.

But very soon the exploits of Maltazard the glorious ceased to interest people.

Maltazard found himself more and more alone—confronted with himself, struggling with his past.

Miro advised him to read *The Great Book of Ideas*, but Maltazard would hear nothing of it, let alone read it. He did not understand how they could have written such a book without waiting for his advice.

He had traveled through the Seven Lands—up, down, and across. He had battled the most fearsome people, survived indescribable storms, defeated animals that even a crazed imagination could not invent. None of this experience had been taken into consideration for the *Great Book* and Maltazard was extremely angry about it.

"It was not a guide to warfare that we were trying to write

but a guide to good behavior!" Miro told him. This response put Maltazard in a black rage. He left the village and began to get drunk in neighboring bars, reciting his tales of war to anyone who would listen.

Every day, he buried himself deeper in bad living, consorting with the worst insects, often poisonous, including one rather pretty young coleopteron who . . .

"Be quiet!" Maltazard suddenly cried.

Selenia smiled at him. Judging by the beads of sweat on Maltazard's forehead, there was a good chance that her version of the story was much closer to the truth than Maltazard's.

"I met that young woman for only a second," he defended himself, sounding very guilty.

"You gave her your powers and she gave you hers!" replied the princess sharply.

"That's enough!" screamed Maltazard, mad with rage. Such fury was not good for him, since, as soon as he became angry, the wounds on his face oozed open, smelling horrible, as if the pressure that was inside had to find a way out.

Selenia was not impressed, but she was moved by the pain that she could read in Maltazard's face. While he did not like to be contradicted, he liked it less when he was looked straight in the eye, and still less when it was with compassion.

He turned around and began to walk back into his immense marble salon.

"I did celebrate my victories in several neighboring bars,

People were so interested in my exploits that it would have been cruel to deprive them of a chance to hear them!"

"There, you see!" muttered Selenia between her teeth.

"And one memorable evening I met a remarkable individual, from a very good family," Maltazard went on.

"A coleopteris venemis, pretty to look at but dangerous to be with!" Selenia specified.

"I know! I know!" Maltazard replied, annoyed by Selenia's common sense. "I let myself go, carried away by memories. She had me wrapped around her little finger. She drank in my words. And in the night, in colors of the shadowy half-light, she probably stole a kiss . . ." he admitted with some sadness. "A poisonous kiss. In the days that followed, I began to decompose, eaten away by the poison that attacked my body. That is how a single kiss ruined my entire life."

"A single kiss is enough to bind you to someone for life. As a Minimoy you should have remembered that," Selenia reminded him, but Maltazard was no longer listening. He was overcome with nostalgia and sadness.

"I left the village in search of healers capable of stopping this evil spell. I was a guinea pig for all kinds of potions. They made me eat all kinds of disgusting dishes, covered with the most repulsive creams. I even had to eat worms, raised to feed on this poison. They all died before even reaching my stomach. In the Fifth Land, I encountered several wizards who took a lot of my money in exchange for ridiculous charms. I ate every kind of root that can be found in the kingdom, but nothing could ease my pain. A life completely ruined because of a simple kiss."

Maltazard sighed, overcome by the sadness of his life.

"Next time, be more careful in choosing a partner," Selenia said.

Maltazard gave her a dark look. "You are right, Selenia," he said, pulling himself together. "Next time I will choose the most beautiful partner—one like a magnificent flower, one that I have seen grow and that I have always dreamed of picking."

Maltazard smiled and Selenia began to worry.

"A healing tree told me the secret that will free me of this sickness that devours me."

"Trees always give good advice," admitted Selenia, instinctively taking a step back.

It didn't matter because Maltazard, without even being aware of it, had taken one toward her.

"Only the powers of a royal flower, young and pure, can free me from the spell and restore my Minimoy appearance. A single kiss from this flower and I will be cured!"

Maltazard was slowly advancing.

"The kiss of a princess has power only if it is unique!" replied Selenia, who knew a lot about this subject.

"I know, but if my information is correct . . . you are not yet married," he said confidently, only too happy to see his trap snap shut.

"Your information is somewhat out of date," she said.

Maltazard stiffened. If this news was true, it was a catastrophe, condemning him to spend the rest of his life in this miserable carcass.

There was a little cough from the doorway, and Darkos entered the room.

It would have to be a real emergency for him to disregard protocol, which normally required him to be announced and to wait until his father deigned to see him.

Maltazard signaled for him to approach with a slight nod of his head, sensing that this visit must be of the utmost importance.

Darkos approached his father with care—he never knew what Maltazard was capable of doing—and murmured several words in his ear.

Maltazard's eyes widened to twice their size. It was true. The princess had married . . . without any announcement, without even sending out invitations.

Maltazard was shocked. Any hope for a return to his normal life had vanished—just like that—in a few seconds, with this confirmation. He was groggy for a few moments, like a boxer surprised by a left hook. His knees weakened and he swayed in place, but soon he regained control of himself.

For so long, he had held on to hope, being patient. He had absorbed more blows in his life than a punching bag. Now he let out a sigh, suffering this latest bitter and irrevocable defeat.

"Well played," he told the princess, who was watching him warily. "You are more intelligent than I thought. In order not to succumb to my charms, you offered your heart to the first person who came along."

"It was actually the last one," she replied with a bit of humor.

Maltazard turned his back to her and slowly approached the cart filled with fruit.

"You have given this young child an inestimable gift, the value of which he himself is unaware, and so he will do nothing," he said. "You had the power to save my life and you didn't. Don't count on me to save yours."

He seized an enormous raisin. "And to make you understand what my suffering has been like, you are going to suffer, too, before dying," he added, with a touch of true cruelty. "You will watch as your people are exterminated in the most horrible pain."

Selenia's blood ran cold.

Maltazard looked at his raisin, as if he had already moved on to something else. Or perhaps he was imagining that the fruit was one of his innocent victims.

A tear ran down Selenia's cheek. A burst of heat, of hatred, was rising inside her and she could do nothing to stop it. She seized her sword, lifted her vengeful arm, and threw the blade with all her might. The sword cut through the air like a bolt of lightning and sliced right through Maltazard. Unfortunately

the cursed prince was so eaten away by poison that his body
was mostly holes, and the sword ended up flying through one
of these and nailing the raisin to the cart. Maltazard looked at
the sword that had passed through his body without even
touching it.

For once my mutilated body has been good for something! he thought,
amazed to see how destiny was playing with his life. He who,
only a few minutes before, had cursed this body, was now glad
to still have it.

He regarded the red juice that flowed from the fruit and
put his finger under it to collect a few drops.

"I will drink the blood of your people as I drink that of this
fruit," he said evilly.

At these words, Selenia no longer heard her fear but only
her heart, which was racing furiously.

She ran toward Maltazard . . . but she was too late. Henchmen were pouring in from everywhere and surrounding
Darkos, who had placed himself in front of his father to protect him.

The guards grabbed Selenia. It was impossible to escape
from these mountains of steel and muscle. The princess was
lost and disarmed.

Maltazard pulled the sword from the wood and turned
toward Selenia. He looked delighted for a moment at her help-
essness.

"Have no regrets, Selenia," he said slyly. "Even if you had married me, I should tell you . . . I would have exterminated your people just the same!"

Selenia burst into tears. "You are a monster, Maltazard!" she sobbed.

The prince of darkness smiled grimly. He had heard this insult so many times.

"I know. I get that from my first wife," he answered, his humor as black as his look. "Take her away!"

CHAPTER
9

Arthur was on his knees in front of the prison bars. He had exhausted himself shaking them.

"I am barely married and I already have the feeling that I am a widower. A widower and a prisoner," he noted, sick to his stomach.

This thought was enough to give him a bit more courage. He got up and began to shake the bars for the millionth time. Nothing happened, of course. Prison bars are made to resist all kinds of assaults.

"We have to get out of here, Beta! We have to come up with something," he cried.

"I'm thinking, Arthur, I'm thinking!" Betameche assured him. The Minimoy prince was comfortably curled up on a minuscule bed of grass. He seemed more in search of sleep than anything else.

"How can you sleep at a time like this?" said Arthur angrily.

"I'm not sleeping!" the little prince responded grouchily.

"I am pulling together all the energy that I normally use for walking, talking, and eating, and I am reorganizing it . . . into a single force . . . in order to . . . better be able . . ."

"To fall asleep!" Arthur concluded, as he watched his friend slowly nod off.

"That's it . . ." answered Betameche, who was finally asleep. Arthur kicked him in the shins, which was almost as effective as a cold shower. Betameche was on his feet in a second.

Arthur grabbed his shoulders.

"Beta, the powers! The powers Selenia gave me when she kissed me?" he said.

"Yes, a very nice kiss, very sweet," commented Betameche.

"What exactly are these powers?" Arthur persisted.

"Oh, that!" the prince answered. "I don't know."

"What do you mean you don't know?"

"She is the only one who knows what she has given you," Betameche replied, as if it were obvious.

Arthur was crestfallen. "That's fantastic. She gives me powers, in case I have to use them, but then she doesn't tell me what they are. Your tribe has a very strange idea of sharing!" Arthur grumbled.

"That's not exactly the way it works among us," Betameche replied maliciously. "Normally when you marry someone, it's because you know her and appreciate her gifts. When the marriage takes place, she doesn't need to tell you what she has to offer. You already know it."

"But I have only known her for two days!" cried Arthur, completely infuriated.

"Yes, but you still married her, didn't you?" replied her younger brother.

"A sword was being held to my throat!" Arthur defended himself.

"Oh? Do you mean that if you didn't have a sword at your throat you wouldn't have married her?"

"Of course I would have!" Arthur replied angrily.

"And you did! It was a beautiful wedding!" concluded Betameche with his own mysterious logic.

Arthur looked at him the way a chicken would look at a remote control. He felt a bit like an old knight battling windmills. He didn't think his nerves would be able to stand it much longer.

"Yes, it was a beautiful wedding. And I promise you a beautiful funeral if you don't help me to get out of here," he cried, going for Beta's throat.

"Stop! You're strangling me!" Betameche yelled.

"I know I am!" Arthur yelled back. "So at least there is one thing we can agree on!"

"Stop that petty quarreling," said a voice from the back of the dungeon.

It was a gentle voice but worn out, probably from unhappiness and age.

"It is useless to mistreat this poor boy or these faithful prison bars. No one has ever escaped from a prison in Necropolis," added the stranger from the darkness.

Arthur searched the shadows for the owner of the tired voice. He could see a silhouette: a man lying down on his side at the very back of the cell, with only the curve of his back visible. *Probably a poor madman*, thought Arthur, because you would have to be in order to stay in this place and not try any escape. He headed back toward the bars.

"Don't tire yourself out. Save your strength if you want to eat," the old man interjected again.

Arthur was forced to admit that he was not making much progress with the bars. He approached the old man instead, intrigued by his advice.

"What do you mean? Eating is not that complicated. Why is it necessary to conserve energy for it?" asked Arthur.

"If you want to eat," explained the old man, still keeping his back turned, "you have to teach them something new. If you don't, you don't eat. And it's impossible to cheat! I have tried to give them old inventions, even a full year later, but it doesn't work. Those morons really have good memories. It is probably their only good quality.

"But that is the rule. They will fill your belly on the one hand, and empty your brain on the other. Knowledge is the only thing of value here, and sleep, the only luxury," he added before trying to find a more comfortable position in which to continue his nap.

Arthur scratched his head, intrigued. There was something about the old man's voice which, while not entirely familiar, reminded him of something or someone. . . .

"What kind of things do they want to know?" asked Arthur, hoping for both an answer and a chance to listen again to that voice.

"Psht! They aren't very observant—they will take anything!" said the old man. "From the laws of physics and mathematics to how to cook green peas. From theorems to mint tea," he added with humor.

This glimmer of a joke surprised Arthur. He had known only one person capable of keeping this kind of perspective in a similar situation . . . a person who was very dear to him and who had disappeared a long time ago.

"I have taught them how to read, to write, to draw—"

"To paint?" added Arthur, who hardly dared to believe it. Could this old man be his grandfather Archibald, who had disappeared four years ago? How would he recognize him, if not by his voice?

Arthur had been only six when his grandfather had disappeared, and the picture in his memory was somewhat fuzzy with age. Now that Archibald was half an inch tall and resembled a Minimoy, it would be almost impossible to recognize him.

The old man was clearly intrigued by Arthur's last words.

"What did you say, my boy?" he asked politely.

"You taught them how to draw and to paint giant canvasses

to fool the enemy, didn't you? Also how to transport water, to direct light using large mirrors—"

"How can this snip of a boy know so much?" the old man wondered aloud. He turned around to see his questioner's face.

Arthur looked at the old face, with its overgrown beard, two funny dimples, an eye that still twinkled, and small wrinkles in the corners of his mouth from smiling too much. There was no doubt—this somewhat crumpled Minimoy was none other than Archibald, his grandfather!

"Because I am the grandson of this great inventor," replied Arthur, beginning to feel a rush of emotion.

"Arthur?" the old man asked tentatively, as if he were asking for the moon.

His grandson smiled a big smile and nodded.

Archibald could not believe his eyes. Life had just sent him the most beautiful of all presents. He rose and threw himself into Arthur's arms.

"Oh! My grandson! My Arthur! I am so happy to see you again," he cried between outbursts of emotion. They hugged each other so tightly that they could hardly breathe. "I have prayed so long to see you again, just once! What joy to finally see my prayers answered!"

A tear rolled down his cheek, disappearing into the wrinkles on his aged face. Then he held Arthur at arm's length to have a better look at him. He stared at him with enormous pride and happiness.

"How you have grown, Arthur! It's incredible!"

"I feel more like I have gotten smaller!" Arthur answered.

"Yes, that's true!" Archibald agreed, and the two began to laugh.

The old man had to hug his grandson again, since he still could not believe what was happening. He wanted to be sure it wasn't Maltazard's idea of a bad joke, one of his famous magic tricks—that this wasn't all an illusion.

But Arthur's arms were really flesh and bone, and now well-muscled. He was no longer the child Archibald remembered. Now he was a handsome young boy, made mature for his age by this adventure. Archibald was really impressed by his grandson.

"But how did you get here?" he asked finally.

"Well, I found your riddle!" Arthur replied.

"Oh, yes, of course! I had completely forgotten I left it for you."

"And the Bogo-Matassalai came to help me with the passage," Arthur added.

"They came all the way from Africa, just to save me?" Archibald wondered.

"Why, yes. I think they like you very much. They entrusted me with the mission of freeing you."

"They did the right thing." Archibald was delighted. "This is wonderful! You're a real hero! I am so proud of you!" He pulled his grandson toward his cot and made him sit down, as if they were in his own living room. "All right, tell me everything! What is new? I want to know everything about you!"

Arthur didn't really know where to start when everything was so complicated. He decided to begin at the end.

"Well, I'm married."

"Really?" Archibald replied with astonishment. This was not at all the news he was expecting. "How old are you?"

"Almost one thousand years old!" Arthur replied.

"Ah, yes! It's true," said Archibald, smiling.

This reminded him of the young Arthur who, at the age of four, had wanted a Swiss army knife, believing that he was old enough to cut his own meat all by himself. His grandfather had replied that at four years, he was already very big, but to have your own knife, you had to be very old.

"And what age do you have to be, to be old!" little Arthur had asked him, who even then would not allow himself to be tricked.

"Ten years!" Archibald had replied, to give himself some time.

Time had now caught up with them.

"And who is the lucky girl?" Grandpa asked.

"Princess Selenia," Arthur said, hardly daring to reveal his pride.

"I couldn't ask for a more adorable granddaughter-in-law!" Archibald rejoiced. "Have you met her family?"

Arthur pointed to Beta, who was sleeping by the bars.

"Ah, brave Betameche!" said Archibald. "I didn't recognize him. I have to say that this is the first time I have seen him so quiet. You must be a good influence on him."

Arthur shrugged.

"My little Arthur, married to a princess!" Archibald couldn't get over it. "That means you are the future king, my son! King Arthur," he said solemnly.

Arthur was embarrassed. He was not used to receiving so many compliments.

"A king in prison is not much of a king," he said. "Come on, Grandpa! We've got to get out of here!"

Arthur jumped up. With his energy and his grandfather's genius, how could they not manage to escape from this blasted prison? But Archibald didn't move.

"And your grandmother? How is your grandmother?" he asked, ignoring Arthur's request.

"She misses you a lot. Now come on!" Arthur answered.

"Of course, of course . . . and the house? How is the house? And the garden? Has she taken care of it?"

"The garden is perfect! But if we are not back by tomorrow noon with the treasure, none of it will be ours anymore—not the garden, not the house!" Arthur insisted, pulling him by the sleeve.

"Of course, my son, of course . . . and the garage? You haven't made a mess, have you? You loved to tinker when you were little!" Archibald remembered. Arthur stood in front of him, grabbed him by the shoulders, and shook him like a sleepwalker.

"Grandpa? Didn't you hear what I said?"

Archibald sighed. "Of course I heard you, Arthur, but . . . no one escapes from the prisons of Necropolis. It has never happened," he said sadly.

"We'll see about that! In the meantime, do you know where the treasure is?"

Archibald nodded. "The treasure is in the throne room and M. the cursed sits on top of it."

"Not for long," promised Arthur, whose spirit had returned. "Selenia went to take care of him and, knowing her, there won't be much left of that terrible Maltazard when she's through!"

Betameche awoke with a start upon hearing the evil name, with all its bad luck. Why was it always when he was asleep that Arthur put his foot in his mouth?

Archibald said a silent prayer, hoping to ward off the bad luck, but it was already too late. Misfortune never waits. The door of the prison opened, and Selenia was thrown in, landing flat on the ground.

One of the henchmen quickly locked the door, and the patrol moved off.

Arthur hurried over to Selenia and hugged her. He wiped her face, which was covered with dust, and fixed her hair.

Selenia was touched by this attention, and she allowed him to continue.

"I failed, Arthur. I'm sorry," she said with infinite sadness

Never had the princess felt such despair. "All is lost," she added, letting her tears fall where they wanted.

Arthur wiped them away gently with the tips of his fingers.

"As long as we are alive and we have each other . . . nothing is lost," he said.

Selenia smiled at him, impressed by his relentless optimism. She had obviously made the right choice in selecting a husband. Arthur had goodness, generosity, courage, and tenacity—all those qualities that make someone a real prince. Selenia looked deep into his eyes.

The problem was that when Selenia looks at you like that, nothing else in the world matters. Arthur looked at her and melted like a lump of ice tossed into a fire. He leaned forward without even realizing it. Their mouths came closer while their eyelids closed gently.

Just as their lips were about to find each other, Betameche slipped a hand between them.

"Sorry to bother you but . . . I think it would be a good idea, despite the situation, to respect protocol and tradition," he said, annoyed at having to be the grown-up here.

These few words awakened our young princess, who instantly emerged from the dream into which she was slipping. She cleared her throat, stood up, and arranged her torn clothing.

"He is a thousand percent correct! What was I thinking?"

The real princess, the official one, was back. Arthur was

frustrated, like a kitten that has lost its ball.

"But . . . what tradition?" he asked, lost.

"It's an ancestral tradition, a basic rule of protocol that all marriages must follow," the princess explained.

"Yes?" said Arthur.

"Once the first kiss has been given, the one that seals the destiny of the young couple forever, you have to wait a thousand years before the second kiss," recited the princess, who knew protocol better than anyone. Knowing these sorts of things was part of the requirements of being a princess.

"The second kiss will thereby be even stronger, because that which is rare is valuable," she added, completing the picture for Arthur, who was feeling a little overwhelmed by this news.

"Uh . . . yes . . . of course," he muttered.

The door to the prison opened suddenly, so violently that everyone jumped. Darkos was very fond of this kind of theatrical entrance. He loved to play villains who came onstage always at the worst moment, throwing a monkey wrench into the plot.

"How are you all? Not too hot?" he said, detaching a piece of ice that was hanging from the ceiling and putting it into his mouth.

"The temperature is perfect," replied Selenia who, in spite of the cold, was seething inside.

"My father has prepared a little celebration for you. You four are the guests of honor," announced Darkos.

As usual, several henchmen cackled. The guests knew perfectly well what kind of spectacle was awaiting them.

Arthur leaned toward Selenia. "We must provoke a fight. During the confusion, some of us might be able to escape," he whispered into Selenia's ear.

"Comments, young man?" interrupted Darkos, who was following his father's instructions to remain vigilant.

"It's nothing! Arthur just made a relevant observation," Selenia replied.

It was as if she had thrown a worm in front of a fish and asked him not to eat it. Darkos took the bait without hesitation.

"And what was the subject of this relevant observation?" he asked.

"*You* are the subject, obviously," the princess replied.

Darkos beamed. Without his even realizing it, his chest expanded with pride.

"Now that I know the subject, may I have the verb?" he said with poetic spirit.

"Interest. There's the verb that goes with your subject. Arthur was wondering how your father, who is already so ugly, managed to have a son who is even more repugnant than himself. Arthur formulated his sentence in the following manner: 'Darkos's ugliness interests me!' Subject, verb, complement," the princess explained, as if she were an eminent grammarian.

Darkos froze, fixed to his spot. His ice cube fell out of his mouth.

His troop of henchmen began to guffaw, as they often did. Darkos did an about-face and glared at his men. His look was more cutting than a razor blade and the laughter died down quickly.

As best he could, Darkos contained the anger within him, even though it was waiting to explode like a bottle of soda about to be uncapped.

The cursed son took a deep breath.

He turned toward Selenia and smiled, very proud of not having reacted to this insult.

"The pain that awaits you will be nothing compared with the pleasure that awaits me when I see you destroyed," Darkos promised her. "Now, if Her Highness would please take the trouble to follow me."

No fight in sight . . .

"Good try," whispered Arthur to Selenia, who looked disappointed at having failed again.

The little troop lined up and all left the prison together.

"This impromptu ceremony doesn't sound good!" commented Archibald, who was disturbed and impressed by the number of guards.

"At least we're out of the prison—that's not too bad!" Arthur replied, always positive. "We must keep watch for any mistake on their part. That is our only chance."

"This is not exactly the kind of house to make mistakes!" interjected Beta, as worried as Archibald.

"Everyone makes mistakes. Even Achilles had heels!" replied Arthur confidently.

Arthur, Archibald, and now Achilles. Betameche wondered about this new member of the family that he had not yet had the honor of meeting.

"Is he your cousin?" asked Beta.

Archibald felt he should explain. "Achilles was a brave hero of antiquity," he said, "known for his strength and courage. He was almost invulnerable. Only one part of his body was weaker than the others and could be harmed: his heel. So you see, every man has his weakness, even Achilles . . . even Maltazard," Grandpa whispered in Beta's ear. Beta shivered at the sound of the name. He hoped they were right.

CHAPTER
10

At least ten henchmen were needed to push open each of the two doors that led into the large royal hall. The little troop of visitors stayed together as a group and watched with interest as the two enormous metal plates grated mechanically and revealed the entryway.

The hall was gigantic, impressive. It resembled a cathedral. Two huge tanks were attached to the ceiling, like twin clouds caught between mountains. These were, in fact, the double tanks containing subterranean reservoir water that supplied the house. From this perspective, they seemed monstrous. The reservoirs were pierced with dozens of holes, each holding one of Arthur's stolen straws. The multicolored tubes were connected to each other and joined at the center like an enormous pipe system.

Maltazard's plan was now all too clear: he was going to use the straws to guide this vast amount of water into the system of pipes leading to the Minimoy village. He was going to drown them all. The flood would quickly wipe them out since, as everyone remembers, Minimoys do not know how to swim.

"To think I was the one who taught them how to transport water. And now they will use it against my friends," Archibald said sadly as they were marched past his work.

"To think I was the one who provided the straws!" added Arthur, who felt just as responsible.

The little group crossed the monumental, endless pathway.

On each side stood an impressive army of henchmen, standing attentively at their posts. At the end of the esplanade was a pyramid, almost transparent and tinted red. Up close, it proved to be hundreds of pieces of translucent stone, piled upon each other.

At the bottom of this glass monument was a throne, which was much too pretentious looking to belong to a good king.

Maltazard had placed his hands on the armrests, which ended in enormous sculpted skulls. He held himself straight at the back of his throne, not out of pride, but simply because it was the only position that his sick, mutilated body would allow him to assume.

"You were searching for the treasure. There it is!" Archibald whispered into his grandson's ear.

Arthur did not understand. He looked all around them, then at the strange pyramid. He realized he was looking at a pile of precious stones: a hundred rubies, each more perfect that the other, placed scientifically in order to form a perfect pyramid.

Arthur's mouth dropped open. He couldn't believe his eyes.

"I *found* it!" he cried jubilantly.

"Finding it is one thing. Transporting it is another story," said Betameche with unusual common sense.

In fact, the treasure was resting on a large platter-shaped disk, and each stone probably weighed several tons to someone Minimoy sized. Arthur thought about it. If only he were his normal size, carrying this saucer full of rubies would be child's play. What he really needed was a way to remember the location of the treasure in the real world, so he would be able to find it again once he had returned to his normal size.

Unfortunately, everything was disproportionate in the world of the Minimoys, and the signs were unrecognizable. Nothing that he saw around here reminded him of anything.

Darkos brought him out of his reverie by pushing him violently in the back. "Advance. Don't keep the master waiting!" Darkos barked, like a good watchdog.

"How sweet, my good and faithful Darkos," interjected Maltazard, like an understanding master. "Forgive him, he is a little nervous right now. His mission was to exterminate your people and, unfortunately, he failed to do so on many occasions. This has made him a bit . . . very bad. But everything will be back in order soon. Papa is here." Maltazard was all too aware of his superior situation and he was savoring it, the way one takes one's time when eating chocolate icing from a cupcake.

"Now . . . let the festivities begin," he exclaimed. He snapped his fingers, and the music began. It was booming, royal music.

Archibald put his fingers in his ears. "If I ever return to prison, I promise to teach them music theory," said the old man, yelling in order to be heard.

Maltazard gestured with his arm. To the side of the ruby pyramid stood a console and a control panel with a dozen large wooden levers. In front of the console, ready to activate the levers, stood a sad little mole.

"Mino?" exclaimed Beta, recognizing his young friend. It was Miro's son Mino, who everyone believed to be lost. He was alive!

This news greatly cheered up Selenia and her brother, who, when they were little, used to spend whole days playing with the little mole. Their favorite game was hide-and-seek, even though Mino would always win because of his ability to dig tunnels. The three had often spent nights stretched out on sele-nielle petals, organizing the stars in order to give them names. They had been inseparable until the day that Mino fell into a trap laid for him by Darkos.

Betameche tried to signal to him now, but the little mole, like all members of his family, did not have very good eyesight. All he could see was a vague form gesturing in the distance. Luckily, his sense of smell was much better than his sight, and soon Selenia's perfume reached his nostrils.

His face lit up and a smile appeared. His friends were there! They had come to his rescue at last. His heart pounded with the promise of freedom.

"Mino, are you awake? I've been signaling you for the last hour," cried Maltazard, as impatient as a hungry shark.

Mino panicked. "Oh, yes! Of course, master! Right away, master," he replied, bending over the controls.

Darkos leaned toward his father. "He can't see very well. They are all like that in his family," he explained. His father gave him an angry look. You do not explain things to Maltazard. Darkos had forgotten. He took a step back, and bowed his head in apology.

"There is nothing that Maltazard does not know. I *am* knowledge, and, unlike yours, my flawless memory has no limits!" his father said to him sternly.

"Excuse me, Father, for that moment of forgetfulness," his son responded, overcome with shame.

"Send," Maltazard bellowed at Mino.

The little mole jumped, hesitating over which lever to use. Finally, he pulled on one that sent a mechanism into operation—a complicated system involving gears, cords, and pulleys.

"I am so happy to see him alive!" whispered Betameche, his face full of joy.

"When you work for Maltazard, you are not really alive—

only on probation!" replied Archibald, who knew what he was talking about.

Slowly a small trapdoor swung open at the top of the gallery, revealing a glimpse of the outside world above ground. A ray of sunlight shone through, forming a well of light. It illuminated the very top of the pyramid, where the largest ruby of all was placed, and began to spread, reflecting off each of the gems' facets. It was as if magic were lighting the pyramid, little by little, from top to bottom, turning it a luminous red . . . like translucent blood traveling through crystal veins.

The show was magnificent, and our friends, despite their precarious situation, couldn't help but appreciate it.

The ray finished its course by lighting the last ruby, the one in which Maltazard's throne was carved.

His whole body was lit up like a divine apparition.

A murmur rose from the assembled army. Some of the soldiers even fell to their knees. This was the kind of magic trick that always impressed weak minds, and Maltazard, as a good dictator, knew them all.

Only Archibald, the old scientist, was unimpressed.

"Well, Archibald! Are you proud of how we have used your knowledge?" Maltazard inquired.

"It's very pretty! It doesn't do much except give you a little color in your cheeks, but it's very pretty," Grandpa answered.

The prince of darkness stiffened, but decided not to get angry.

"Perhaps you prefer my new irrigation system?" he said ironically.

"It is actually very clever and well executed," Archibald confessed. "It's a pity that you plan to use it so wrongly!"

"What? Isn't it designed to transport water?" asked Maltazard, pretending to be naïve.

"Transport water, yes, to irrigate plants and cool people off, but not to flood them!" said the scientist.

"Not only to flood them, my dear Archibald. Also to drown them, pulverize them, liquefy them, do them in, and *annihilate them forever*," said Maltazard with great excitement.

"You are a monster, Maltazard," the old man told him calmly.

"Your granddaughter-in-law said the same thing! Who do you think you are? What gives you the right to divert nature from the path that it is given, but no one else? How dare you claim that nature can be improved by your inventions?"

Archibald was struck speechless. Maltazard had made a point.

"That's the problem with you scientists—you invent things without even taking the time to think through the consequences!" Maltazard went on. "Nature takes years to make a decision. It causes a flower to grow and tests it for millions of years before knowing if it has its place in the grand scheme of things. You invent things and you call yourselves 'geniuses' and you engrave your names in the stones of the pantheon of science!" Maltazard emitted a scornful laugh.

Darkos did also, to imitate his father, even if he had understood nothing of what was said.

"It is pure arrogance!" added the dictator with disdain.

"Arrogance is dangerous, but not fatal, my dear Maltazard. Fortunately for you, because otherwise you would already have died a thousand times per day," Archibald shot back.

The sovereign didn't react, but these insults were beginning to get to him.

"I'll take that as a compliment, since arrogance is a requirement for every great ruler!" Maltazard said.

"Being a ruler is not only about a title. You must know how to behave like one, to know how to be good, just, and generous," Archibald said firmly.

"What a portrait! It sounds exactly like me," joked Maltazard. Darkos laughed. For once he had understood the joke. "Well, I am going to prove to you that I *can* be good and generous. You are free to go," he announced, accompanying his words with a sweeping theatrical gesture.

Several henchmen had raised the grille that blocked the main pipe system. These pipes led directly to the Minimoy village, and it was here that all the straws were aimed. Archibald understood the trap before any of the others.

"You offer us freedom—and the death that goes along with it!" Archibald said.

"Yes, two gifts at a time. Aren't I ever so generous?" answered Maltazard.

"The minute we step through that gate, you will release tons of water on us!" exclaimed the princess, who had just realized his evil plan.

"You should think less, Selenia, and run more!" he answered cruelly.

"What's the use of running if there is only one chance in a million of surviving?" the princess added.

"One chance in a million? I find that somewhat optimistic. I would say, perhaps, one chance in one hundred million," the dictator specified with humor. "But it's better than nothing, isn't it? Go on! Bon voyage!" Maltazard lifted his arms again and signaled to the henchmen to push the Minimoys into the pipe.

As Betameche began to tremble like a leaf, Arthur finally found the idea he was looking for.

"May I ask your Serene Greatness for one last favor before dying? A very small favor that will only serve to highlight your majesty's extreme graciousness?" he said, bowing low.

"I like that little one!" Maltazard said. He was always easily swayed by flattery. "What is this favor?"

"I would like to leave my only treasure, this bracelet, to my friend Mino, who is over there."

The little mole was completely surprised by the interest that everyone suddenly had in him, especially this young man, who he did not know at all.

Maltazard looked at the watch that Arthur was holding up.

He sniffed, but could not smell a trap of any sort. Finally he announced: "Granted."

The henchmen began to applaud the generosity of their master.

While Maltazard waved happily at his admirers, Arthur walked over to Mino.

"Your father sent me," he whispered into the mole's ear.

He took off his watch and handed it to Mino. "Once I am outside, I need you to send me a signal, so that I will be able to find the treasure. You must send the signal precisely at noon. Is that clear?" Arthur asked urgently.

Mino was astounded. "But how do you want me to do it?"

"With your mirrors, Mino!" Arthur insisted. This was his last hope. "Do you understand?"

Mino, completely lost, agreed with a nod, but it was more to please Arthur than anything else.

"That's enough now. My mercy has its limits! Take them away!" exclaimed Maltazard.

The henchmen grabbed Arthur and hustled him back to his group, now standing at the entrance of the enormous pipe.

Mino watched his new friend move away, bewildered.

"At noon!" whispered Arthur.

The guards pushed the small group inside the pipe. The grille immediately came down behind them, separating them from the square. There was only one exit now.

In front of them was the long pipe that led to freedom . . .

freedom they would never reach. This pipe would also be their tomb.

The idea of inevitable death completely depressed the entire group. No one wanted to run. What for? To delay their suffering by a few seconds? Better to have it over with quickly, so the little group stayed there, worn out, behind the grille.

The spectacle was not a very interesting one and Maltazard sighed.

"All right. I will give you a one-minute head start. That will add a little spice," he said, trying to liven up the game.

Darkos was very excited by this news.

"Bring the timetables," cried Darkos.

Two henchmen brought in an enormous panel. In the center was a nail on which a package of dried leaves had been attached. On the first leaf was the word "sixty."

Selenia, clinging to the bars, glared at Maltazard. There was so much venom in her eyes that she hoped a drop of it could reach him.

"You will pay for this," she murmured between her clenched teeth.

"He already is!" Arthur replied, taking her by the arm. "Hurry, now!"

"What's the use of running?" the princess said, and pulled her arm away. "So we can die a little bit later? I prefer to stand here and die with dignity, staring death in the face!"

Arthur grabbed her more firmly by the arm. "One minute,

That's better than nothing! That gives us the time to come up with something," he cried with conviction.

This was the first time he had been so decisive, and Selenia was quite impressed. Was her awkward prince growing up? she wondered. She allowed herself to be pulled along behind him.

Maltazard was happy to see his four captives start running.

"Finally a bit of sport! Begin the countdown," he ordered with pleasure.

The henchman removed the first leaf, marked "sixty." Underneath was another, marked with a magnificent "fifty-nine."

The clock was so simple and crude it would make a Swiss turn pale, but Maltazard was greatly amused. He even nodded his head in time with the discarded leaves.

"Prepare the valves," he ordered, between two nods.

Darkos left to take his place, wiggling with delight like a fish, while the henchman timekeeper unveiled a new leaf marked with a "fifty-two."

CHAPTER
11

The Minimoys ran as best they could through the garbage and the layer of filth that time had deposited at the bottom of the tunnel. But Archibald tired quickly and he began to slow down. The old man had spent four years in M.'s prisons without any exercise, and the muscles in his poor legs were weak.

"Sorry, Arthur, I can't do it," said the old man, as he came to a stop, breathing heavily. He sat down on some sort of round object, which was attached to another, much bigger object. Arthur turned back and ran up to him.

"Go on! I'll stay here and wait for the end with a bit of dignity," Grandpa sighed.

"That's not possible! I can't leave you here! Come on, Grandpa, give it one more try," Arthur said.

He tugged him gently by the arm, but the old man pulled away.

"What's the use, Arthur? Look at the facts, my boy. We're lost."

With these words, the rest of the group immediately fell

apart. If a scientist thought that the chances for survival were now zero, why bother struggling?

Beta and Selenia slumped to the ground, overcome by sadness.

Arthur sighed. He didn't know what to do.

Maltazard, on the other hand, was in fine spirits, collecting his dead leaves. The one marked "twenty" pleased him a lot. He was practically singing.

"All of this has made me hungry. Is there something to eat? I like to snack during a show," he said, amusing himself like a king.

A henchman immediately brought a large platter of small grilled roaches, His Highness's favorite dish. There was always a plate of these appalling tidbits in every room of the palace. It would probably have been easier for a servant to follow him around all day, carrying a platter, but Maltazard had always refused to have this done. He liked to see his minions scurry around whenever he demanded his treats. That was part of his pleasure—knowing that they would be rushing to bring him his plate as quickly as possible, on pain of death. More even than these small, grilled insects, the suffering of others was his favorite dish.

He did not know that, behind his back, Darkos had hidden plates all over the palace, so that his father would never have to wait too long.

"Cooked just right!" Maltazard pronounced as he nibbled on a roach, which was crusty exactly the way he liked it. Darkos took this as a compliment.

The timekeeper revealed a new leaf: a magnificent "ten."

"Slow down a little!" Maltazard ordered. "I need time to chew!"

Arthur could not concede defeat. He wanted to die a hero, to fight until the end, until the last moment. It had nothing to do with dignity.

So he walked in circles, trying to come up with an idea. "There must be a solution! There is always a solution," he repeated constantly.

"It's not just an idea that we need now, Arthur—it's a miracle," replied Archibald, who had abandoned all hope.

Arthur let out a big sigh. He was seconds away from giving up like the rest of them. He lifted his eyes upward, as if to call for help, as if to ask for a miracle, no matter how small. Something caught his attention. How was it possible that he could see the sky from where he was? He realized that he was standing below a pipe that rose to the surface. Unfortunately, the opening was too high and the walls too slippery to be climbed.

If only that nice spider could return and drop down her thread. Alas, it was not to be. However, the small blades of grass that he saw all around the opening above reminded him of something. This must be the drain hole in his grandmother's garden.

Arthur searched his memory, but he couldn't pinpoint what it was.

Perhaps he was on the wrong track. He looked down at the object on which his grandfather was sitting.

The object was lying in the light, so it had probably fallen from above. From the garden. That triggered something in Arthur's brain. Garden. Pipe. Object. Fall. He leaped forward and pulled his grandfather up.

Archibald had been sitting on the tire of a car, resting on its side. And it was not just any car. It was the magnificent racing car, the red Ferrari, that Arthur had just gotten for his birthday on Saturday, a day which now seemed like ancient history. He remembered now that the dust from Davido's car had knocked the toy into the opening of a drainpipe on Sunday. In all the excitement of searching for the treasure after Davido left, Arthur had forgotten to rescue his present.

"Grandpa! *You're* the miracle," he shouted with joy.

"Explain yourself, Arthur!" Selenia said, astonished.

"This is a car! It's *my* car. Grandma gave it to me. We are saved!" he crowed enthusiastically.

Archibald knit his brows. "Your grandmother has lost all sense of reality. Aren't you still a little too young to be driving this kind of car?"

"When she gave it to me, it was much smaller, I assure you," Arthur replied with a smile from ear to ear. "Help me!" he cried to his partners.

Selenia and Betameche joined him on the other side of the car, which was standing up on its side like a wall. They began to push with all of their strength. With superhuman effort, the car at last fell back on its four wheels. Their cries of joy echoed down the tunnel.

Maltazard was amazed. How could they be happy, when they had only a few seconds left to live? This puzzle disturbed him and he decided not to take any risks. He was too close to victory.

"Open the valves," he ordered suddenly.

"But . . . the counter is not at zero. There are still three leaves," said Darkos, always a little slow on the uptake.

"I know how to count to three!" Maltazard yelled. "Open the valves!"

Darkos ran to the valves to execute his mission before his father decided to execute him.

The henchman timekeeper was quicker than Darkos and he tore off the last leaves all together. "Zero," he cried, with a big smile.

Arthur put the little key, which had become enormous, in the top of the car.

It was so hard to move that beads of sweat began to appear on his forehead. Selenia climbed up beside him and helped him turn the key around and around.

"Are you sure you know how to drive this kind of car?"

Betameche asked. He was uncomfortable with unfamiliar transportation.

"It's my specialty," Arthur answered quickly to avoid further discussion.

Betameche only half believed him.

Darkos came up to the henchmen posted along the cistern. "Go ahead," he ordered.

The henchmen swung their mallets and knocked loose the wedges that were temporarily blocking the holes.

Once the wedges were removed, Darkos took a sledgehammer and, with all his strength, slammed it into the tap, which gave way immediately.

The water instantly began to pour through the straws, as if they were large veins, and rushed like a torrent through the pipe taken by our escapees.

Arthur made another attempt to turn the key. Selenia was blowing on her hands, which were hurting from the effort she'd put in.

Suddenly the rumble of rushing water reached their ears. Selenia jumped.

"That's it! They have opened the valves. Arthur, hurry!" she cried.

"Get in the front. I'll be right behind you," Arthur ordered as he continued to lean on the key.

Betameche scrambled in and joined Archibald in the back of the car. They both turned and saw, through the back window, the mass of water that was rushing upon them.

"Hurry, Arthur," his grandpa pleaded, frightened by the sight of the enormous wave.

"If we want to be able to reach the end, I must turn the spring as tight as I can," replied Arthur, grimacing with pain. He drew on his last bit of strength, emitting a Herculean cry to give himself courage. He managed to turn the key one more time, under Selenia's watchful—and admiring—eye.

Arthur held the key in place with his shoulder and tried to grab a bit of wood on the ground. He needed something to block the key so he would have time to get into the car, but the wave would wait for no one and it was dangerously close now.

Beta sat with his mouth open and his hands pressed over his eyes. He would have liked to scream for help, but no sound would come out—his jaws were so strained with fear.

Arthur finally managed to plant a stick to temporarily block the key. He jumped into the car, behind the steering wheel.

The interior was rather basic, but Arthur quickly found his bearings. The Ferrari could not be much more complicated than his grandma's Chevrolet. He hoped *this* car wouldn't end up wrapped around a tree. He adjusted his rearview mirror and saw the liquid wall pounding toward them, ready to swallow them up.

"And we're off," he sang, pulling loose the stick that was blocking the key.

The rear wheels immediately began to spin in place, finally free. Fortunately, the wind generated by the movement of the wave pushed the car forward.

Then the tires finally began to find some traction and the Ferrari doubled its speed. The car flew through the tunnel, fleeing the torrent.

Arthur clutched the steering wheel with both hands. Selenia's back was glued to her seat. Betameche muttered that he would never again take public transportation of any kind; while Archibald, intoxicated by the speed, watched the scenery pass by with delight.

"It's amazing what progress cars have made in only four years," he mused.

The speed had become so fast that the straight line of the pipe now seemed to be a series of successive turns. Arthur concentrated harder. It was no longer a matter of only holding the steering wheel but of actually driving.

Betameche, despite the pressure of the speed, managed to grab on to the back of the front seats, and he pulled himself forward to address Arthur. "At the next intersection, make a right," he said.

He had no sooner finished his sentence than the fork appeared in front of Arthur. He turned the steering wheel sharply to the right, which threw the passengers against the doors.

The car straightened itself up in this new pipe. Arthur breathed a sigh of relief.

"Beta? Try and let me know a little sooner the next time," he said.

"Okay. Left!" cried Betameche.

But the new fork was already there. Arthur yelled with surprise and reflexively spun the steering wheel to the left. They just barely avoided crashing into the beveled wall that separated the two paths.

Arthur let out an even bigger sigh of relief. "Thanks, Beta," he said. He was so tense that sweat from his forehead was dripping into his eyes. Selenia noticed and leaned over to wipe his face with her sleeve. The two lovebirds exchanged smiles.

"Right!" hollered Betameche, making them jump.

Arthur, entranced by Selenia's smile, could barely distinguish his right from his left, and he spun the steering wheel in all directions. It was mere luck that Arthur managed to steer the car into the tunnel on the right.

Their screams echoed throughout the entire network of pipes.

CHAPTER
12

The sun had risen on a sad-looking garden, and it shone in the sky as the minutes ticked along toward noon. Arthur's father, for the thousandth time, put his foot on the shovel and pushed. This was his sixty-seventh consecutive hole.

His wife watched from a distance, hoping to avoid any new catastrophes. All at once she thought she heard something—a small cry that came from somewhere far away and resounded in the air. But it quickly vanished. Arthur's mother continued to listen for a moment, then decided that it was probably her imagination playing tricks on her. She went back to peeling oranges for her husband.

But now another noise could be heard in the air. It was a dull, seething rumble. Arthur's mother listened again. This one was only getting louder.

"Honey, do you hear that strange noise?"

Arthur's father, half asleep on his shovel, stood up. "What, where?" he asked with the expression of a bear emerging from hibernation.

"There, in the ground. It sounds like water spreading underground." She got down on her knees and bent over to better pinpoint the sound that was gurgling deep down inside the earth.

Arthur's father laughed. "Now you're hearing things?" he joked, his elbow on the handle of his shovel. "Just wait a bit and maybe you'll see little angels and spirits everywhere."

He had no idea how right he was. Strange silhouettes suddenly appeared, outlined behind her laughing husband. Arthur's mother saw them and her smile froze.

"Spirits and little monsters, like in your father's old books," Arthur's father added with a chuckle. "With short fur and ugly faces, along with their brothers, the sorcerers."

He began to laugh stupidly, and then to mimic a tribal dance. His wife looked at him, her face contorted with fear. She tried to point toward the shapes behind her husband and ended up fainting into the oranges.

Arthur's father was quite surprised. He turned around to look where she had been pointing and found himself nose to nose, or rather nose to belly button, with five Bogo-Matassalai. They were all dressed in simple loincloths, and each carried a pointed spear in his hand.

Arthur's father instantly turned to jelly. His teeth began to chatter like a typewriter that was printing his last will.

The Bogo-Matassalai chief carefully leaned down to him, which took some time since there was an almost three-foot difference between the two men.

"Do you have the time?" the giant African man asked politely.

Arthur's father nodded rapidly, like a marionette at the end of a string. He looked at his wrist. He was afraid he wouldn't be able to read the watch hands; and, as it happens, he couldn't, since he was not, after all, wearing a watch.

"It is . . . it is . . ."

He tapped on his wrist pointlessly. There was no way he was going to be able to give them the time.

"I—I have another in the kitchen that works better," he stammered, staring at the point of the nearest spear.

The Bogo-Matassalai said nothing and simply smiled.

Arthur's father concluded that he had permission to leave. "I'll—I'll be back," he stuttered, before taking off like a rabbit in the direction of the house.

Darkos proudly read from a small piece of paper in his hand. "According to my calculations, the water should reach the Minimoy village in less than thirty seconds," he announced to his father, who was immensely pleased by the news.

"Perfect, perfect! In less than one minute, I will be the

absolute and uncontested master of the Seven Lands, and the Minimoy people will be nothing more than a mere paragraph in the history books."

Maltazard rubbed his hands evilly.

The king Sifrat de Matradoy paced up and down at the main door to his village, where our brave adventurers had set out not so long ago. Reports had come in that the Maltazard situation was serious and that the chances of saving his kingdom were infinitesimal. But the loss of a kingdom was nothing compared with the loss of his children. Selenia and Betameche had still not returned and that was the cause of his great concern.

"What time is it, my brave Miro?" he asked the faithful mole.

Miro took his watch out of his pocket, looking unhappy, and squinted at it. "Ten minutes until noon, my king," he replied.

And here there was no question of stretching time, as Maltazard had with his leaf chronometer. In the land of the Minimoys, seconds were regular and led inevitably to an end that in this case would most likely be tragic.

The king sighed. "Only ten minutes left and we still have no news," he noted sadly.

Miro approached and placed his hand affectionately on the king's shoulder. "Have faith, my good king. Your daughter has exceptional courage. And as for young Arthur, he seems resourceful and full of common sense. I am convinced that they will think of something."

The king smiled slightly, comforted by these kind words. "May the gods hear you, my good Miro. May the gods hear you."

Despite his fatigue, Arthur still clutched the steering wheel. He had become used to the speed, and his eyes were glued to the road ahead.

The Ferrari had succeeded in outrunning the wave that was following them—so far.

"Thanks, Grandma," he said softly. Arthur knew he would never have managed without this magnificent gift. His grandmother could not have imagined that a toy would one day be so useful or that it would save the lives of the people most dear to her.

Betameche suddenly turned around. He seemed to have recognized the place in spite of their speed. "I think we are almost there," he said. "That was the border that marks the entrance to the dandelion field."

Selenia peered down the tunnel ahead of them. "There, the door! That's the door to the village!" she screamed with joy.

This news was welcomed with great emotion in the car, and everyone congratulated one another and jumped about. But their happiness was short-lived. The car had begun to slow down.

"Oh, no!" whispered Arthur. The Ferrari slowed down more and finally rolled to a complete stop. There was consternation onboard.

"Do you want me to get out and fix it?" Selenia asked.

Arthur did not think it could be fixed, but he barely had time to say that before Beta cut him off in mid-sentence.

"Hurry! We have to wind the spring before the water reaches us."

"Impossible! It will take too much time. Besides, my arms are still aching all over—I don't think I *could* move it again," Arthur replied.

"Then I hope your legs are in better shape than that," Selenia said, throwing open her door.

In a few seconds, the group had left the car and begun to run down the tunnel toward the Minimoy village. It was no more than half a mile, but it seemed like the ends of the earth. The Ferrari would have covered the distance in a few seconds . . . and so would the wave, whose rumbling could be heard once again.

"Quick! The water is catching up to us," Arthur yelled to his grandfather and Betameche who, overcome with fatigue, were lagging behind.

Inside the city, the sound of the water was beginning to be heard.

"What is that rumbling?" the king asked Miro.

"I have no idea," the mole replied, "but I can feel waves in my feet. This vibration can mean no good."

The little group had only twenty yards left to run. Arthur turned and slipped his arm under his grandfather's. "One last push, okay, Grandpa? I know you can do it," the young man urged.

Arthur had developed a phenomenal and unexpected energy. He, who at home had always had a tendency to avoid household chores using never-to-be-finished homework as an excuse, had now become a completely unrecognizable young man, one who was brave as any warrior.

As they got closer, they could all see that the huge gates to the village were open—waiting for their return—but that there was another layer of secondary safety doors in front of it that was closed and barred. It was the worst possible situation: with the great doors open, the water would destroy the village for certain. But with the smaller doors closed, the four of them would not be able to get in to warn the Minimoys . . . or to escape the flood.

Selenia was the first to arrive at the door, and she began to pound with all her might. "Open the door!" she cried with all the strength she could muster.

A few yards away, the king perked up his ears. He could pick her sweet little voice out of a thousand. It was his beloved daughter, his princess, his heroine who had returned from her mission! He ran back toward the main gate.

The guard slid open the little window into the tunnel. Even though the wave was not yet visible, its wind was already there, and the watchman caught a gust of air right in his face.

"Who goes there?" he asked in a deep voice, hoping it showed he was unafraid.

Selenia put her hand into the opening, then stood on tiptoes to show her face. Betameche ran up and pushed his sister aside to show his.

The watchman looked at them for a moment, expressionless, then slammed the window in their faces.

This made Selenia furious, of course, and she knocked even louder. Arthur and his grandfather joined them, and they all began to pound on the door.

The king arrived at the entrance to the village and was surprised that the watchman was not reacting to this din. "What are you doing? Why haven't you opened this door?"

"It's another trick," explained the watchman. "But they won't do that to me a second time! This time, they made a drawing—an animated one—of Princess Selenia and Prince Betameche. The one of the princess is particularly well done, but the one of Betameche has a few mistakes and you can tell right away that it's a fake."

The little group outside continued to pound with all their

strength, while the wind preceding the torrent became stronger and stronger.

Archibald turned to estimate how much time they had left. He was amazed to see that the wave was already visible. A wall of furious water was headed in their direction at rocket speed.

"Open the door, for goodness sake!" Archibald cried out suddenly, his survival instinct finally awoken.

The king heard this urgent cry. If his memory served him correctly, it was the voice of Archibald! The king approached the door. He wanted to be sure.

He opened the little window and instantly saw the faces of Selenia and Betameche. "Help!" they cried in unison, their faces distorted with fear.

The king, furious, turned quickly toward the watchman.

"Open this door immediately, you triple gamoul," he cried with all his powerful authority. The watchman ran toward the door and, with the help of his comrades, unlocked the sliding latches.

"Hurry up!" urged Betameche, who was watching the monstrous wave swallow the Ferrari in less than a second. The wind was now so strong that it plastered our heroes against the door.

The last lock was finally removed and the guardians began to open the door, but the wind surprised everyone by bursting the doors open all of a sudden. Our friends ran inside and quickly placed themselves behind the enormous main doors.

"Quick! The wave is coming! Help us close the gate," cried Arthur without taking the time to greet anyone.

The watchman was somewhat annoyed. "Open, close—they don't know what they want!" he muttered.

Just then he saw the wave, seething with foam, hurtling toward them. His attitude changed immediately, and he ran to Arthur's side. "Come on! Help!" he cried to his fellow guards, who immediately came to his aid.

There were ten of them to push the doors, ten who were sorry that it was so heavy and that the wind was so violent. As for the wave, it seemed delighted to have finally found its destination and thrilled at the idea of drowning everything.

Miro threw himself against the door with the guards. The little mole was more accustomed to digging tunnels than to pushing doors, but, in the event of an extreme emergency like the present one, any assistance was welcome.

"Come on, my good Palmito, put me down!" the king instructed his animal carrier.

With its powerful hands, Palmito took the king carefully by his head and placed him delicately on the ground.

"Come on, Palmito, close this door for me!"

Palmito looked at him for two seconds with his gentle look.

It always took the animal two seconds to understand what was being said. The Minimoy language was not its native tongue. People had a tendency to forget that.

Finally the animal put its enormous hand on the door and pushed with its huge muscled arms. The wave was getting closer. It was only a few yards away.

Arthur jumped on the first latch and pushed it through the rings.

The wave began to crash against the door with an unexpected violence. The shock could be felt everywhere, and our little friends were thrown to the ground.

Arthur struggled up and reached the second latch, which he wrestled to close.

On the other side, the water filled the entire tunnel. Not a bubble of air remained.

The second bar finally slid into the rings and held the door fast. Everyone kept their hands on the door just in case, to give added support. This was necessary, since the pressure from the water on the other side was enormous.

Water is powerful but also clever. It could take advantage of the smallest crevice to infiltrate the interior.

The king saw that the door was completely and firmly closed.

"Let us hope it will resist," he said with some concern.

* * *

Darkos looked at his abacus. The last round ball rolled gently on the two rods that guided it, indicating the end of the cycle.

"That's it," he said with a great deal of pleasure. He turned toward his father. "From this moment on, Your Majesty, you are the one and only emperor. You rule as absolute master over all of the Seven Lands."

Darkos bowed more deeply than usual. Maltazard savored his success. He slowly expanded his chest, as if he were breathing for the first time, then sighed with pleasure.

"Even though I do not care much for honors, I must acknowledge that it does mean something to know that you are the master of the world," he admitted with due modesty. "But what pleases me most of all . . . is to know that all my enemies are dead!" he added with glee.

Our little heroes weren't exactly dead yet, but the situation remained precarious.

"Do you think the door will hold?" asked the king, who liked to be reassured.

"It will hold for now," Miro replied. "We should get everyone to hold the door later, when the pressure starts building up. But for now, we are safe."

Coming from an engineer as well-known as Miro, this response satisfied everyone.

Selenia and Betameche slowly let go of the door and ran into the waiting arms of their father.

"My children, what joy to know you are safe and sound!" the king exclaimed, overcome with emotion. He hugged them close to his chest and raised his head toward the heavens, his eyes full of tears.

"Thank you! Thank you for having answered my prayers!" he said with deep humility.

CHAPTER
13

Grandma would also have liked to have her prayers answered. She was on her third since morning, with no results yet.

She gave a small sigh at the same moment Arthur's father chose to burst into the living room, babbling like a Martian.

"There! There! They are giants! Too many! Five! In the garden! Warriors! Very tall! And they don't know what time it is!" he shouted as if he were delivering a telegram.

He whirled around, gasping for air.

"Quick! Very angry! No time to lose!" he added before heading toward the door.

He had not come to find out the time, as he had led the Bogo-Matassalai to believe. He had come to find an escape route.

Arthur's father peeked through the window curtain and saw that the visitors were still in the garden. It was the perfect moment to flee.

"I'll . . . be back," he managed to say to Grandma, before

sprinting to the front door on the other side of the house. He opened the door and jumped again. There was another visitor, or rather three visitors, to be exact.

The first one was actually fairly elegant. Arthur's father calmed down a bit as Davido doffed his hat. The other two wore rather frightening-looking uniforms—police uniforms.

"It is noon!" Davido said with a big smile, as if he had just won the lottery.

Arthur's father looked at them without understanding. Davido took out his watch, carefully chained to his vest.

"Five minutes *to* noon, to be precise," he added with humor. "This is the limit of my patience."

Betameche led the group as they bolted into the Hall of Passages.

The old watchman was once again disturbed and had to leave his cocoon. This did not put him in a very good mood.

"Hurry up! I've already turned the first ring," he grumbled. "You have less than four minutes!"

Archibald positioned himself in front of the giant mirror, behind the lens of the magic telescope. The king was there to say good-bye. He had come without Palmito, who was too big for the Hall of Passages.

The king approached Archibald. The two men smiled knowing smiles and shook hands.

"No sooner have you returned than you have to leave us," said the king with a sadness that was difficult for him to hide.

"It's the law of the stars and stars don't wait!" Archibald answered with a regretful smile.

"I know, and it's a real pity. There are so many things that you still have to teach us!" the king said with great humility.

Archibald placed his hand on the king's shoulder. "You have your own wealth of knowledge in addition to what I have taught you," he said. "The two of us, we form a whole, the knowledge of one complementing the knowledge of the other. Isn't that the secret of teamwork? The secret of the Minimoys?" Grandpa said gently.

"Yes, that is true," admitted the king. "'The more we are, the more we laugh.' Fiftieth commandment."

"See, it is you who taught me that," Archibald said with a big smile.

The king was greatly moved by this mark of friendship and respect. The two men, small in size but great in heart, shook hands vigorously.

The gatekeeper turned the second ring, that of the mind.

"Take good care of my son-in-law," the king said with a smile.

"With pleasure. And you, take good care of my grand-daughter-in-law," Archibald replied.

The gatekeeper finished turning the third ring, that of the soul.

"All aboard," he cried, like a conductor.

Archibald waved one last time and threw himself on the glass, which immediately absorbed him. The old man disappeared, like a piece of toast under jelly.

Arthur watched as his grandfather, tossed by magic, passed through each of the lenses, becoming larger each time. The end of the telescope spit him out like a piece of dust that expands when it makes contact with the air and the light.

Within three rolls in the thick grass, Archibald had resumed his normal size.

He took a deep breath and decided to remain for a few moments on the ground, trying to put his emotions in order. The Bogo-Matassalai chief stood over him. The man greeted him with a magnificent smile, showing all his beautiful white teeth.

"Did you have a good trip, Archibald?" asked the chief.

"Magnificent! A little long but . . . magnificent," Grandpa replied, comforted to see his old friend.

"And Arthur?" wondered the African.

"He's coming!"

Our Minimoy friends were not too eager to see their brave Arthur leave, and he also was not keen to disappear into the gelatinous mass of the telescope lenses. But that was the price he had to pay if he was to return to his family and tell his grandma all about his adventures.

Betameche approached him, visibly moved. "It will be so

boring without you! Come back soon," begged the little prince.

"As soon as I can—at the seventh moon next year. It's a promise," Arthur replied, raising his hand as a pledge.

Betameche was somewhat surprised by this custom, but it pleased him and he immediately adopted it.

"Promise," said Betameche, raising his hand in a mirror gesture.

Arthur could not help but laugh.

"We have to hurry," the gatekeeper reminded him. "The passage will close in thirty seconds!"

Arthur stood in front of the enormous lens that distorted his reflection.

Selenia approached, somewhat shyly. She had a hard time containing her emotions. "It took me a thousand years to choose a husband and then I only had him for a few hours," the princess said, trying not to cry.

"I have to go back. You know that. My family must be so worried, just as yours was," Arthur said.

"Of course, of course," Selenia agreed without much conviction.

"And twelve moons isn't so long," Arthur added, trying to be reassuring.

"Twelve moons! That's *millions* of seconds that I will spend without you," said Selenia, who could no longer hold back her tears.

Arthur's eyes were also swimming. With the tip of his finger he collected her tears and kissed them.

"Millions of seconds. It will be a good test of our love," he said. "The people who wrote your rules would approve."

"You know what?" the princess said. "I don't give a hump-backed gamoul about protocol." She leaned forward and her lips met Arthur's in a second kiss, even more real than the first.

Then Selenia placed her hands on Arthur's shoulders and pushed him back.

Arthur disappeared, absorbed by the glass that was waiting for him. "Selenia," he managed to call before his voice was muffled by the glass and he was tossed to and fro by the uncontrollable currents.

Now he understood what mountain climbers feel, caught in monstrous avalanches. Arthur struggled and did not stop moving, as was recommended in *The Guide to Mountain Climbing*, his favorite book before he found his grandfather's accounts of his African adventures.

The lenses that he was passing through became smaller and smaller, harder and harder. The last one was like a wall and Arthur's head hurt passing through it.

As soon as he emerged, his lungs filled with pure air. His entire body inflated like a balloon, like a car's air bag after an accident. He was thrown to the ground, and he rolled away. He ended up on all fours in the grass, face-to-face with a dog's nose.

Alfred, delighted to see his master, licked Arthur's face and wagged his tail vigorously. Arthur burst out laughing and tried to protect himself from these dribbling assaults.

"Stop it, Alfred! Let me breathe for a few seconds," said Arthur, thrilled to see his faithful friend again.

Archibald came to the rescue and offered him a hand.

As soon as Arthur stood up, he saw his mother, still passed out nearby. Arthur ran toward her and bent over her. "What happened?" he asked worriedly.

"She saw us and fainted into the oranges," the Bogo-Matassalai chief explained simply, holding up the fruit as proof.

Arthur gazed at his mother's face with affection. "Wake up, Mom! It's me," he whispered in a voice so irresistibly charming that his mother awoke at once. She slowly opened her eyes and saw the face of her son right in front of her. At first she thought that she must be dreaming, so she smiled blissfully and lowered her eyelids again.

"Mom," Arthur insisted, tapping her on the cheek.

His mother's eyes flew open. "This isn't a dream?" she asked with a look of amazement.

"Of course not! It's me, Arthur! Your son," he said, shaking her lightly by the shoulders.

Arthur's mother realized that her son had really returned, and she immediately burst into tears. "Oh, my dear little boy," she said and promptly fainted into the oranges again.

At the other side of the garden, Grandma was unaware of the drama that was unfolding as she came out onto the front steps, where Davido was standing. The loathsome landlord peered with exaggerated care at the small road winding off toward the horizon. He looked again at his watch, like an official timekeeper.

"Noon on the dot," he gleefully declared to his audience of one. "Noon on the dot and still *no one* on the horizon," he added, to twist the knife in the wound.

He let out a big sigh before adding with false desperation, "I am afraid that even on this beautiful day, there won't be any miracle!"

He took advantage of the fact that his back was to Grandma in order to laugh stupidly. He would have made an excellent henchman for Maltazard.

The two policemen stood by, helpless. They wanted so much to help this poor woman, but today the law was on Davido's side and the policemen, unfortunately, had to do their job.

Davido's villainous smile faded and he became serious. Clearing his throat, he turned toward Grandma and discovered that she was no longer alone. Archibald and Arthur were on either side of her, each holding her by the arm. They had appeared as if by magic.

Davido was speechless. His jaw dropped.

Grandma, on the other hand, looked radiant. Her two most beloved people in all the world had returned to her at last.

If Harry Houdini himself had made an entire village disappear in front of his eyes, Davido could not have been more astonished. This was more than a magic trick. It was more than a miracle. It was a catastrophe.

Archibald smiled. It was not a friendly smile but a polite one. "You are right, Davido. . . . It is a very beautiful day," the old man exclaimed.

Davido, paralyzed by surprise, could not move.

"I believe we have certain papers to sign?" Grandpa asked him.

Davido took a few seconds to respond. The shock had obviously damaged his poor mental capacities, which were already rather limited.

"Let's go into the living room. It's cooler there and we will be more comfortable," Archibald suggested with exaggerated courtesy. As he turned toward the house, he whispered a few words into Arthur's ear, as discreetly as possible.

Here is what he said: "Now is when we need the treasure. I'll create a diversion and try to gain some time. You take care of finding the rubies!"

Arthur was not sure that his was the easier mission, but thi mark of confidence made him very proud. "You can count o me," he answered just as discreetly. He headed toward the back of the garden, his head held high.

He had only gone a few yards when he tripped and fell into one of the holes dug by his father, landing face-first.

Alfred poked in his nose to check out the damages.

"It's not over yet," Arthur sputtered through a mouthful of dirt.

CHAPTER

14

In the great square of Necropolis, the time had come to prepare for war.

The army of henchmen was lined up, forming an immense M on the ground.

There were thousands of soldiers perched on their mosquito mounts, preparing to invade new lands.

Maltazard came slowly out onto his balcony, which overlooked the enormous square where his perfect army had assembled. For the occasion, he had put on a new cape, in deep black with hundreds of shining stars, each glittering more brightly than the other.

The noise of the army greeted their powerful ruler, who reached out his arms toward his people.

The Prince of Darkness is savoring his overwhelming, disgusting victory, thought Mino, still standing near the pyramid, as he wondered what to do. Could Arthur have survived such a tidal wave?

It was practically impossible, but it was not the "impossible" that bothered him, it was the "practically." Even if there wa only one chance in a million, there was still a chance and Mino did not want to waste it.

Mino looked at the watch again. Although the little mole was perfectly able to tell time, he was, unfortunately, incapable of reading something so close to his face. He panicked. It didn't even work to hold his arm as far away from his body as possible. He was blind as a mole.

Arthur paced up and down the garden in every direction. It was impossible to recognize anything from the land of the Minimoys at the moment, except the tiny stream that he had traveled on aboard his nutshell. He followed it, along the little wall, only a few bricks high, and arrived at the foot of the windmill.

There must be a minuscule grille, somewhere, buried in the grass, but try as he might, Arthur couldn't find it. Alfred, on the other hand, had found his ball, the new one he had just given to Arthur for his birthday. He placed it at the feet of his master, who, as far as the dog could tell, was looking everywhere for it.

"This is not the time to play, Alfred," said the boy, who was concentrating very hard. He picked up the ball and threw it far, which is not the best way to tell a dog that the game is over.

Down below, Mino approached one of the henchmen guarding the treasure. He coughed slightly. "Excuse me for bothering you. Could you tell me the time, please? I can't see very well!"

The henchman had the face of a brute. It was a miracle that he had allowed the mole to finish his sentence. The guard leaned over and looked at the watch.

"I don't know how to tell time," he barked like an ogre.

A brute *and* a moron.

"Really? Oh, too bad. Well, it's not important," the little mole replied.

"Come on, Mino! Hurry up," Arthur prayed.

Alfred brought back the ball, wagging his tail. The dog definitely did not understand the tragedy that was unfolding before him. He only saw his ball and the game that went along with it.

Arthur, annoyed, grabbed the ball and threw it as hard as he could to the other end of the garden.

Well, that was the plan, anyway. Unfortunately, a tired arm and a light wind decided otherwise. The ball swerved off course and crashed through the living room window.

Inside, Davido jumped up, spilling coffee all over his beautiful cream-colored suit. He began yelling insults that pain transformed into gibberish.

Grandma hurried over, a towel in her hand, while Grandpa pretended to look bothered.

"Oh, I am so sorry! You know how it is! Children!" he said

Davido grabbed the towel out of Grandma's hands and wiped himself off.

"No, thank goodness! I have not yet had the pleasure," he sputtered through clenched teeth.

"Ah! Children!" marveled Archibald. "A child is like a lamb that fulfills your life and, in my case, has saved it," he confessed.

"Can we leave the lambs alone and return to the business at hand?" suggested Davido. He pushed the papers that needed to be signed under Archibald's nose.

"Of course," Grandpa replied, looking at the papers. He needed to find another way to buy more time. "First let me make you another cup of coffee," he said, standing.

"Don't bother," Davido replied, but Grandpa pretended to be deaf and headed for the kitchen.

"The coffee comes from central Africa. You are really going to like it!"

Maltazard still had his arms outstretched, facing the jubilant crowd.

"My faithful soldiers!"

The crowd fell silent.

"The hour of glory has arrived," cried their sovereign in a voice that would freeze your blood.

The henchmen screamed with joy. You had to wonder whether they understood what was being said or were blindly obeying the sign that Darkos held up on which was written the word "Applause." But since most of them couldn't read, they were happy just to cheer.

Maltazard waited for silence and continued his speech. "I

promise you wealth and power, grandeur and eternity!"

The henchmen cheered again, not really understanding what their king was promising and what they would never be receiving. There was little chance that he would share any wealth and power, much less grandeur and eternity.

"We are now going to invade and conquer all the lands that were promised to us," he added, sending the crowd into a frenzy. This they understood, and mosquitoes and henchmen alike stamped their feet with excitement at the size of the mission being entrusted to them.

Mino's mission was much less ambitious. He simply had to read the time on the watch Arthur had given him. He plucked up his courage and tried again.

"Excuse me—it's me again," he said politely to the henchman. "I'd like to give this to you," he added, handing him the watch.

The henchman was so stupid, it was very unlikely that he would know what a gift was. Mino did not give him time to think—that could take hours. He quickly strapped the watch around the henchman's wrist.

"There! It looks very good on you," he said.

The henchman looked at the watch for a moment, like pineapple would look at a television.

"What am I supposed to do with this? I don't know how tell time."

"No problem! When you want to know what time it is, all you have to do is hold up your arm in the direction of someone who does know how. Me, for example. Lift your arm— you'll see, it's easy."

The henchman, dumber than a fish that has never seen a hook, listened to Mino and raised both his arms. The little mole could finally see the time on the watch from a distance that was comfortable for his eyes.

"My goodness! Five minutes past noon," he cried in a panic, and ran off toward his levers, leaving the henchman planted like a scarecrow.

On the surface of the earth, Arthur was still waiting for the little mole to work his magic. But nothing had happened yet, and Arthur began to despair.

Down below, Mino was trying his best. The animal made his calculations as fast as possible—and you have no idea how fast a mole can calculate. He pulled on several levers, which immediately adjusted the position of several rubies. As a result, the light, which had been illuminating the pyramid, slowly began to fade without anyone realizing it. Everyone in this world was absorbed by Maltazard's speech, which he ended with the following words: "Let the festivities begin!"

The army screamed with joy. They threw their weapons into the air in perfect unison and, for a few moments, as swords and knives spun and glittered above them, the show was impressive. Its end was less so, however. Weapons fell every which way, raining down on the soldiers. The wounded numbered in the dozens.

Maltazard rolled his eyes, appalled by the stupidity of his army.

Mino took advantage of the temporary chaos to pull one last lever. All of a sudden, the light came together and was transformed into a magnificent red beam. It burst out of the top of the pyramid and climbed directly toward the outside world.

The audience let out an admiring "Oooohhh!" They obviously thought this new play of light was part of the show. "What a beautiful red" was heard here and there.

Mino pulled a lever and the beam intensified. Like a bolt of lightning, it sliced through the sky of Necropolis.

"It's magnificent, O divine sovereign," rejoiced Darkos, applauding quietly in order not to drown out the clamoring crowd that idolized his father.

Maltazard had no idea what was happening, but he didn't want to admit it.

In the middle of the garden, a magnificent red ray shot out of the ground and climbed practically to the sky. Arthur screamed with joy and threw himself down so that he could look into the hole.

Alfred, who had succeeded in finding his ball, also came

over to investigate. Arthur thrust his hand into the hole, but his arm was not long enough to reach into the cavern.

Mino looked up and saw Arthur's shadow at the edge of the opening. Maltazard had also seen these shadows, and even if he did not really understand what was happening, he could still feel the impending danger.

"We must find the idiot responsible for this! Arrest him at once," he screamed at the guards who were positioned around the hall.

Arthur scratched his head. "I have to come up with an idea, Alfred! Right away!" the boy said as he looked at his dog.

Alfred pricked up his ears, as if he wanted the statement repeated.

Arthur sighed. There was nothing he could learn from this dumb dog. All he knew how to do was chase after the ball he was holding in his mouth.

Arthur paused. He had an idea.

"The ball! Of course!" he shouted. "You have saved my life, Alfred! Give me your ball!"

Alfred was thrilled. His master did want to play after all! He seized the ball and took off to the other end of the garden, his tail wagging happily as Arthur ran after him.

Arthur took off after his dog, but with only two legs against four, he could not catch him.

* * *

Meanwhile, the guards had regrouped and were marching toward Mino, spears at the ready. Mino trembled with fear, desperately searching for a way to defend himself.

"Alfred, STOP!" *yelled Arthur, as he had never yelled before in his life, so* loud that he hurt his throat. It was not exactly a shout that could kill, but it could certainly paralyze.

Alfred stopped cold in his tracks, transfixed by this awful cry that seemed to come from deep inside his master, as if a monster were living within him. He opened his jaws, the ball fell to the ground, and Arthur picked it up.

"Thanks," the boy said to him, once again calm, patting him on the head.

This was one game of catch that Alfred was not likely to forget.

CHAPTER
15

Mino was not likely to forget this day, either, since it was beginning to look like it would be his last.

The guards were massed in front of him, and Mino, as a last recourse, assumed a position of self-defense, Bruce Lee–style, mole version.

"Watch out," Mino warned, his hands in front of him. "I can be bad!"

Maltazard, fuming, pulled out the magic sword that he had stolen from Selenia. He swung the sword with a broad gesture and threw it, with all his might, in Mino's direction.

Although the mole had bad eyesight, his other senses were excellent, and he could tell there was a missile flying directly at him. Mino jumped slightly to the right. The blade planted itself noisily in the stone a few inches from Mino's contorted face.

Maltazard was furious at having missed his target, especially in front of his son.

"Seize him!" he shouted.

"I warned you! I am going to get angry," insisted Mino, step-ping back carefully.

The henchmen laughed in disbelief. Too bad for them. A tennis ball, two hundred times bigger than they were, had just appeared in the tunnel above them. The object, as big as a meteorite to them, blocked the light from the surface, and the henchmen looked up to see this shadow rolling down on them. They didn't have long to wonder.

Barely a second later, the ball landed with a crash in the middle of the henchmen.

Maltazard bent over his balcony in a speechless fury.

"Arrest that ball," he cried.

The henchmen couldn't hear him. They were being swept away like dead leaves. With each bounce, the giant ball crushed, destroyed, and mowed down everything in its path.

Straws and pipes flew in all directions, like bowling pins. Released from the elaborate system of pipes, water now flowed from dozens of holes in the cistern. The square was full of sudden geysers that spit water released from the two enor-mous tanks. The torrent, which before had been pouring only into the tunnel to the Minimoy village, now was released to flow through the entire underground.

The ball rolled and bobbed on the water as far as the entrance to the tunnel, where it got stuck in the hole and began to block it, like a bathtub stopper. Very quickly, water filled the whole square, causing panic in the army of henchmen.

"Do something," Maltazard ordered his son. Darkos was at a loss.

Mino didn't have any idea what to do, either. He had climbed into the saucer holding the treasure and hid himself between two rubies. Now the water lifted the saucer and its treasure, and the little plate climbed gently inside the pipe that led to the surface.

Mino was completely terrified. Drifting on the surface of the water is not really a mole specialty, and our little friend quickly felt sick to his stomach.

The spectacle he saw before him was disastrous. Water had conquered the great square of Necropolis, carrying off the small merchants' stalls in all directions.

Some mosquitoes had remained on the ground and were already in water up to their saddles. Others flew around the royal hall, which now had no exits that were not completely underwater.

The henchmen who fell into the water sank very quickly, thanks to their heavy armor.

Entire sections of wall, eaten away by the water, collapsed into the square, causing monstrous waves. The same waves carried off the little groups of huts that came crashing into the palace walls, under Maltazard's balcony.

The sovereign saw this catastrophe climbing quickly toward him. Soon it would engulf his balcony. He couldn't believe it.

How could that little nothing of a mole cause such a cata-clysm? How could an empire as powerful as his own fall so easily?

Sometimes all it takes is one grain of sand to stop a huge machine, a small stone to fell a giant, and a few courageous men to start a revolution. He would have known that if he had read *The Great Book of Ideas*, as Mino had advised him to do a hundred times. Commandment two-hundred and thirty would have reminded him that "the smaller the nail, the more it hurts when it is in your foot."

Maltazard understood the lesson now, but it was too late. He was lost, destroyed, just like his kingdom.

The water had now reached the balcony, and there were no longer many options for him. He chose the first one that came to mind: he jumped onto a mosquito.

The henchman who was piloting it was obviously very proud to have his master aboard but, as he soon discovered, there can only be one captain on any ship.

Maltazard grabbed the henchman and carelessly threw him overboard. The poor pilot didn't even have time to cry out before tumbling straight down into the tumultuous water.

Maltazard took the mosquito's reins, which were a little small for him, and prepared to leave.

"Father?" cried Darkos.

Maltazard pulled on the reins and stopped his mosquito.

His son was on the balcony, looking lost, up to his knees in water. "Don't abandon me, Father," he said in a voice that was almost childlike.

Maltazard moved in front of him, hovering.

"Darkos! I appoint you commander of all my armies and all these lands," his father said in a solemn voice.

Darkos was only vaguely flattered by this, for in order to take advantage of his new appointment, it would have been better to be dry. He extended his hand toward his father, hoping for a small spot on the back of the mosquito.

"And a captain never leaves his ship," his father added, annoyed at having to remind him of the most basic military rule.

Maltazard pulled on the reins, did an about-face, and disappeared into the vaulted sky of Necropolis.

Darkos, disappointed, bruised, and abandoned, lowered his head. He noticed that the water had already reached his waist and that his face was reflected in the water. He looked at the tired face rapidly rising toward him, like a brother looking to find him. This thought made him smile. Immediately, his reflection put on the same smile. Darkos was very moved by this. It was the first time that anyone had ever approached him with a smile.

It would also be the last. His reflection came closer and gave him a kiss good-bye.

Arthur was still stretched out on the grass, his ear planted to the ground so he could hear the gurgling sound rushing through the belly of the earth. The little hole into which he had tossed the ball still remained desperately empty, and Arthur began to wonder whether he had failed in the last part of his mission.

After having crossed the Seven Lands at a height of half an inch, fought henchmen, married a princess, found his grandfather and a treasure, he felt that to fail so close to the end would be too terrible. There was a kind of injustice here that Arthur could not allow. Why would his good fortune, which up to now had accompanied him, fail so suddenly? The thought gave him new courage, and once again he bent over the little hole. He clearly heard the water gurgling. The fact that it was getting louder meant only one thing: the level of the water was rising!

Arthur peered into the hole once more.

Suddenly, an object glistened. The first ruby at the top of the pyramid had just found the light. Little by little, the saucer rose, carried by the water, and the pyramid became increasingly illuminated.

Arthur was amazed and astounded. He had tears in his eyes.

His mission had been a success. A perilous mission, during which he had risked his life a hundred times, braving all kinds of dangers. An adventure that had forced him to go beyond anything he knew about himself. A path that he had begun as a small boy and that he had finished as a young man.

Arthur reached out his hands and caught the saucer full of rubies. He gazed at the treasure for a moment, the way a student looks at his diploma at the end of the school year.

The audience congratulated him by wagging its tail and barking its compliments.

Arthur hurried into the garage and turned on the bright fluorescent light, which hesitated a moment, as always, before working. The boy gently placed the saucer on the table and rummaged through the drawers of the workbench. Finally he found what he was looking for: a magnifying glass.

Arthur carefully examined the pyramid of rubies, in search of a little mole.

"Mino?" whispered Arthur. He knew his normal voice would sound monstrous to a Minimoy.

Mino had heard, but this strange noise worried him. How would he be able to recognize his friend Arthur, now that the tone of his voice had become so low? The little mole plucked up his courage and decided to show himself. As he scrambled free of the rubies, he slipped on a wall of glass and realized that the lens reflected a giant eye, bigger than a planet.

Mino let out a shriek and fell into the rubies, which is much better than fainting into oranges.

Half the Minimoy people had their hands and backs pressed against the door when they realized that the water pressure wasn't getting stronger anymore. In fact, it had started to weaken. Miro announced the good news, putting his ear to the door to listen.

The king stopped pushing but still did not dare to remove his hands.

Palmito asked fewer questions. He stepped back a few steps and stretched hugely, cracking his back. He had probably been responsible for two thirds of the work.

The king, alone with his hands on the door, began to feel a little ridiculous.

"You can let go, Father! I think it will hold," his daughter said, amused.

The sound of the water was receding, like a bad memory.

Miro opened the little window located at eye level and peeked outside. "The water is gone! Arthur and Archibald have succeeded," cried the mole.

The news was greeted with unparalleled joy, and hundreds of little hats were thrown into the air to the sound of screams, cries, songs, and various kinds of whistling. Everything that made it possible to express the joy of being alive was heard at that moment.

Selenia threw herself into her father's arms. Huge tears rolled down her cheeks and, at the same time, she burst into uncontrollable laughter.

Betameche was intoxicated by all the hands that wanted to shake his. He made sure to say thank you to everyone. The entire Minimoy people were jubilant and they spontaneously began to sing their national anthem.

Miro watched all of this wistfully, for his heart wasn't fully in it. The king approached and placed an arm on his shoulders.

He understood the unhappiness that was preventing Miro from celebrating.

"How I would have loved to have my little Mino here, to enjoy this spectacle!" Miro said sadly.

The king felt great sympathy for his friend. There was nothing to do, given the situation, and even less to say. But a new noise was beginning to disturb the celebration, stronger even than the noise of the water.

The ground began to tremble slightly and the ceremony immediately came to a halt. Worry could again be seen on everyone's faces.

The trembling of the ground grew more pronounced, and several chunks of earth fell from the ceiling, like bombs falling from the sky, that exploded, making huge craters.

Who other than a demon would attempt to destroy the vault over the city?

A jolt, much stronger than the others, detached an enormous stone from the ceiling.

"Watch out," cried Miro.

The Minimoys scattered, leaving the enormous stone to dig a hole in the ground in a cloud of dust. The shock was so violent that the king fell back.

At last the trembling stopped and a gigantic multicolored tube appeared from the ceiling, descending to the ground.

The king could not believe his eyes. *What diabolical thing has that demon Maltazard invented now?* he wondered.

The impressive tube steadied itself and, since it was transparent, it was now clearly possible to observe a ball sliding down the inside, toward them.

"A ball of death," cried Betameche.

That was all that was needed to cause total panic.

Selenia was the only one who stayed calm. The horrible tube reminded her of something . . . what was it? "It's a straw," she cried suddenly, smiling from ear to ear. "It's one of Arthur's straws!"

The ball finished its descent, hit the ground, and rolled to the side. It was Mino the mole! He stood up, aching all over, and spit the dust out of his mouth. He held Selenia's sword tightly in his arms, having rescued it from the wall before hiding in the pile of rubies.

"My son!" cried Miro, overcome with emotion.

"My sword!" rejoiced Selenia, crazy with happiness.

Miro ran to his son and hugged him tightly.

The Minimoy people, covered with dust, once again shouted for joy.

The king approached Miro and his son.

"All's well that ends well," he said happily, not at all sorry that the adventure was finally over.

"Not just yet," replied Selenia with authority.

She left the little group and walked to the center of the square, where the rock of the ancients stood. She brandished her sword and, in a single movement, planted it in the stone. The stone closed immediately, imprisoning the sword forever.

Selenia let out a sigh of relief. She glanced at her father who, with a nod of his head, indicated his approval. This adventure had taught her many things—especially one, which was essential for being a good queen and for succeeding in life in general. She had learned wisdom.

Very gently, the straw rose like a silent rocket, leaving the village square.

CHAPTER
16

Arthur pulled up the straw and checked to make sure that Mino was no longer inside. He placed a small stone over the hole he had made and recovered the saucer filled with rubies.

Archibald had run out of ways to stall for time. His hands were covered with ink and he was toying with his pen, which he had separated into three parts.

"It's incredible! This pen has never let me down before! And now, at the worst moment, when these important papers are to be signed, it falls apart!" Grandpa explained talkatively. "It was a Swiss friend who gave it to me and, as you probably know, the Swiss are not only specialists in clocks and in chocolate but they also make excellent pens!"

Davido, exhausted and suspicious, stuck his own fancy pen under Archibald's nose.

"Here! This one comes from Switzerland, too! Now, sign!

We've lost enough time as it is."

The landlord would not tolerate any more diversions. You could see it in his face.

"Ah? What? Yes, of course," mumbled Archibald, who had run out of ideas. He tried to gain a few more seconds by admiring the pen. "Magnificent! And . . . does it write well?"

"Try it yourself," Davido answered shrewdly.

Archibald had no other choice. He signed the last paper.

The landlord immediately grabbed it from his hands and put it in his file.

"There! Now you are the owner," said Davido, his expression somewhat strained.

"Wonderful!" answered Archibald, who knew that it wasn't so simple. He had filled out all the papers, but he had not paid the principal.

"So—the money!" Davido demanded, holding out his hand.

He knew that this was his last chance to steal the property. The deed would be invalid until Archibald had paid the sum due, and Davido was almost certain he did not have it. The old man looked at the two policemen on either side of Davido with a beseeching smile. Unfortunately, the two representatives of the law could not do much for him.

Davido felt the wind change direction in his favor. It was already a miracle that the old man had reappeared at the last moment. There could not be two miracles in the same day.

Davido opened the file, grabbed the deeds, and prepared to tear them up. "No money . . . no documents, no house," said the evil landlord.

The front door opened, and everyone turned toward it with the natural curiosity you have when you are waiting for a miracle.

On this occasion, the miracle was very polite. He entered by the door and wiped his feet before crossing the room.

Arthur came up to the table, where the audience was waiting for him with bated breath. He carefully placed the saucer full of rubies in front of Archibald.

Grandma held back her emotions, Grandpa his admiration.

As for Davido, he held his breath. Was it possible?

Arthur was beaming with happiness.

Archibald rejoiced. He would finally be able to enjoy himself a little. "Well," he said, looking at the rubies, "good accounts make good friends. That is commandment number fifty-nine. . . ."

He chose a ruby, the smallest one. "That should cover it. Now you are paid!" he said, placing the tiny stone in front of Davido, who was mesmerized.

The two policemen breathed a sigh of relief. They were quite pleased by this happy ending.

Grandma placed a small jewelry box on the table. She picked up the saucer and emptied the rubies inside.

"They will be safer in here, and, besides, I have been looking for this saucer for four years," she said with humor, picking
it up.

Archibald and Arthur laughed. Not Davido. Davido was not
laughing at all.

"Sir, I bid you good-bye," said Archibald, standing up and
indicating the exit.

Davido felt as though his legs had been cut out from under
him. He could barely stand.

The two policemen saluted Arthur's grandparents by putting their hands to their caps and heading toward the door.

Davido, devastated, felt his nerves snap, one after the other.
A nervous tic appeared at the corner of one eyelid and his eye
began to wink, as if it were about to pass out. The road that
leads from hatred to madness is not very long, and Davido now
seemed ready to follow its path.

He opened his jacket and took out a pistol, a gesture that
left no doubt as to its meaning.

"Nobody move," he cried.

The two policemen reached for their weapons, but Davido's
madness had made him very sharp.

"Nobody, I said," he shouted again, even louder than before.

The others were speechless. No one had imagined that this
villain would go so far.

Davido took advantage of the general astonishment to slip

the little box full of rubies under his arm.

"This is exactly what I was hoping for," he gloated.

"Is that why you absolutely had to have our property?" asked Archibald, who was beginning to understand.

"Of course! The desire for wealth! Ever and always." He laughed with a crazed look on his face.

"How did you know that our garden hid such a treasure?" Grandpa asked, mystified.

"It was you who told me, you stupid idiot," said Davido excitedly, his weapon still pointed at them. "One evening we were both in the Two Rivers bar. We were celebrating the end of the war, and you shared your stories of bridges and tunnels, of Africans, big and small, and of treasure! Rubies that you had brought back from Africa and carefully buried in the garden. They were so well hidden that you couldn't remember where. That made you laugh, but I have cried every night since then! I could not rest, knowing that you were sleeping peacefully on top of a treasure without even knowing where it was!"

"I am sorry to have disturbed your sleep so much," Archibald replied, as cold as ice.

"It's not important! Now that I have the treasure I can catch up on my sleep. You are the one who will never rest again," Davido assured him, beginning to step back toward the door.

"Davido, it was not the treasure that prevented you from

sleeping. It was your own greed."

"Well, today my greed is satisfied, and I promise you I will sleep well. I am thinking of the Caribbean. Africa is not really my style," replied the villain.

What he did not see was the five spears of the Bogo-Matassalai, now aimed at his back.

"Money doesn't buy happiness, Davido. That is one of the first commandments, and you will learn it soon enough," said Archibald. He was pained to see this poor madman fall into a trap that he himself had unwittingly set.

Davido took another step back and froze. He could feel the five lances pressing into his back, and he realized that his luck was changing again, like storm clouds rolling into a clear sky.

The two policemen jumped forward as he stood, paralyzed with fear, and disarmed him quickly.

The African chief recovered the jewelry box while the policemen handcuffed Davido and pushed him toward the door without time to say another word. Not even "farewell."

The Bogo-Matassalai chief gave Archibald the jewelry box.

"Next time, be more careful where you put the gifts you are given," said the chief with an enormous smile.

"It's a promise," replied Archibald. He was smiling, but he had learned his lesson.

Arthur ran into the arms of his grandma and took advantage

of some well-earned cuddling.

Meanwhile, out in the garden, Arthur's mother was slapping herself, not very hard, but still slapping. She knew it was the only thing that could wake her. Her husband came up and slipped his arm behind her back to help her sit up.

The first thing that she saw, upon opening her eyes, was Davido, handcuffs on his wrists, being thrown into the police car by the two officers.

Arthur's mother knit her brow, convinced that she was still in a dream.

"Are you feeling better, dear?" her husband asked gently.

She did not respond right away. She was waiting to see if the police car, with its sirens blaring, would fly up into the air.

The car raised a lot of dust, but it remained wisely on the road.

She was really in reality.

"Yes. Much better," she responded finally, as she stood and straightened her dress. She looked at all the holes her husband had made around her in the garden. "Everything is very good," she continued vaguely. She had obviously not completely come to, and her various falls must have rattled her brain.

"I'm going to straighten up a bit," she said, as if she were in the kitchen. She grabbed her shovel and began filling up the holes.

Her husband watched her, helpless. He sighed and sat down at the edge of one of the holes. There was nothing to do but wait and hope that his wife's condition was temporary.

CHAPTER
17

One week had passed since the amazing adventure. The garden was almost as good as new, the gravel in the driveway had been raked, the windows repaired, and the electricity and telephone turned on again.

The only difference was the delicious smell that was floating through the kitchen window.

Grandma lifted the cover of the pot. It had been simmering for hours and smelled absolutely wonderful. This probably explained why Alfred the dog was sitting quietly next to the stove.

Grandma dipped her wooden spoon into the pot, then took a tiny taste. Given the smile of satisfaction that appeared on her face, there could be no doubt: it was ready. She lifted the dish with the help of two towels and headed for the dining room.

"Ahh," everyone hummed with pleasure.

Archibald pushed the bottles aside to make room for the

beautiful new dish. "Oh! Giraffe neck! My favorite," he exclaimed.

Immediately, his daughter began to get up from the table, but her husband stopped her in mid-flight. She had recovered, but she was still somewhat fragile.

"I'm only joking." Grandpa guffawed.

Grandma served, and the delicious aroma of beef stew filled the room. Everyone was served—Arthur's mother, Arthur's father, the two policemen, the five Bogo-Matassalai—and they all waited politely until the mistress of the house finished going around the table.

The last plate was filled, but one chair was empty.

"Where is Arthur?" asked Grandma suddenly. She had been so busy with her stew that she hadn't noticed he was gone.

"He went to wash his hands. He'll be right back," Archibald replied.

Arthur had not really gone to wash his hands. He was upstairs. He came out of his grandma's room, the famous key in his hand, and tiptoed down the hall, making sure, this time, that Alfred wasn't following him.

There was no chance of that. On beef stew day, Alfred was never more than a few feet away from the kitchen.

Arthur arrived at the door to his grandfather's study and slipped the key into the lock.

The room was full again. The desk had been put back in its place. Each trinket, each mask, had found its nail and once again cluttered the room. The books also had the pleasure, once again, of piling on top of each other.

Arthur moved slowly, as if to prolong his pleasure. He touched the cherrywood desk, the large buffalo-hide trunk, and all the masks he had loved to play with before this story began. He glanced up at the banner that read WORDS OFTEN HIDE OTHER WORDS, which had started him on his adventure. He felt happy and sad all at the same time.

He opened the window and let summer fill the room. He put his elbows on the windowsill and sighed as he looked at the big oak tree and the garden gnome under it. Above, in the azure sky, a pale crescent moon offered itself timidly to the sun.

"Only eleven more moons, Selenia . . . eleven more moons," he said.

Arthur remained in the silence for a moment, hoping that an echo might send him a response. But none came. All he could hear was the whisper of a breeze in the leaves of the big oak.

Arthur kissed the palm of his hand, then blew on it to show it the path to take.

The kiss danced in the direction of the oak tree, passing nimbly through its branches and landing on Selenia's cheek.

The little princess was sitting on a leaf, looking up at Arthur in the window. A tear slid down her cheek.

"I'll be with you soon," whispered Arthur, with an air of melancholy.

Selenia knew he could not hear her, but she answered anyway.

"I'll be waiting."